MANI SEMILLA
finds HER
QUETZAL VOICE

MANI SEMILLA
finds HER
QUETZAL VOICE

Anna Lapera

LEVINE QUERIDO

MONTCLAIR · AMSTERDAM · HOBOKEN

This is an Arthur A. Levine book

Published by Levine Querido

LQ

LEVINE QUERIDO

www.levinequerido.com · info@levinequerido.com

Levine Querido is distributed by Chronicle Books, LLC

Text Copyright © 2024 Anna Lapera

Jacket art copyright © 2024 Rosa Colón Guerra

Library of Congress Control Number: 2023938684

ISBN 978-1-64614-371-9

Printed and bound in China

Published in March 2024

First Printing

This book is dedicated to Annika & Sofia . . .
And to anyone stepping into the power of their voice

MANI SEMILLA
finds HER
QUETZAL VOICE

ONE

*Seventy-three days until my world
crumbles like burnt quetzal feathers*

WHEN YOUR DAD is Chinese-Filipino-American, and your mom is Guatemalan, it's really annoying trying to explain why you don't speak Mandarin or Tagalog. It's even more annoying trying to defend yourself in your broken Spanish why you can't roll your *r*'s. It leaves you making stuff up like, "In Guatemala they don't really roll their *r*'s. That's why so many people go to learn Spanish there. It's like an easier type of Spanish." That only fools rich people, especially I-took-French rich people—the kind my tía nannies for—who never want to offend you by challenging you on your own cultural knowledge.

It also leaves you making up even weirder stuff like, "When you grow up with a ton of languages, your brain gets all cross-wired and stuff and you end up not speaking anything good at all." I sometimes add, "All that knowledge in the language part of your brain needs somewhere better to go, so it just gets pumped into the corner of your brain that does math and logic games."

Now that is false on two levels. For one, I suck at math. For two, my pediatrician told Mami that speaking more than one language

✦ 1 ✦

makes you good at stuff, and I'll see the benefit of all of this one day. Today is not that day. Just saying.

But you can't tell me any of this, 'cause I'm twelve and life sucks when you're twelve. You're not a little kid, but you're also not an adult, and all the grown-ups in your life talk about your body the minute it starts getting a shape. And what sucks even more than being a half-Chinese-Filipino-American half-Guatemalan who can't speak any ancestral language well? When almost every other girl in school has already gotten her period except for you and your two besties, Kai and Connie. And everybody's looking at you like you're still some little girl with no real-life knowledge to go with those big, stupid, purple-framed glasses.

Glasses that have been bigger than my face ever since I was eight and first started wearing them, 'cause I'm myopic, which is a fancy way of saying things look blurry in the distance. Sometimes I wish a big, ugly meteor would come and destroy my glasses so I could get new ones. Like those clear-framed ones, the kind that would make me look like a grown woman, like a writer. Not gonna happen. Mami picked my glasses. (On rebaja, of course. Paying full price is for rich folks and pendejos, and we're neither, even though we got to move out of an apartment and into a house last year.) I mean, I know she's trying. Mami picked the color too, after her favorite bird—the quetzal, which is the national bird of Guatemala.

Manuela, the most beautiful and rare quetzal birds of all have a purple sheen, she said the day she got them. That is if you're lucky enough to see a quetzal, which is almost no one. But still, I think I'd have more luck spotting a real-life quetzal (or rolling my *r*'s better than Abuelita) than getting out of yet another ridiculous homework assignment.

"Ma-nu-hay-la, you're up," says Mr. Jones, who teaches first period health and never says my name right. (My cousin C.C. told me that mispronouncing someone's name is an attack on their alma, and she's real smart and goes to college and says words like "self-sustaining," "consent," and "Latinx," so it's gotta be true. Not to mention she can switch between English and Spanish so smooth like that first Takis dusting on your fingers three seconds after you open a new bag and no one else's hands have been in it.)

"Ma-nu-hay-la, you must not have heard me," he says.

Except I did. I just didn't do this stupid homework. Who gives seventh graders an assignment to describe their ideal partner? Really?

"Who, me?" I point to myself and turn around, even though I'm in the last row. All I see are the "healthy relationship" posters the quarter three health kids made for the Valentine's Day competition a few months ago, except they look like they cut and glued them together with their teeth or something.

A'niya from the third row picks off her nail polish, turns around and side-eyes me. I try to do it back, but she's like twelve thousand times closer to becoming a woman than I am. I mean, she started wearing a real bra in fourth grade. *And* she can recite the Spanish alphabet backward. (I heard her do it once during a fire drill back in fifth grade.) So there's that. She turns her head back toward the front of the class, sneaks out her phone and checks her teeth on the reflection of the home screen. Must be nice to get to have boobs *and* a phone.

In front of her is Hector, who looks at me like I just took his chocolate milk and french fry cafeteria money and he's too scared to ask for it back. Uy, I should have told him earlier about the jalea and peanut butter on his upper lip from this morning's cafeteria breakfast, 'cause it's all dry and crusty now.

Connie kicks the side leg of my chair with the bottom of her Converse, all loud and obvious, careful not to mess up the lightning bolts she sewed on by herself. Shoes are her thing. (That, and chewing her nails.)

"Mani," Kai whispers, all concerned every other sentence, like Mami.

But I don't want to go up there, even though my abuelita says I'm a Guatemalan quetzal bird—you know, rare and powerful and stuff—and that I need to find my *quetzal voice*. Except I don't really know what that means. *Manuela, be a quetzal like your Tía Beatriz*, she says on days she has her memory. (But also on the days she doesn't.) What she means is be like her other daughter—Mami's sister— apparently a real quetzal of a woman, who got on a bus one day in Guatemala and never came home. (That was way before they moved here. Before I was born. I don't know exactly what about that makes her a quetzal woman—just 'cause she took the bus alone? Mami won't even let me go to the mall alone.)

Mr. Jones scratches the back of his head, clearing his throat in that we're-all-waiting kind of way. But I don't like being forced to speak up in front of people, ever, and I didn't do my stupid homework.

"Ma-nu-aiii-la," Mr. Jones repeats, this time stretching it out like he's got something stuck between his teeth.

I sit up straight. "Um . . . this one was hard for me to do. I don't know if I even want to get . . ." I don't finish 'cause my quetzal voice gets all tangled in my throat. But that's the thing—quetzales barely even sing. (At least not like they used to.) Abuelita told me that according to a Mayan legend, quetzales *used* to sing all beautiful back in the day, until the Spanish came all uninvited and stuff and tried to destroy everything. The legend says quetzales are never going to find their voice and sing again until Guatemala is free. Hasn't happened yet. They still don't sing like they're apparently capable of, *and* (like I said) it's rare to ever see one. I don't know what a mysterious songless bird has to with me, plus—

"You don't want to get what?" Mr. Jones asks, interrupting my thought.

"Married," I say quietly, after a few seconds. Maybe now he'll let it go.

Giggles rip through the room, and I swear I hear someone fart. Seventh graders are opportunists like that. Connie starts biting her nails (which is gross), and Kai pulls her hair in front of her face like a curtain—hair her parents won't let her cut, 'cause then she wouldn't look like a lady, according to them.

Kai and Connie always have my back—no one gets me like they do. We call each other Las Nerdas, though we would never tell anyone else that. If we tell people that, they're less likely to notice how much our boobs grew over spring break. Fact: if you introduce yourself as *una nerda*, no one looks down at your boobs. (If Mami ever let me wear my own size clothes instead of always buying me two sizes too big, they'd be noticeable.) We've been inseparable since Kai stood up to bullies who were bothering me and Connie for my glasses and her shoes. I can't even remember what Kai said to them, but ever since then, I've been comfortable hiding behind her voice.

The three of us are on a mission. One of those real important journeys, but into womanhood. We're about to turn thirteen. Kai's older sister told us that once you get to your teens, you're pretty much a woman, 'cause you get your period, and you can get pregnant any time. I think there's probably more to it than that, but Kai's sister is real smart and gives good advice. Even though on her bad days, she can be real mean to Kai. (Like once, we barged in on her in her room after she had come back from her piano class, and she bent Kai's finger back so far she almost broke it. But they're sisters and sisters are like that, I guess. I wouldn't know.)

"We're waiting," says Mr. Jones as he points to the front of the class.

I squirm in my chair, but then I'm saved by an intercom announcement from the principal. Something about the weather changing and it being the first warm day and "Ladies, please remember we still have a dress code."

Connie rolls her eyes and cleans the soles of her shoes with an eraser for the fifth time since class started.

"What are the boys supposed to remember?" says Kai.

Kai always has a comeback, even for the intercom. And she's right. It's annoying that Mr. Dupont only addresses the girls, but I have other problems to deal with right now. As if I didn't have enough to worry about with not having my period, this morning Mami told me we are going to Guatemala for my thirteenth birthday this summer. And for some unknown reason, we have to leave the last week of school, ON my birthday.

Punto y final, she said. Like, tickets-bought-and-seats-assigned *punto y final*. But I don't want to go. Scratch that.

I WILL NOT GO.

When I get my period, I'll officially be a woman, and then I'll get treated with more respect. What I want will matter, like not wanting to go to Guatemala.

Last week my history teacher, Ms. Martinez, announced the end-of-year Speak Up competition that all seventh-grade history classes in every middle school across the county are doing. All we have to do is think of a social justice-y project. One group from each school will be chosen as the winner. If we win, we get to spend two whole weeks in New York at some youth activist camp, where you learn how to be an activist, how to start a fire and set up a tent. That's what the brochure says. Plus, FREE. (And that's better than rebaja.) We have to win. What if Kai and Connie go to New York without me and they forget about me while I'm in Guatemala all summer? What if this is the summer I get my period and become a woman, and instead of being with Kai and Connie finishing our Nerda Manifesto, I'm surrounded by people who will just make fun of my horrible Spanish?

But I couldn't say any of this to Mami this morning. I couldn't find my quetzal voice like Abuelita told me to do, as she warmed the quetzal coin against her palm before setting it next to the Santa Ana statue, the saint of mothers and daughters. But, if a whole country I've never even been to can't figure out how to make the quetzales sing again (or even appear), how am I supposed to figure it out? What does it even mean to have a quetzal voice?

"So, you're choosing to take a zero," Mr. Jones says.

He isn't going to let it go. Uy, just get it over with, I say to myself.

I start to walk down the aisle between desks. It's so narrow that I have to turn my body each time I pass someone, and my butt cheek rubs against the tops of desks.

"Get your nasty butt off my notebook!" says Mason, a boy from my bus and history class.

"Shut up! *Your* butt is nasty," says Connie.

"As if you even take notes," says Kai (in a voice more quetzal than mine).

My words don't come out steady and strong like Kai's, and I can't come up with real wild thoughts and put them into expert five paragraph essays like Connie.

Mr. Jones rolls his eyes so hard I think they might get stuck in the back of his head. (That's what Mami says will happen if you roll your eyes too hard.)

My butt squeezes past the last two desks. The smell of Abuelita's coffee that danced in my nose all morning is replaced with first-warm-day feet and cafeteria chocolate milk breath.

Mr. Jones looks at his watch every three seconds like Mami on Saturday mornings and Wednesday nights when I'm in the bathroom stalling for every possible minute ('cause you know, church in Spanish is a long time, even when you get there late).

The folded-up piece of paper is warm in my hands as I look up and face the class. I feel like when you eat too much too fast and everything gets stuck in that place between your throat and stomach.

The longer I stand there, the more people start to look up at me. I feel like I'm about to throw up every last champurrada I ate this morning.

"Still waiting," says Mr. Jones.

I can't mess this up. If I get another C, Mami will make my summer even worse than what it's already going to be. I open the piece of paper, but it's blank.

I take a deep breath. I look at Kai and Connie. I can do this.

"For one," I say. "I don't even know what I want to do or be like as an adult, so I don't have space in my brain to think about an 'ideal partner.' For two, my abuelita says I have to focus on ME before I can focus on someone else. She says she learned that the hard way. I don't know exactly what she means by that, but it sounds like real good advice."

Mr. Jones is clearly ready to fail me, so I try again, even though the paper I'm fake-reading is blank.

"But if I *did* have an ideal partner, I *guess* his name would be Freddy," I say. "He will have two huskies. His passion will be graffiti art, but due to family pressure, he will end up working in finance. He will read at least three days a week. He will do the dishes."

That's just what comes out of my mouth; I don't even know where I got the name Freddy. If I'm speaking from the heart, like Dad tells me to do, well, my ideal partners are Las Nerdas, and my cousin C.C. Maybe even Kai's sister, Lani, on her good days. Can't I just live with them when I grow up?

Mr. Jones doesn't seem impressed, but I technically answered every question, so he can't give me anything less than an A. Maybe a B but definitely not an F.

I quickly walk back to my seat, minimal butt cheek on the desk this time.

"Listen up, boys and girls," Mr. Jones says as he lifts up a stack of paper. "Now that we *finally* got through our presentations, we can begin our final unit. Everyone's favorite: the body systems, starting with the reproductive system. Let's see how much you already know. To end today's class, you are labeling the female body, specifically parts of the female reproductive system."

There are a few giggles, but mostly kids are all head on desks, or checking phones.

He passes the papers out. "Fill in whatever you can and turn it in when the timer goes off. You might get a pop quiz tomorrow."

I want to tell him that if he tells us we might have a pop quiz, then it's not a pop quiz, but I don't, 'cause I'm gonna hold on to my *maybe* B. I look down at the worksheet. I turn the paper upside down, but it still doesn't make sense. There are arrows pointing to squiggly lines I didn't even know existed and a giant word bank with more words of stuff that's harder to pronounce than some of the Spanish words Abuelita makes me practice Thursday nights when we watch *La Rosa de Guadalupe*. It's a soap opera with a new story every week, where some people make bad decisions, and then someone (usually a girl) gets in trouble and has to deal with consequences.

A kid from the back left shouts, "Am I ever going to have to actually know this?"

I suck my teeth at him, but I kinda want to know too.

"Congratulations, Corey," says Mr. Jones. "Because of that question, whatever you guys don't finish is now homework."

Now everyone is sucking their teeth at Corey.

"You have ten minutes, so no excuses," he says, and looks directly at me (kinda like during my first communion when the priest told the boys they could be astronauts, doctors, or lawyers, and then told the girls they could sing in the church choir. Like, what if we wanted to do more? The priest looked right at me, just like Mr. Jones is looking at me now). He turns a dial on the giant timer on his desk, except it makes this annoying ticking sound and I can't concentrate.

"This is an infringement on my rights," says Connie.

Connie always has a way of taking things too far. Like last week she told Ms. Martinez that if we didn't win the Speak Up competition, she'd run away and decompose into the exosphere. Her words exactly.

"I can't take this home," Connie says. She has two mostly annoying brothers who always go through her stuff 'cause, you know, no boundaries. That's what Kai says anyway.

"Chill," Kai says. "We have ten minutes. Let's just be efficient."

Kai always comes up with the best ideas and uses action words.

"OK, nipple, check." I say, all low like it's a bad word, 'cause it kind of feels like it.

"What?" Connie says.

"Homework," Kai says.

We label and laugh. Some kids are laughing too, and others sneak out their phones to take pictures of the worksheet.

We breeze through most of the upper body stuff. Who doesn't know this? I look up at the timer Mr. Jones set.

"We only have a few more. What's next?" Connie asks.

"V-ulva," I say. "Wait, what's the vulva?"

"I think it's part of *you know what*," says Connie. Her mom's a nurse so she knows a lot more than we do, except that's obvious, 'cause almost everything we have to label is part of the *you know what*.

Kai is the like the muscle of our group, and Connie is the brains, even though what she says is real out there sometimes. She gets it from her mom. I don't really know what I contribute. I don't know what or where the vulva is, and neither do they. Not really anyways. We've definitely never learned this one.

Mr. Jones forces the timer off even though we have two minutes left. "Start packing up, people! The rest is homework, and graded for accuracy. Every blank space is a zero!"

Maybe it's Mami and the Guatemala meteor she threw on me this morning, or 'cause I had to stand in front of everyone and present that stupid homework, but this isn't fair. I hear Abuelita's warm crinkly voice in my head—*Be a quetzal, chula*—even though real quetzales can't even figure out how to sing. My quetzal voice feels stuck inside me (kinda like my feet trapped in these fuzzy socks and sneakers on this first hot day of April, sneakers with Velcro that can't decide if they're yellow or beige, sneakers that look like I stole them from Abuelita's closet). I can't take *this* work sheet home.

Kai, Connie, and I look at each other in that do-something kind of way. Then they look at me. It's my turn to help us out for once. I'm not gonna let them down. I raise my hand.

"What now, Ma-nu-hayla?" he says, like I just asked to go to the bathroom for the fifth time or something.

"Where's the vulva?" I say, all loud like a quetzal. (I think.) I look at Kai for approval, but her head is turned up to one side in that I-don't-know-you kind of way.

"Excuse me?" Mr. Jones says, like he didn't hear me.

Only I know he heard me 'cause he gets all mad thinking I'm joking or making fun of the worksheet. But I really can't take this home. None of Las Nerdas are allowed to have phones, so our only option is to search answers to our "vulva" homework on our school computers. (What if my computer breaks and I have to take it to Mr. Dave, the school technology guy? Mr. Dave is also Gonzalo's dad, and Gonzalo is the hot nerd in my history class who rides my bus. What if the computer finally starts working and up pops my last search: *Where's the vulva?* Can you imagine how embarrassing that would be? Would he tell Gonzalo?)

"Young lady, I've had a long day," he says, even though it's only first period, so it's kind of a weird thing to say. "I don't know what you think you're doing, but—"

I start to get mad, mad at adults smooshing down my questions and feelings like chicle stuck on the bottom of your shoe. I'm mad at myself for not saying anything to Mami when she tried to change my life's destiny this morning. I have to prove to Abuelita that I DO have a quetzal voice. And I have to prove to Kai and Connie that I *can* stand up for us. I snap.

"I'm not kidding! WHAT'S A VULVA?"

Kai and Connie's eyes go all wide like they just saw La Llorona, and La Llorona mistook them for her lost children. I mean, the last time they heard me yell was, like, never. Some kids behind me start to laugh. Three girls in the hallway peek their heads in to see what's happening. Mr. Jones slams a gray pad of paper on his desk.

"That's it, you can serve lunch detention with the principal and tell him what you asked me," he says.

My lip trembles (like the time in first grade when Mami told me if I peed in my pants one more time, she'd bring them in for *show and tell*). I try to tell Mr. Jones that this is unfair—that if it's such a bad word, why is it on a worksheet?

But I open my mouth, and nothing comes out. I squeeze my eyes tight and call on my quetzal voice, the voice that every woman in my family seems to have except for me.

If I have a quetzal voice, it's buried deep in my intestines alongside the champurradas I swallowed this morning like they were the last ones on earth. Maybe they were, if Mami ever finds out about this.

TWO

No hay mal que por bien no venga.

THAT'S WHAT ABUELITA's always telling me, on the days she loses her memory, but also on the days she doesn't. I'm pretty sure she plagiarized it from the internet. Plus, I don't think it translates well, but Mami told me it means you should look at the good in any bad situation.

That's what I've been trying to do since I had to spend all of lunch plus a class period in Mr. Dupont's office. Well, the only good thing about having to hear Mr. Dupont crunch on his chips and slurp his Pepsi in between lecturing me while I quietly ate my frijoles sandwich is that I got to miss English class and mean Mr. Lewis.

When I finally get to leave, there are only two more periods in the day but none of them are with Las Nerdas, so I'm like a lost bird. That's what Abuelita is always telling me *not* to be: *No seas pájaro perdido, chulita.*

I'm mostly unscathed but the note I have to take home is burning a hole in the pocket of my dark green pants—green 'cause Mami says it reminds her of the rainforests of Guatemala. She's always trying to write songs about them on Viernes de Canto, when Mami only works half a day at her job and the rest of the afternoon is her songwriting time, where nothing can put her in a bad mood. (It's the one night of the week she doesn't dedicate to telling me what to do.) She sits in a big closet that my dad turned into a "creativity room." But who wants to hear songs about rainforests and birds? Plus, she sucks at guitar, if you ask me. She tries, I guess. And she loves it. She has lyrics written on sticky notes that she actually pastes on the wall. It's literally the only room in the house that's allowed to be messy.

Soon as I walk out to the bus loop and run to my line, Kai and Connie see me and leave their spots, even knowing they won't get their safe seat up front and will have to sit in the back with all the loud and annoying guys.

They hug me.

"Girl, where were you?" says Kai.

"We were sure Mr. Dupont called your mom," says Connie.

"Did he—call your mom?" asks Kai.

"OMG, what did she say?"

"It's worse . . . ," I say.

Reaching down, I pull out a blue piece of paper. They gasp 'cause they know it's bad. Mr. Dupont has this real mean thing he does where instead of calling your parents, he writes down what you said or did on a piece of paper. And then you have to take it home and your parents have to sign and date it. Cruel, right? At least it's Friday, and she'll be in a good mood. And if I don't show it to her tonight, I'd have to do it Saturday, but that's Saturday morning misa. I'd take guitar-playing Mami over church Mami *any* day.

"How am I going to show the blue note to my parents? To my mom? I mean, the note says *vulva*. She's totally going to look that up on the computer. This is so embarrassing," I say.

"Your mom's a medical interpreter. Don't you think—"

"Not now, Connie," I say.

Kai and Connie stare at the note like it's a booger on a desk or something. Kai reaches for it, unfolds it, and reads it out loud.

"Manula—" She stops and looks up. "He didn't even get your name right."

Connie throws her hands up, mid-chew of her thumbnail.

Kai continues, "Anyways, as I was saying. 'Manula demonstrated disrespectful behavior toward her teacher today. She disrupted class by asking her teacher where her vulva was. Twice.'"

"He didn't have to put *twice* in there," Connie says, shaking her head.

"Don't think about this now," says Kai. "Take the Nerda notebook out. Work on the Manifesto on the bus, because if we stand here and whine, they win. Remember, they can't break us."

Connie nods 'cause Kai's real good at making us feel better. Plus, she never whines or cries, about anything. I don't know what I'm really good at. Definitely not being the daughter Mami wants. (I can barely roll my r's or find my quetzal voice.) And I'm definitely never, *ever* going to sing along to her sucky songs about pájaros like she wants me to. I'm tired of being compared to birds.

A group of eighth grade boys pretend punch each other while looking at me and laugh.

"OMG, do THEY know . . . about health class?" I ask Kai and Connie.

"Everyone knows, Mani," says Connie. "Even the library kids during lunch were—"

Kai elbows Connie to stop talking.

"At least no one filmed it," Connie says, rubbing her arm. "At least I don't think anyone did."

"It's Friday," Kai says. "It'll pass over the weekend."

Kai and Connie's bus pulls up. Kids swarm the front door.

Connie puts out her pinkie finger, and her nail is all jagged from chewing on it all day. "Hurry up. I'm not missing the bus. My mom works late tonight, so she canNOT pick me up," she says.

Kai and I put our pinkies out, and we do our Nerda handshake. Our pinkies lock together. We flap our other fingers like quetzal wings and flick our thumbnails against our teeth.

They run off, their backpacks bouncing off their butts. They make it just when the doors are closing. I wish I could run after them 'cause then I wouldn't have to face the nightmare that is my bus alone. Ever since my family moved out of the apartments and into the house, we don't take the same bus anymore.

My bus pulls up all fast like Mr. Sanchez doesn't care if he hits us. Everyone starts pushing each other to get on first. Kind of like Sunday mornings when I'm with my abuelita at Sabor de Mi Tierra when the pan francés comes out hot. The afternoon bus smells twenty million times worse than the morning bus, and the morning bus is already bad. It smells like Friday sweaty gym clothes and Axe body spray. All the safe spots toward the front are taken. I look at a couple of kids with glasses in the front, but they don't even squeeze in to make room for me. You'd think glasses kids would help each other out, but I guess not.

I walk past Corey and Mason from my health and history classes. They're taking turns burping at each other across the aisle to see who burps the loudest, and it smells so gross I get dizzy—like the time Tía Gladys turned the air conditioning off last summer when she read on the internet that sweating opens your pores and makes you younger by seven and a half years or something.

I find a seat three rows from the back, which isn't as bad as the very last row.

The doors start to close, but Gonzalo skip jumps the steps. I see him mouth *Lo siento* to Mr. Sanchez and extend his arm for a fist bump. Mr. Sanchez returns it but shakes his head and tells him something in Spanish that I don't understand. Gonzalo smiles, and I swear his eyes sparkle. His hair is all colocho like he slept with neatly wrapped old lady tubos—the kind my abuelita sleeps in the nights before church when she wants to give her hair *curls the doctor ordered* (again, doesn't translate well). He hugs his skateboard so close to his body it wrinkles up his faded T-shirt.

"Gonzo!" Mason and Corey yell at the same time, and wave him over. But he just silently nods at them and sits in the row across from Genesis, who is in almost all my classes but never says anything. She reminds me of *me* before I met Kai and Connie. I start to sink into the seat and take out the Las Nerdas notebook; it's a giant, white, spiraled sketchbook with a Polaroid of the three of us from last year, the title "NERDA MANIFESTO" written in tacky red Sharpie, and pencil sketches of our secret handshake (out of order so no one figures it out and tries to copy us). It's basically a book of life rules (fifty-nine of them so far), ideas, dreams, and a whole bunch of doodles. It's my month to carry it around and come up with ideas only a Nerda would understand, so I fan the pages till I get to the very end, where we all have pages dedicated to each of us where we can include really personal stuff.

Mr. Sanchez starts to drive away. Corey takes a plastic water bottle out and tries to drink it all in one gulp. Mason and some other guys cheer him on while filming it for social media.

"Drink! Drink! Drink!" they say.

They high-five each other when he almost spits it all out, but manages not to. When the bottle is half empty, he starts flipping it onto the ground to see if it will stand up.

"Corey is sooo cute," says Jordyn from health class, who is in the row right next to mine.

"Yeah, but he's kind of a jerk," says Mia, a girl next to her, not looking up from her sketchbook.

"I bet he would be nice to me," Jordyn says, and giggles.

I want to throw up my garlic frijoles sandwich all over her. (It's like my cousin, C.C., said once, *If a guy is mean to his friends or a dog, don't date him because he'll be mean to you.*)

I think about telling Jordyn that, but she's all stupid smiles and crushed out.

I open Las Nerdas notebook to my page in the back and try to ignore her. I draw a stick figure of C.C. with exclamation points all around her, 'cause she's coming from college to stay with us next week. Other than Kai's sister, C.C. might be one of the smartest women who isn't kind of old like Ms. Martinez or old-old like my abuelita. I'm making a list of smart things C.C. has said when something small hits my forehead. I look up and Corey and Mason are rolling up pieces of paper—probably their homework—into tiny balls and throwing them. They're aiming at girls' shirts and trying to get the tiny paper balls to fall into their cleavage. The next one they throw hits Jordyn, and it falls right down her shirt. She's not smiling anymore, at least not like before. She reaches her hand in her shirt and tries to pick the paper ball out of her bra but doesn't get it.

Corey and Mason start to high-five and yell and argue about whose point that was. Gonzalo looks back, but just puts his head-phones in and looks out the window.

Corey reaches into his backpack and opens a tissue and there's a hot dog that he's had wrapped in it probably since lunch, 'cause that's usually what they have on Fridays. The tissue already melted into part of the hot dog, but he just picks out the melted flimsy parts. His friends try to grab it out of his hand. One of them manages to rip off a piece. The actual sausage falls on the ground.

"Quit it, bro!" Corey says to his friends, and he grabs it off the floor and stuffs it back into what's left of his bread. He doesn't even brush the shoe grime off.

"Hey, what's going on back there!" Mr. Sanchez yells. He's real caring and doesn't put up with kids being mean on the bus, but a few months ago they got rid of all the bus aides (Dad said the bus aides made our school district one of the safest in the country, so I don't know what that means for us now) and it's unfair for Mr. San-chez to drive AND try to control everyone.

Corey takes a big bite. He wipes his mouth with his sleeve, and then wipes his ketchup fingers on the back of the seat in front of him, the seat where Genesis is sitting. She hasn't looked back once. Gonzalo in the next seat over just hugs his skateboard against his chest and flicks the wheel with his finger.

Corey takes his two fingers and rubs them on Genesis's hair, wiping the ketchup right off of them. She doesn't seem to notice. Maybe she doesn't want to. Maybe she's like me and has trouble speaking up and finding her quetzal voice. Corey and his friends start laughing. So do a lot of girls around me, even Jordyn with the paper ball stuck in between her boobs. Then I look over at Gonzalo again, who's watching it all with his side-eye. But he just sits there, acting like it's nothing. And it isn't nothing and I want to say something. But the bus stops and Genesis gets up. Corey and Mason laugh even harder.

My jaw clenches. Then Mia looks up from her sketchbook and says, "Hey, that wasn't nice." She says it so confident (like someone who's been wearing a real bra since like fifth grade or something).

Corey turns around and looks straight at me, as if I said it.

"Um, hey," he says in a fake high-pitched voice, as if I sound like that. "I heard you don't know where your vagina is."

Everyone around me starts to laugh, even paper-ball-in-her-bra Jordyn next to me.

Why is he saying vagina? I asked about the vulva. Who doesn't know where their vagina is?

"Obviously I know where *that* is," I say in a voice so tiny it fades into the crunchy fake blue leather of the bus seats.

"You're not my type, but I can help you find it," he says.

My face gets hot and it feels like the bus is spinning in circles. Mason and his other friends start laughing. They try to high-five each other, but most of them miss. Then one of the boys says, "Gross, dude. She's so flat," and I realize they're talking about my boobs. I'm red and angry and his words hurt like when someone kicks the ball right to your stomach during kickball day in PE. I look at Gonzalo who's all eyes out the window, finger flipping his stupid skateboard wheel. I even look at Mia who's all eyes down and sketching in her notebook, again.

I hate it when people talk about my body. What I hate almost as much is not having Kai or Connie here 'cause without them I'm not good at saying stuff. Not really. I wonder if that's something you get better at when you're older or when you get your period.

Thankfully Corey gets off at the next stop. With Corey gone, his friends don't bother anyone. And I just sit there feeling the shame of flatness and not knowing where my vulva is and the burn of the blue note in my pants pocket. I look out the window and squint at the sun of the first warm day—wondering if there's a meteor on the other side and if it will at least crash into my house before dinner.

THREE

WALKING INTO MY HOUSE, the familiar smells of cafecito and spices dance in my nose. But something's different. Mami's choppy Friday guitar strumming and songs about pájaros and who knows what else are gone.

Mami's on a ladder, wiping the blades of the ceiling fan with a wet, old T-shirt. Dad's mixing and flipping things on three different sartenes all at the same time, like he learned from his great-aunt Linda, who he lived with during college to save money. Apparently, she was an architect turned owner of a Filipino fusion food truck before food trucks were a thing. Anyway, that's where Dad learned how to cook three things at one time. Says that's what won Mami over. Ew. Anyway, his family history has a lot of *This person moved here, and then I think this person moved here*, but he was born here so I think he gets why I don't want to go to Guatemala. Plus, he's the one who says, *My story starts right here in the US*.

Tía Gladys is home too. She isn't at work nannying for those kids a few neighborhoods away. She's pinching tiny yellow chilies with her fingers and letting pieces fall into a bowl. Abuelita is wiping down all the Santa Ana statues in the corner of our kitchen that she's set up like an altar.

This could only mean one thing. Someone is coming over. They always go into limpieza extreme mode when someone comes over for dinner. I squeeze the blue paper in my pocket, and hear it crinkle like plantain chips from Sabor de Mi Tierra. But I don't take it out.

"Puchica, vos. No seas malcriada, saluda," says my tía.

I fight hard not to roll my eyes, but I have to go around the room and saludar *everyone* with a kiss on the cheek, even though I just saw them all this morning before I left for school. (I feel like there should be a once-per-day maximum rule.)

"What's going on?" I say.

"We have invitados," Mami says.

"Charlie is coming," says Tía Gladys.

(Charlie is her boyfriend of the month.)

"And C.C. is coming too," she adds.

"C.C.!?" I yell. "I thought she wasn't coming until next weekend!"

"Pues, I convinced her to come a week early. I want her to meet Charlie, and he's going away next week. On *business*," she says, like it's something real important. "It was going to be a surprise for you, pero ya sabes."

I do know. Tía gets real excited and can't keep secrets. I guess that's not a bad thing, until it is. (Like once, Doña Marta, the fortune teller who sits outside of Sabor de Mi Tierra, told her that an hombre fuerte with dark hair and a full mustache would ask Tía to marry her. That just happened to fit the description of her boyfriend that month, so one night at dinner, Tía just extended her hand right in front of the guy, waiting for the ring. Right in front of everyone. I think that scared him off. We never saw him again.)

My smile is so big my face hurts thinking about C.C. I walk over to Abuelita, who hasn't really noticed that I'm home. She's sitting off in a corner wiping down all the Santa Anas with a Q-tip that she dips in a cup of holy water. I don't know if she knows that it's the holy water bottle, and even if she does, I don't know if that's allowed, but no one can really tell Abuelita what to do. Her hair is wrapped in tubos like she's getting ready to go to misa. I put my hands around her shoulders and give her a kiss on her cheek.

"Buenas tardes, Abuelita," I say with my weak *r*.

I'm not embarrassed to talk to her in Spanish 'cause she's the only person in the house, other than Dad, who doesn't give me a hard time for having an accent.

Her eyes get all wide. "Beatriz," she says, and I know she thinks I'm her other daughter, the tía I never met, the one whose bus never made it, which I guess is code for *died*. That's all they've ever told me. But she's also the reason that I can never do anything!

Ten cuidado; do you know what happened to your Tía Beatriz?

But I thought she died on in a bus—

Puchica, no seas malcriada. Don't take the bus; remember what I told you about Tía Beatriz?

Puchica, puchica, puchica. That's all I hear. That's Guatemalan for "Oh, shoot" or something like that. Anyway, that's usually how the conversations go, and they've been warning me a lot about life's dangers this year, now that my boobs are getting bigger.

"It's me, Manuela," I say.

Abuelita looks sad and I try not to take it personally. Helping her unwrap her hair out of the tubos, I try and think about what it's like to be Abuelita. For her daughter to take a bus and never come back. I guess I'd be sad.

"Apurate a ayudar, niña," Mami says. She steps down from the ladder and over to a box filled with papers, frames, books, and other random stuff.

"OK, but can I talk to you about what you said this morning?" I say.

I know that once C.C. and Mr. Boyfriend-of-the-Month come, I won't get a chance to talk alone with Mami.

"De Guatemala? Puchica, that's final. There's nothing to talk about," she says.

"But this is so unfair! Why do we have to leave *on* my birthday?" I say, about to stomp my foot on the floor, but I know better.

She sets the box down and gets closer to me and starts talking just as much with her hands as with her mouth, so I know she's getting mad. Like, *enojada*-mad, which is way worse.

"Manuela, you are going to turn thirteen this summer. Ya vas a ser una señorita and you should know where you came from. There are people I want you to meet that day. We're going, punto y final," she says, and picks up the box again.

"On my birthday? You want me to meet *your* friends on *my* birthday?"

That's the other problem: I was born at the very start of the summer. So unless there's an epic snowstorm that adds days to the end of school, my birthday is usually the last week of school, even though it's been a while since snow in general (you know, global warming). So I always have to compete with end-of-the-year stuff. At least I always celebrate with Kai and Connie. I know, being born in the summer is no one's fault. The universe chooses when and where you'll be born. Unless you're my favorite Mexican singer, Chavela Vargas, who was actually born in Costa Rica. She once said, *Nosotros los Mexicanos nacemos donde nos dé la gana.* (I read that online somewhere.)

I think that means *We Mexicans are born wherever we feel like it.* (I just know that 'cause Mami is always telling me how I need to get more ganas, like it's something you buy at a store.)

"Toma," she says, putting the box in my arms. "Take this upstairs and put it in the attic above your room. Grab the ladder from the closet."

"What? You never let me go up there. You said the polvo caused Abuelita's memory to go away, and I don't want—"

"Apurrate, tenemos invitados," she says. "Go!"

I catch a glimpse of Dad looking our way from the kitchen. I give him a silent get-me-out-of-this-one look, but he just shakes his head.

Upstairs I go.

THE ATTIC ENTRANCE is on the ceiling of my room. I grab the ladder from the hallway closet and head up. It's all Pine-Sol smelling, like someone comes up here often to keep it clean. There are two dark green bookshelves, and a yellow circular carpet in the middle. I set the box down on the carpet, and I see our boxes from when we moved from our apartment in sixth grade. I'm about to head back down, but something stops me. In the corner of my eye, I see a big square tin box with a colorful quetzal bird and pyramids and volcanos in the background, like the ones on pretty much every

Guatemalan tourism brochure. I know, 'cause Tía prints them out from the internet at the library for Abuelita sometimes.

The tin box is sandwiched between books in Spanish and maps so wrinkly like they've been opened and closed a million times. On the bottom, it says, SEREMOS MILLONES and UN DÍA CANTARÁ in black Sharpie, and I recognize Mami's handwriting. I open it. There're pictures and stacks of envelopes and letters. Like, written by hand. Who does that anymore?

I take out the stack of envelopes and open the one on top. There's a letter and some newspaper clipping. It's addressed to our old apartment.

Querida Isabela

That's Mami. I look at the envelope more closely, but there's no name, only an address from Guatemala. I get confused at first, but then I remember that the date is written differently in Guatemala, with the day written first, and then the month. It's dated a few months before I was born. I skip to the very end of the letter. (That's like reading the last page of a book; you can't do that, but I do.)

It's from her sister, Beatriz. I read it slowly. There are words I am not sure of, since it's all in Spanish.

I'm sorry it took me so long to write. I made it to San Marcos. They advised me not to write at first, because of what we are reporting on. The work is dangerous, but we knew that, right? I didn't know if I could do it without you. I didn't know if I was strong enough, but I met a photojournalist, Mirabel, and we have kept each other company. I asked her how long she will work here, and she said until all the disappeared come home. Her words

float in my chest and flutter against my rib cage like wings. You
wrote that in one of your songs right before you left.

I am including my first article that got published in La Patria.
I cried and laughed when I saw my name. My head still hurt
from when the police descended down on us with their fists
and ends of guns, but my heart is filled with the beautiful
sounds of all those women standing firm and risking so much.

What work is dangerous? Police? Guns? I look at the article
stapled to the letter: "Thousand March Against Femicide." I don't
understand it, and plus, femicide sounds like a cleaning product. I
make it a point to look it up later. In the picture, there's a giant
group of mostly women. They all look like they're shouting over
each other, but saying the same thing. They're holding signs that I
can barely see 'cause the paper is so faded, but I think they say, "Tengo
Miedo," which means *I'm scared.* Then I see a woman who looks like
she could be Tía Beatriz, based on a few wallet-sized pictures Abuelita keeps in her coin pouch. She's holding a microphone up to someone and has a notebook under her armpit. Her eyes glitter, even in
the faded paper of the picture, like Abuelita's when she gets stuck
in the old times and starts dreaming and singing in Spanish. I keep
reading.

I am not mad at you, Isa. I miss you. Please write to me at
the address on the envelope. You must be having your baby
any day now. One day I will meet her. One day we will sit
around a big round table in a house full of light, and Santa

Ana statues and quetzales, and Mamita's singing. I'll prepare us coffee, just the way we like it, with powdered milk that's always sweeter. Around us will be all the women we've ever known, and all the women who haven't made it home yet. I know we will one day be at the same table again, perhaps when all the disappeared return.

> *Primero una voz, y luego seremos millones,*
> *Beatriz.*

I don't understand the last part, but it's what's written on the box. Something about a voice and a million of something. I recognize it from one of Mami's Friday night songs. I remember 'cause her singing kept me up real late one night when she thought everyone had gone to sleep. I look at the envelope again. My parents moved here before I was born. The letter was sent here, to this country, but that can't be. Tía Beatriz had already died in a bus accident—the bus that never made it home. That's what Mami told me.

I read it and reread. Maybe I misread the date. But each time I read it, it's the same. My whole life I've been told that she died on a bus, or that the bus never came home. Did Mami respond? I start to look through the stack of envelopes and dates. They don't stop till I'm five years old. How could—

"¡Apurrate, niña!" Mami shouts. "What are you doing? ¡Ya vienen los invitados!"

Stuffing the picture in my pocket, I put the envelope back and head down the ladder. I open the Nerda notebook to my personal page at the back, and slip in the picture, making a note to myself to tape it down when I go back to school on Monday. I look up at my ceiling, and the little room of lies and secretos that has existed above my head all this time.

I can't ask Mami about it, 'cause I wouldn't even know where to start. I hold my own secreto on my tongue and keep it there like it is the last bit of flan.

FOUR

Tía tells me to put a plate at the head of the table for Charlie, as she fluffs out Abuelita's hair at the kitchen table. Usually no one sits at the ends, unless we need more space. I don't know why they are treating him like a king when he's only the novio of the month. But I don't say anything.

"Chuliiiiiiiiiiita," Abuelita says as she looks up at me and reaches up to grab my face and force it into a smile. "Sonrie que si no, vas a tener arrugas."

She tells me to smile 'cause if not I'll get wrinkles. For one, that doesn't make any sense, but for two, I can't smile. I can't get Tía Beatriz's letter out of my head. It's swirling in my brain like one of those mystery licuados Abuelita makes in the blender when we leave her alone for two minutes.

Two slow knocks on the door, then super fast knocks, then three slow ones.

Our secret knock!

I run to the door, open it, and throw my arms around C.C. to give her the biggest hug. I breathe in real hard 'cause this is what college, being a woman, and independence must smell like. We step back and look at each other, then giggle, then hug again.

C.C. is wearing a white bra *over* a baggy "This is what a FEMINIST looks like" shirt. She has jeans that Mami would never let me wear. They hug her legs and they're torn in all the right places. Her hair's in a messy black bun and she has a big purple streak in it.

"I'm home!" she yells and looks past me at everyone at the table and sets down her backpack and suitcase by the door. Abuelita does the sign of the cross and Mami and Tía whisper about her outfit.

"What are you wearing?" says my tía, pointing to C.C.'s bra over her shirt. "You're lucky nothing happened to you on the way, wearing *that*."

I want to tell her that what people wear isn't an invitation for anything, 'cause I heard C.C. say that once, but I stop myself. Abuelita, Tía, and Mami all look at C.C. like all the rosaries and the Santa Ana statue they just finished cleaning are going to catch on fire. Dad says, "Good to have you home, C.C." and gives her a kiss on the forehead. C.C. moves around the table to give everyone a hug and kiss 'cause she has to saludar everyone too.

Then Mami tells her to take her stuff upstairs and to please change and start to unpack since we just finished cleaning and Tía's invitado is coming.

Dad helps carry the suitcase upstairs, but then leaves us alone in my room to catch up. "Just come back down in ten minutes, OK?" he says. "The *invitado* is coming." He makes quotes with his fingers around "invitado" and laughs. We laugh too.

C.C. opens her suitcase and it's an explosion of books and colorful clothes.

"Check this out, Maní." She says my name with an accent on the *i*, which means peanut in Spanish. I used to not like it, but then she told me that you can crack your tooth on a peanut, so then I felt a little more powerful. She holds a white dress that looks like she rode her bike through a puddle of red paint or something. "I threw paint on it and wore it at this reproductive rights protest," she says, and puts her hands on her hips and sways side-to-side as if pretending the dress is still on her.

I don't really know what those two words mean together, but C.C. is real smart, so I just let her talk. The more she talks, the more I just want to be in her skin and live in the world the way she does.

"I'll be right back. I need to go to the bathroom," she says, and leaves my room, her suitcase wide open.

Mami is always telling me not to be a metida, but I notice a lime-green lacy bra buried under some socks and books that all have *feminist* or *feminism* in the titles.

I grab on to the strap but it's stuck underneath everything. The strap doesn't give. I pull harder and it bounces into my hands like when you stretch a rubber band with your other hand and let it go. It's soft and the color is even brighter up close. I can't picture C.C. wearing such a girly lacy bra. There's a wire like the ones Kai and I found in her sister's room once, and soft boob pillows that seem like they'd be real comfortable. I hear C.C. opening the bathroom door, so I quickly stuff it under my pillow.

C.C. lets me look through pictures on her phone while she separates the dirty and clean laundry in her suitcase. But then I remember the word "femicide" from Tía Beatriz's letter. I open Google on her phone and type in *what does femicide mean?* I scroll through the different things that come up and land on the sentence that catches my eye. "Femicide: the killing of women and girls." How is that a thing? Suddenly, it's like there's a rock in my stomach. Is that what Tía Beatriz's article was talking about? Does that happen in Guatemala? Where else? Does Mami know?

A few minutes later, we hear the doorbell and three knocks. C.C. and I look at each other and scream, "El invitado!" and fall on the bed laughing. I'm having so much fun with C.C. that for a moment I forget about the secret letters and the gross boys on the bus and the wrinkled blue vulva note in my pocket.

We run downstairs as Dad gets up to the open the door.

"Those are knocks of an hombre bien, pero *bien* fuerte," says Tía as she follows right behind Dad.

I expect a big strong man with muscles ripping out of his shirt, but instead, he's just a regular guy, except the first two buttons of his shiny, light blue collared shirt are open and his tie is undone. And he's got epic sweat stains that run almost halfway down his body. He looks like he's some guy in one of those real bad gringo sitcoms that I see when I'm clicking through channels trying to find *La Rosa de Guadalupe* for Abuelita.

After a bunch of *mucho gustos* and *nice to meet you's*, Tía takes his briefcase and leads him to the table.

"Chicas, this is Charlie. He's a lawyer," she says, glaring at C.C.'s bra over her shirt, 'cause she didn't make herself more *decente* for the invitado.

I don't know why adults always introduce themselves by what they do. It's real annoying. Maybe I should say, *Hi, I'm Mani. I get in trouble for asking about weird body parts that no one seems to know. Oh, and I don't want to go to Guatemala.*

"¡Hola!" he says a little too loud, like we're not right in front of him. I notice his *h* is way heavier than mine. "I'm Charlie, but you can call me Robert-o."

I don't know how you get Robert-o from Charlie, but I don't ask him. I just say hi 'cause I don't want Mami to call me a *malcriada*.

"No sean malcriadas, saluden," my tía says.

We each go in for the obligatory kiss on the cheek, but he kisses both cheeks, 'cause he learned Spanish on a college spring break trip to Spain or something.

C.C. and I settle in our chairs, and he sits right across from us. He turns to C.C. and says, "Carolina, your mother has told me you are a very independent young woman with a mind of her own," but he says it all weird like he's saying, *Carolina, I heard you have a wart on your toe.*

C.C. doesn't say anything, 'cause there's no real question. Then he starts asking Mami where the bathroom is in Spanish, like she doesn't speak English, except his Spanish is worse than mine.

A few minutes later, Dad whistles as he moves the chicken from the pot to a big bowl. He closes the oven door with his foot. Mami gives him a look 'cause it's malcriado to do anything with your feet, but he winks at her and she smiles. (He's the only person who Mami doesn't get mad at. No sé, but maybe it's 'cause he lies and tells her she's a good singer.) He brings the chicken to the table. Mami starts to get up to help, but he puts his hand on her shoulder like he's telling her to stay where she is. He comes back with more plates in his hand. Mami nods and smiles. They talk in all smiles, nods, and touches, and I don't know how that works. I guess she saves all the cuchillo-sharp words for me.

"Can you please pass the Rosa de Jamaica juice?" I ask my tía, who is passing all the chicken and plátanos to Robert-o who's serving himself like there's no one else at the table. We're all watching and waiting for him to hurry up, but he just sets the plates next to himself when he's done.

"Total gringo move," says C.C., real quiet in my ear.

I almost laugh out loud, except then he takes the biggest, crispiest piece of plátano that's still dripping in oil—the one Dad always leaves on the sartén extra-long for me—and I want to tip my Rosa de Jamaica juice all over Robert-o's lap.

"Dilo en español," says Mami.

She's always trying to get me to show off my busted Spanish to people who suck even more than I do. I do my best, but I hate being put on the spot. But maybe if I do what she says and say it in Spanish, she'll at least be nice enough to hear me out later about why going to Guatemala on my birthday is the worst idea ever.

But before I can say anything, Abuelita stands up, and we all look at her, 'cause we never know what she's gonna say.

"Did everyone forget their manners? No somos gringos malcriados. Let's give thanks for the food. It didn't grow in the supermarket," she says.

Robert-o puts down his fork and looks at us to see what he should do. He's so still he doesn't even swallow the crispy plátano he just stuffed in his mouth. (The one that was meant for me.) We all clasp our hands and bow our heads like we're in church.

"¡Señooooooooor!" she says, almost yelling, and puts her hands up above her head.

Here we go.

My stomach starts to growl and Mami and Tía look at each other. This is going to be like that time she prayed for fifteen minutes and all the food got cold. I look at the plátanos. They won't be hot anymore. Even the second crispiest one (also meant for me) will be soggy. Mami tells Abuelita that we already graced the food, thinking she might be able to fool her, which is kinda messed up if you ask me, but I hope it works. Robert-o is looking around like he's waiting for someone to explain, but no one bothers to let him in, so he stabs the next piece of plátano with his fork.

"OK, hijitas. I'll keep it short," says Abuelita. "I know we have guests."

She asks God to watch over us and to guide C.C. and me on the right path. We fist-bump 'cause we get a shout-out, but then Abuelita gets sad and weird. It happens sometimes.

"Y seguimos luchando, Jesusito, hasta que regresen todas las desaparecidas," she says.

Hasta que regresen las desaparecidas. Until all the disappeared return. That was in my dead tía's letter. I feel a chill, I feel—

"¡Wow, que delicisiooooso!" Robert-o says with his mouth now full of chicken and beans. Then he gets some black bean on his work shirt and Mami hands him one of the nice cloth napkins. He rolls up the end, dunks it in his glass of water and starts to dab his shirt. C.C. kicks my foot under the table, and I bite my lip to stop myself from laughing.

"¡Compórtense!" Mami whisper-screams.

Robert-o doesn't seem to notice that he just interrupted Abuelita (which is almost as bad as interrupting the priest during misa. You just don't do that). He starts telling us about riding his motorcycle through Central America back in the 90s even though he didn't speak

Spanish. "Not as good as I do now," he says, and winks at Tía. She blows an air kiss his way, and I want to throw up.

C.C. and Abuelita side-eye him. My eyes want to roll at him so hard, 'cause C.C. says that gringos always have annoying stories about riding motorcycles through Latin America. But to be honest, I kinda like his story. I've never heard of anyone who didn't seem afraid of Central America, except for Abuelita. I'm wondering if he's making it up.

But then Abuelita looks up from her plate and stares at him as if just noticing him for the first time. We all look at each other.

"Mamita," Mami says to her. "Estás aquí con nosotros," like that's code for *don't say anything embarrassing*.

Abuelita looks straight at Robert-o and points her finger at him. "And you? Who are you?" she asks. She looks him straight in his eyes. Then she looks around the room. "What do you all have to say for yourselves? Who is this man eating at my table?"

"Doña Lota, it's me, Robert-o. I'm practically your son-in-law," he says.

I bite my lip. Abuelita totally forgot she just met Robert-o like fifteen minutes ago. I don't know what's worse, I think—to be Robert-o right now, or to be me with the crinkled vulva note in my pocket.

"My son-in-law? Well then whiten and straighten those teeth, Roberto, porque nosotros los guatemaltecos somos gente guapa," Abuelita says, catching a glimpse of herself in the big mirror above the table opposite to her almost as proof, and then starts singing a song about a beautiful girl from a *rancho grande*.

Rosa de Jamaica juice squirts out of my nose a little with each giggle I can't control. Mami pinches the side of my thigh under the table. Then she says, "Sorry, Roberto. That's just part of the song," which is a lie.

I don't know if he believes her. But then Abuelita looks straight at me.

"And you, chulita. Get that hair out of your face. Pareces La Llorona," she says.

C.C. starts laughing, for real this time. Mami gets up and lowers Abuelita's pointing finger and helps her sit back down. Then it's silent except for the sound of Robert-o scraping the frijoles with his fork (which is awkward, like when someone farts during a math quiz that no one studied for).

Dad must feel bad for Robert-o, 'cause he starts asking him boring questions about his job.

"Sentate recta, niña," Tía says. She tells me to sit straight, 'cause no boy is ever going to notice me all hunched over like a vieja. Gross, I think. Why would I want any boy to notice me? And then I think about Corey on the bus and the other boys calling me flat-chested and I get real mad all over again.

I stand to clear the plates, 'cause I'm the youngest at the table, and that's how it works when you have invitados.

Robert-o keeps scraping the leftover frijoles juice on the plate with his fork, even though the pan francés is sitting right in front of him, getting colder and harder by the second. He looks up at Mami. "Excuse me, Isabela, do you have any butter for the bread?" he says.

Puchica, I know I'm not good at being Guatemalan or anything, but I don't think you need to have an ounce of Guatemalan blood to know that the bread is for soaking up the frijoles, not for decoration or for putting butter.

"Roberto, isn't my niece getting such a nice cuerpecito?" Tía Gladys says.

All the mad feelings boil up in me and start to push against my ears and eyes all over again, and I want to drop the plates right there on the floor; the one they just triple mopped that still reeks of lemon-scented cleaner. I don't want plate-scraping Robert-o to look or think about my body. But he doesn't look at me, which is good.

I want Mami to tell her to stop, to get mad at her.

But instead, she says, "Así es. We need to go get new clothes. Her chest has grown a lot. I don't want her to have any problems at school."

How did she just agree? How did she just say that? And why would a large chest size mean problems? I turn around and look at her.

"You're not a little girl anymore," she says. "Maybe we'll get you a real bra too."

"Stop it," I say, in a voice tinier than the one I managed to squeak out on the bus.

It's so unfair that adults think they can just talk about how your boobs have grown right in front of you like you're not even there. First, they're all proud calling you a woman, but then they're giving themselves the sign of the cross and talking about it like it's a big nasty disease or something. Puchica, they're such hypocrites, I think.

Dad tells them to stop 'cause I obviously don't want them to talk about my body, but his voice is no match for two quetzales. My face burns. They're talking about my body like it's a piece of fruit, like I'm not even there. They have no right. And I want to say something so bad, but my throat feels tight and like it's on fire, just like earlier on the bus, and nothing comes out.

"Ay Dios, y esas caderitas," Tía says.

"Mamá, ya, para. Maní doesn't like that," C.C. says, trying to stop them.

Now they start talking about my butt like it's a balloon at my old neighbor's quinceañera party, talking about how it just keeps filling out.

Just stop just stop.

I think about the bus, and disgusting Corey telling me he can help me find "it," and the other boy calling me flat. I think about the ketchup in Genesis's hair, and the boys throwing paper balls down girls' shirts. I think about all the times just today when my voice was so tiny that I couldn't find my quetzal voice.

I slam the plates down in the sink, and some crack.

With all eyes on me, I shove my hand in my pocket and pull out the principal's vulva note. It's warm and crinkly and now greasy from my dirty plate fingers. I hold it out and lift it in the air.

"Stop it!" I yell. "I need you to sign this. I got in trouble because I didn't know where in the vagina the vulva was . . . well, because I asked my teacher where it is, and I still don't know, and today sucked. And I don't want to go to Guatemala! Why do we have to go? And stop talking about my body!" I say, crying now and my voice all angry and choppy. I'm desperate. *Anything* to get them to stop talking about my body. Maybe they won't be as mad, 'cause somatando platos and breaking them on purpose is like way, way worse, right? Or maybe I'll tell everyone about the letter I just found in the attic, and expose Mami and her secrets. Call her a liar, that I know Tía Beatriz didn't die before they moved here. Maybe then they'll stop talking about my body. But I stop myself. Maybe 'cause the letters were folded away in a tin box up in the attic, and I get the feeling I wasn't meant to find them. Plus, then I probably wouldn't be able to read the rest.

Everyone's staring at me, and the words don't form. Dad walks toward me and puts his hand on my shoulder. For exactly three seconds it's comforting, like when you've had the worst itch at the bottom of your foot and you finally scratch it. But now I wish I could shove each word back into my mouth, syllable by syllable, and go back in time. The color flushes out of Mami's face. I think maybe she'll say sorry, maybe she'll hug me, but she doesn't.

She stands slowly and starts walking toward me. "Te dije. That's the best week to go visit. There are people you need to meet. And don't talk *porquerías* at the dinner table," she says.

"Why do I have to meet people I have nothing to do with? And why is vulva a *porquería*?" I say, tripping on my *r*'s and feeling tears come to my eyes. "It's part of the female reproductiveness system!"

I feel emboldened to raise my voice at her. But just then Dad puts his arms around both of us, and my almost-words get muffled in his sleeve. Usually, he can solve any problem between me and Mami. (It's what he does all day at work. He mediates environment conflicts, whatever that means.) But before he can say anything, Abuelita's over at the window and she's crying. We all look at her, confused.

Then she walks back over to me and grabs my right hand with the note with both of her warm hands. "Manuelita, I wonder about all the things I could have done if I had just known some things. If people had just told me. Two generations later, and you still don't know what your vagina has."

There's a part of me that wants to laugh 'cause Abuelita said "vagina," but her cries get louder, and I realize that this is about much more. "Mi Beatriz," she starts to say, softly, between tears, and walks back to the window. I think it's weird how she can remember me one second and think I'm her other daughter the next.

Mami goes to hug her. Tía gets up and puts a hand on her back and just starts to rub. Then Abuelita starts to call them by other names, and they start to cry a little too, because it's hard when her mind goes from sharp to all mushy like the plantains that are left after Robert-o took all the crispy ones, and there's nothing you can do to pull her back from the past, except hug her.

"Don't you feel bad? Now she's talking about Beatriz," Mami says.

I don't want Abuelita to cry, but why should I feel bad? All I've ever known about Tía Beatriz is that she got on a bus that crashed or never made it, and then everyone had to up and leave, and they've never been back since. I always thought that was the end of the story. Basta.

But I know from the letter that it's not true, at least not the part about her dying or never making it, before I was born. My words drown in my tears, snot, and hiccups. I can't think of anything that will make my abuelita feel better.

"Is this what you wanted?" Mami says. Her words stomp on my heart.

No, I think. All I want is my period and to be a woman already. I don't want people to talk about my body like it's a bunch of different pieces of a puzzle. I want to sit at a table and be like one of the women, but not at some Guatemalan table—at a table where everyone knows I can't roll my *r*'s and can't really understand jokes in Spanish and *doesn't* make fun of me for it.

Dad puts his arm around my shoulder again, but this time I push his hand away, which I never do. Abuelita stares out the window like Tía Beatriz is somewhere outside and will walk in any minute and everything will be OK.

I try and think about how she must feel, staring out the window like that.

I go to hug her, but Mami's look makes me stop. She yanks the blue paper out of my hand. "We're not done talking about this."

I sit down next to C.C., who can't seem to get a word in. Angry-sad snot bubbles start to form at the tip of my nose, but I also feel relieved, 'cause at least it's not in my pocket anymore.

FIVE

*Seventy days till Guatemala
and my life is ruined,
a.k.a. Guatemala*

ON MONDAY MORNING, I'M WAITING in the cafeteria for the first bell to ring when the intercom blares in my ears. Mr. Dupont is going on about how he hopes everyone had a good weekend, is ready to learn, what beautiful weather, please put backpacks in lockers, and "Ladies, shirts should cover the stomach and skirts should reach the knees." A few girls who aren't all faces-in-their-phones roll their eyes at the speaker above the cafeteria doors.

The morning duty teachers open the doors and we're finally allowed to go to our lockers. When I get to mine, I see a giant V written in Sharpie, the smell still strong like it was just written a few seconds before.

A couple of boys laugh and rush into first period. With the hallways clearing, I quickly lick my thumb and try to rub it off, but Sharpie is strong like the Vicks Abuelita rubs on me if I cough once.

Then the 8:10 a.m. warning bell rings and I see Kai and Connie coming toward me. Soon as they get to their lockers, Mr. Robertson, the seventh-grade administrator, comes out of nowhere.

"Instrument in the locker, young lady. Let's make today a learning day!"

Kai puts her ukulele in her locker, even though the boys are allowed to walk around with their footballs and skateboards, and he doesn't say anything to them. Connie and I look at her in that aren't-you-going-to-say-something kind of way, but Kai just shrugs.

"Pick your battles, Nerdas," she says.

We do our Nerdas handshake and walk to first period health together. That's when I tell them about Mason and Corey on the bus last Friday and Corey telling me he could help me find my vagina, which still makes me feel sick inside like when you drink horchata that's been sitting out in the sun.

Mr. Jones doesn't even say "Good morning" or acknowledge us walking in. A couple of kids put their homework in the bin, but I don't 'cause with everything that happened this weekend, finding the vulva on that stupid worksheet was the last thing on my mind.

The final bell rings, and about one minute later, Mr. Dupont gets back on the intercom to start the Pledge of Allegiance and morning announcements.

Some boys from the front row pretend to cough and say "Vagina" the entire time, but not loud enough for Mr. Jones to hear.

It's VULVA, I want to say, but I stay quiet.

The morning announcements drag on and on, but Kai speaks up before they're done. "Mr. Jones, can you please tell them to sto—"

Mr. Jones cuts her off and looks directly at me. "Ma-nu-hayla, you turned our assignment into a joke and invited this sort of behavior," he says. "Remember last unit we talked a lot about actions and consequences? If you invite someone, don't be surprised if they show up at your door."

I don't know what he's talking about, 'cause I didn't invite anyone anywhere. And I definitely didn't tell them to call me "vagina girl." But the words just get caught in my throat and I feel my jaw clench.

Mr. Jones turns on his screen and there's a collective groan and a lot of eye rolling. We're going to watch those cringey videos of teenagers doing stupid things, and then we have to answer questions about which thing was the stupidest of all.

Five minutes into the video, I look around the room to see who's sleeping. But then I see the "vagina girl" boys. They're looking straight at me, and one of them has a V up to his mouth. I don't really know what it means, but I know it's gross.

"Shut up," I say between my teeth, even though they didn't really say anything.

Mr. Jones pauses the video and turns the lights on.

"Ma-nu-hayla," he says.

"They're doing gross things with their hands," is all I manage to say.

There're a few laughs, mostly among the boys.

"Ma-nu-hayla," he says again. "If you're going to do things that distract boys, don't be surprised if they get distracted." Then he says, "*Ladies* and gentlemen, remember you are here to learn, not to distract those of the opposite sex."

I look over at Kai. I guess she's picking her battles, and didn't pick this one. I want to show her I'm brave enough to speak up.

"But what did I—"

"Now that we're on the subject, look at these, what do you call these . . . spaghetti straps you ladies are wearing?" He looks directly at A'niya, who was just minding her business. "I mean, that's like wearing nothing if you ask me."

No one asked you, I think.

Heads lift and all eyes go to A'niya, but Jordyn who sits next to her is pretty much wearing the same shirt, and no one says anything. I think it's 'cause A'niya's boobs have been adult size since like fourth grade, but that doesn't make Mr. Jones's comment fair. At first Jordyn looks all proud 'cause she didn't get called out, but then she shrinks in her seat. She's real stuck-up and a little mean sometimes, but maybe she thinks this is unfair.

But A'niya doesn't shrink like Jordyn. Instead, she blows a big bubble with her chicle from the fresa Chupa Chups I saw her eating this morning when my bus pulled in. From where I'm sitting, I think she's looking right at Mr. Jones. She doesn't shrink or squirm. The bubble bursts, and a few kids start laughing. Mr. Jones rolls his eyes and wipes his forehead with the back of his hand in that I-don't-know-what-to-say kind of way.

"Remember, you're here to learn," is all he finally manages to say, tripping on his words, as he presses play on the video.

I wonder how you get brave like A'niya. How you can speak up without saying anything at all.

SIX

By THIRD PERIOD SCIENCE, I keep thinking about the mean boys in health, and about A'niya not shrinking at Mr. Jones's unfair words. I'm so distracted that I don't care about the experiment we're about to do where we blow up gummy bears.

Mr. Neimar gives one gummy bear to each student and he doesn't let us even pick the color we want.

"Can I eat mine?" a boy says from the back row all loud.

"For the fifth time, no," says Mr. Neimar, but it's the first time he's saying it.

Then he adds, "I bought an exact amount," which is real confusing 'cause I didn't think you could buy gummy bears individually. We go to Sabor de Mi Tierra for groceries, and there are no gummy bears there, and even if there were, Mami never buys me junk food. She says they're bad for your health, but everyone in school eats them and they're all taller than me, so no sé.

Mr. Neimar asks for volunteers. No one raises their hand, but to be fair, he didn't say what for. He points to Genesis, the girl from my bus, plus my English and history classes. He looks at his roster, even though it's April.

"Gene-Jennifer, come up here, please, and bring your gummy bear," he says.

He gets it wrong, even though her pencil case has her name written in big bold letters: **GENESIS.**

She doesn't say anything and doesn't budge.

"Up here, J-ennifer," he says and points to the front of the classroom. "With your gummy bear."

Nada.

I wonder why she doesn't correct him. Maybe she doesn't have an abuelita to tell her to use her quetzal voice. Maybe—

"Did you eat the gummy bear after I explicitly asked everyone NOT to eat the gummy bear?" Mr. Neimar asks, though it doesn't feel like a question. Not really.

Then her jaw moves, and I think she's about to talk, but she's actually chewing.

He coulda asked the thirty-one other kids in here who *didn't* eat their gummy bears to volunteer, but instead he just gives up and says, "That's it," and starts to pass out the dusty textbooks for random busywork, like he knew he was going to do this all along. I don't really care; I'm just happy he doesn't call on me to stand in front of the class.

"Actually, Jennifer, you can sit outside," Mr. Neimar says.

Genesis's face gets all red and she looks like she wants to crawl into her pencil case with her name on it. But she doesn't move.

"Young lady, out, right now," he says.

This time the whispering stops, and all heads turn to Genesis. It's so quiet I don't even want to blink 'cause for real someone might hear it. Mr. Neimar is waiting. We're all waiting.

"Out!" he says, this time yelling.

But she doesn't get up. Instead, she swallows the last bit of gummy bear, holds on to the cross on her neck like it's gonna speak for her, and gives the tiniest head shake.

Mouths open. No one ever stands up to Mr. Neimar.

He starts to walk toward the back of the room until he's standing right in front of Genesis. He leans over her desk, his lips twitching a little like he's about to say something but can't figure out what. Then he rolls his eyes and walks back to his desk and mumbles something maybe only the front row can hear.

How does a quiet, gummy-bear-eating girl stand up to Mr. Neimar without even saying anything, but I can't even stand up to Mami and tell her what I want? For the rest of class, I think about all the ways I can get out of going to Guatemala, even though I'm in big trouble for the whole vulva thing.

I think about A'niya and C.C. and Genesis. Even Kai, who doesn't have her period yet, but can sometimes speak up no problem. And what it really means to have a quetzal voice even when you say nothing at all.

What it would take for me to be brave like that.

CONNIE AND I CLAIM our usual spot at the empty table with the beanbag chairs in the library while Kai returns books. We rush to sit and laugh as we wiggle into the chairs. They're hidden behind a cart of old encyclopedias, so Ms. Nesbit, the librarian, never sees us sneak in our lunches.

"Do you think we're brave?" I ask Connie in my quietest voice, as Kai starts to walk over.

"Umm, of course," says Connie.

I look back, making sure Kai is still too far to hear. "I mean, do we stand up to, you know, things?" I take the Nerda notebook and open to a blank page, careful not to open the back page with the picture I found in the attic.

But Kai hears, like always. She says she has bionic ears or something, 'cause she's taken music classes her whole life, so that trained her ears to be real sensitive.

"This is about Guatemala, isn't it?" says Kai.

"Maybe?"

"Just look at your mom straight in the eyes and say 'no.' She can't force you on the airplane. That's, like, illegal or something," says Connie.

I doodle on the edges of a paper jutting out of the Nerda notebook. I pull it out a little, and I see it's the graphic organizer for the Speak Up project—the one Ms. Martinez gave us last week that's due tomorrow.

Then it clicks. I know how I can stand up to Mami and get out of going to Guatemala. I hadn't really sold it that hard before. She doesn't know how competitive Speak Up is. If we had a real possibility of winning, how could Mami say no? If we win, I can't actually go to Guatemala. The camp for winners is at the end of June. Mami obviously doesn't care about my impending period and womanhood or ripping me away from my best friends for the summer, but maybe if she knows there are serious academic benefits and it'll look good on college applications and—

But it'll only work if Kai and Connie are on board.

"I have a better idea. Remember the Speak Up thing Ms. Martinez told us about last week?" I say.

They nod. I slide the Nerda notebook to the middle of the table.

"Yeah, aren't we picking our projects soon?" Kai says.

"Yeah. The only way to go is to win. And we CAN win it," I say.

"Really?" Connie says, spitting out the hangnail she's been chewing on.

Kai jumps out of her seat. "Yes! Plus, we can tell our moms it will look really good on college applications a million years from now. What immigrant mom would say no to that?"

"We just have to think about something we want to stand up to, or speak up about," I say. I push my glasses back so they sit snug against that space between my eyes. That's my serious look. But inside I'm glowing and jumping up and down 'cause I came up with an idea they love.

One minute later, our page is still blank other than the squiggly lines I draw when I'm thinking (or thinking about thinking). We start to nod, but the actual ideas don't come. Not for me, at least. We carefully open our lunch boxes. Leftovers, again.

After we finish, I hear Ms. Nesbit talking to someone. Genesis is carrying a wrinkly plastic bag, and I can see her Tupperware poking out of the holes. Ms. Nesbit makes her leave it at the front desk. She's looking around for a place to sit. Most of the tables are taken up by the Magic Card and chess kids. I poke my head over the encyclopedias. We make eye contact for a second, but I quickly lower my head.

I feel bad for her with Mr. Neimar calling her out like that. I want to ask her to sit with us, but no one has ever joined Las Nerdas other than the three of us, and I don't know what Kai and Connie would think. Genesis finds a spot next to the cart overflowing with broken computers and tangled chargers.

We're finally throwing ideas back and forth about what our Speak Up project could be, but nothing feels right, so we decide to go to Kai's place after school to work on it. The only time Mami lets me hang out with friends on a school night is if it's for homework.

We move on. Kai takes out her colorful pens. I flip to the next blank page. Today's a big deal 'cause we're on rule sixty of our Nerda Manifesto, and sixty is a big number.

"I have an idea for rule sixty," says Kai. "I know it's too much to wish that we all get our periods at the same time this summer or on the same day or anything. So, I think whenever one of us gets it first, we have a sleepover, so we can all get it right after."

Connie and I look at each other. I don't really know how that's possible.

Kai sees that we're confused, so she says, "My sister said that tides on the moon control your period."

I think that's the craziest thing I've ever heard, but like I said, Kai's sister is real smart, so it's gotta be true. We all agree and Kai starts writing it down.

RULE #60: WHICHEVER NERDA GETS HER PERIOD FIRST HOSTS A SLEEPOVER SO THAT MOON TIDES GIVE THE OTHER NERDAS THEIR PERIODS TOO.

I've still got questions about timing and moon tide science but it sounds so good, I'm not about to mess up the moment with my negative vibes. Kai writes *moon tide* in eight different colors and starts to draw actual half-moons around the phrase.

"You've got ten minutes till lunch period ends!" Ms. Nesbit yells from her desk.

"I have an idea," says Connie. "For today's closure, let's think of something we are each looking forward to. I'll set the timer on my watch. Then, when it goes off, we each say it at the same time."

It'll be kind of hard to really hear everyone if we all talk at the same time, but I tell her that's a good idea. I look up at the ceiling and really think hard but nothing comes to mind.

"I'll go first," says Connie, even though she said we'd all go at the same time. But that's Connie. "My dad finally agreed to let me try out for the soccer team!"

We lean in for a group hug, 'cause this is huge. Connie could be like the most famous soccer player in the world already if her parents agreed to let her play. They say it's no place for girls to be running so fast and falling down all the time. (Parents can be real sexist sometimes.)

"My mom said they'd let me take ukulele classes, even though I've been pretty good at teaching myself with YouTube," says Kai.

We smile at each other and kick our feet together under the table.

"Any luck on the hair situation?" I ask.

She shakes her head. "They're never going to let me cut my hair," says Kai. "What if I just cut it up to here." She puts her hand up against her ear.

Even though Kai's parents were apparently radical activists back in the day, they have some real backward ideas on how girls have to have long hair, or else they look like boys.

"What about you, Mani?" says Connie.

I keep thinking, but then I remember the green lacy bra I took out of C.C.'s suitcase and put under my pillow. I think of the letter from my dead tía. I could show them the picture taped to my page, but I stop myself. Where would I start? It feels like something I want to keep close inside my heart where no one can see it. I think of Abuelita's words, *Hasta que regresen las desaparecidas*—until all the disappeared return—like she plagiarized it from the letter or something. And even though I always want to be with Kai and Connie, right now all I want is to go home and read more of the letters.

"I know you can think of something," says Kai.

"My cousin C.C. is home," I say. "She was just supposed to come for the weekend, but I think she's staying longer. She brought a huge suitcase."

I think about telling them about the bra, but then A'niya—with the fitted white jeans, grown woman curves, and perfect Spanish—walks up to us out of nowhere. The closer she gets I realize they're the same white jeans from that store in the mall, the ones I wanted so bad but Mami won't let me have.

A'niya's Spanish is real good 'cause she's always leaving in the middle of the year to go back to El Salvador, and then shows up the last few months of school. She's been doing that since like third grade. Even with missing so much school, she's managed to become, every year, one of the most popular girls at school *and* get straight As. She's always nice to us, but she wouldn't exactly invite us to sit with her girls.

Tampoco, she always says.

I don't think there's a good translation for that, but I've heard Mami say it a lot, so I can feel what it means. There are a lot of words like that in Spanish.

I slam shut the Nerda notebook so that she doesn't see everything about periods and moons and sleepovers. Like I said, she got her period in like fourth grade. She leans with one butt cheek on the table, the other leg outstretched to the floor, like she's telling us we're cool enough to talk to, but not enough to sit with. We all straighten up and stick our chests out a little. I shake out my hair and get it out of my face. It's kinda automatic, like we're animals in the wild, seeing the more developed of our species.

"Hey, what are you up to?" A'niya asks.

"Chillin'," says Kai.

"Yeah, chilling," says Connie.

A'niya sucks her teeth and picks at some chipping nail polish so hard that a piece of poppy-red paint goes flying into the air and lands on our notebook. She doesn't notice. Or maybe she does but continues to chip away.

"What are you working on? Revenge of the Feminist Nerds?" she says, laughing and slapping her beautiful skin-tight jeans with the perfect cuts. Only A'niya can make laughing at your own joke seem like a thing you should do.

"Revenge of the Feminist Nerds sounds like an awesome title for our next group story," I blurt out, and realize that maybe it wasn't a good joke, but an insult-joke, but before I can say something smart, Connie chimes in, breaking Las Nerdas rule number thirty-six:

"Mani doesn't want to go to Guatemala, because we're probably all going to get our periods this summer and we want to be together and so we need to win the Speak Up competition so that Mani doesn't have to go to Guatemala, and—"

I kick Connie under the table and give her the stop-talking-now stare, but she doesn't.

"It all started because we don't know where the vulva is," Connie says all awkward, like we're new sixth graders asking for help 'cause we can't ever remember our locker combos. "We don't have phones to look it up, and then Mani blurted it out in class, and now some boys are—"

I twist my neck toward Connie so fast that I think I pull a muscle. "Connie!"

"It's OK," Kai says to me. "Everyone already knows. Plus, she was there."

"You don't know female anatomy?" A'niya says all loud, then laughs. "Yeah, everyone's talking about that."

I don't know why she's got to use fancy words like "anatomy" on top of already making fun of me. And I don't know why everyone talks about me asking about vulvas, but no one talks about what those idiot boys are doing with their hand movements, or how they say *Vagina* each time they see me, even though I tell them to stop.

"But wait, what makes you think you can win Speak Up? The project has to be BOOM! Not just nerdy," she says, moving on to the nail polish on her pinkie.

My ears feel hot and my face is red. I clench my fists. I turn to A'niya, but before I can say anything, the bell rings and she gets up. "Later, putas," she says.

I know we should be insulted 'cause if Las Nerdas had a mission statement or an origin story or one of those important things, it would probably be all feminist and independent and all of that good stuff, but A'niya says "Later, putas" to her *girls*, so we feel kinda special.

Then she turns around and puts her hand on her hip. "Oh, and don't worry about the guys. They're all a bunch of pendejos," she says.

For a second I feel all fuzzy inside, but then I think, It's easy for her to not *worry about the guys*. She's a goddess with boobs who can subtract positive and negative numbers in her head in Spanish and other crazy things like that.

THE LAST FIVE MINUTES of lunch I rush to call Mami from the main office phone, but I spend two whole minutes of those trying to explain to Ms. Wiznitzer why the phone call *is* an emergency. Mami agrees to let me go to Kai's place after school. I tell her we have to come up with an idea for a history project by Wednesday. Of course, she puts me on hold and calls Kai's mom first to make sure someone will be home to supervise us.

We stand in front of Kai's apartment door. Kai combs her hair over her face with her fingers to cover her eyes, just to annoy her mom. She's always trying to get her mom and dad to agree to cut her hair, but they're just like Mami, so they'll never give in.

Kai unlocks the front door, and we're bombarded by Kai's sister, Lani's, high-pitched arguing and at least three "¡Exagerada!" by Kai's mom. It's a regular day at the Espinozas'.

They stop and turn to look at the three of us.

"Kai, cariño, did you look like that all day? Get your hair out of your face, or no one will see your pretty smile," says Mrs. Espinoza.

But Kai doesn't say anything. I think it's weird Kai isn't as out-spoken at home as she is with us and in school. I don't know what that's about. Kai would never let a bully tell a girl she needs to smile and look pretty at school—I know, they tried that day on the bus when Kai stood up for me. Should I stand up for HER now? It's Mrs. Espinoza though, so I let it go.

We cram around Kai's kitchen table, but not before giving Kai's mom a kiss on the cheek and getting our hair messed up by Lani's hand. I know she thinks of us as her sisters, or at least her cousins, so it feels loving.

"OK. Go through high school without ever getting your period, or smelly feet for the rest of your life?" Connie says to us as Lani walks out of the kitchen and to her room.

Obvio. Smelly feet. Kai and I agree.

Mrs. Espinoza brings us each a glass of juice and giant dried corn bits, which basically taste like if you were to turn Fritos into little squares, and then make them ten times crunchier and saltier. She loves it when we come over because she can offer us chicha morada—a Peruvian purple corn juice—and she knows we'll say yes. She asks us about our project, but we give minimal information.

"Middle schoolers are so secretive," she says, and leaves us to work.

Kai rolls her eyes. I don't blame her; it's such a mom thing to say, but I guess it's less annoying when it comes from someone else's mom.

We wait for her to be completely out of sight.

"Now," Kai says.

I take out our Nerda notebook and slide it to the middle of the table. We open to rule sixty, where we left off at the library before A'niya interrupted us.

That's when Lani appears at the kitchen entrance, without warning.

Kai slams our notebook shut and slides it under her butt to sit on it.

We look at Lani, not sure what mood she's really in today. She grabs a folding chair from behind the refrigerator and sets it up next to Connie and me.

"So, what are we working on?" Lani says, motioning for us to take work out of our backpacks, then stuffing a handful of corn chips in her mouth.

We take out the Speak Up planning graphic organizer, take turns reading part of the description and the competition part.

"Oh yeah, I remember that from when I was in seventh grade. I got a good one. Start taking notes," Lani says. She waits till our pencils are out and in hand.

"What's up with the whole limited bathroom pass sheet in schools? People on their periods need to go to the bathroom more. And what if you forget your period products?"

My face must make it obvious I am only 72 percent sure of what period products are, so she clarifies.

"You know, pads and tampons and stuff. Anyway, you forget that stuff, so you have to go to the nurse. So then you go to the nurse to get your stuff, then the bathroom, and then teachers are asking you where you've been. And if you look like me, they assume you've been skipping." Lani flips her hair and messes with the shaved left side of her head, and squeezes her boobs together.

Connie and I look in awe. Kai rolls her eyes.

"You're lucky if they haven't already called security looking for you," Lani says.

We're each taking notes, but she talks so fast it's hard to get it all. Between the three of us, we can put our notes together and get the whole picture.

"How does that impact us menstruators long term, you're wondering?"

I hadn't actually gotten to wondering about that exact part. I was still trying to catch up with writing everything she said, but I nod anyway. So do Kai and Connie. I make it a point to look up "menstruators" later.

"Do the math," she says, this time drinking from Kai's glass and leaving her sticky dark purple lip gloss stain along the edge.

Kai looks like she's about to puke, but knows not to say anything.

"Without period products being readily available, menstruators are forced to spend more time out of the classroom, and—"

Kai and I look at each other. Lani's ideas are like one of those puzzles with tiny pieces that take forever to figure out, but when you start to connect a few pieces, you feel real accomplished. Except I've never been good at puzzles. I'm trying to piece together how bathroom passes connect to period products and girls losing out on school, but Lani said it so there's gotta be a solid connection.

"Wait!" says Connie. "I get it. That means less learning. That means lower grades. That means shorter life spans or something horrible like that." Like I said, Connie is the brains of this operation.

"Whoa, that's extreme, but I like where you're going with that," Lani says.

I hadn't thought of doing a project that didn't apply to us right away, but Lani got me thinking about the greater good and stuff like that. I mean, none of this applies to us right now, but it will, one day.

"Anyway, less time in the classroom means more time in the hallways, where all sorts of things could happen. Not to mention the latest social media challenge, *grope-'n'-go* or whatever they're calling it. Basically, a mob of kids either try to start a fight, and everyone's ready to film it, and—"

"Ugh, what? I thought that was only high school," says Kai.

"No, middle schoolers started doing it too, ever since spring break. My brothers showed me," says Connie.

"Yeah, except instead of just a fight, now they'll grope a girl or knock some random girl down and then post the video. Some kids are even getting paid for their videos! Listen, I don't want to see any of you on any video, understand?"

We all nod at the same time.

"We don't need to worry. We pretty much keep to ourselves," says Kai.

"Oh yeah, definitely," I say, a little too confidently.

The three of us are still nodding, buzzing with Lani's ideas.

Then I think of Tía Beatriz's letter and the article, and the definition I found of "femicide." Missing a few minutes of class to find period stuff doesn't seem that bad, if you compare the two, but I don't say anything.

"What are you waiting for?" says Lani, looking at each one of us dead in the eyes.

We grip our pencils tightly.

Nothing.

We must look real confused, 'cause Lani grabs my pencil out of my hand.

"OK, start with this. Your actionable item is that there should be a free tampon supply box in every classroom," she says.

With my pencil, she writes at the top of our sheet:

Tampons + unlimited bathroom passes = rights for menstruating people and better educational outcomes.

Our faces beam from smiling. It's like a formula. I get it finally, and I'm not even good at math.

"And do you know how expensive this stuff is? Talk about rights. If certain *other* people got their periods, tampons would be raining from the sky," Lani says.

That's when it clicks. Then the ideas just flow. Connie and I set our worksheet aside. This is too good for a worksheet. It needs to go in the notebook.

"Pff, you're welcome." Lani gets up, leaving the chair for Kai to fold back up.

Kai starts picking the edge of her paper, a sign that something is bothering her. Maybe she wanted to come up with the idea without Lani's smothering help.

"But seriously, Kai," Lani says, right before she walks out of the kitchen. "Get your hair out of your face. Not to look pretty, but so you don't look weak."

Kai keeps picking. She hates it when people tell her what to do with her hair. She side-eyes me. I want to tell Lani that everyone should just stop talking about Kai's hair, that she doesn't even want long hair anyways. All she wants is short, don't-mess-with-me hair.

Connie and I exchange no-*you*-say-something glances, but then Kai pulls the Nerda notebook out from under her and we get to working. She draws Lani, with clouds and pads and tampons raining from the sky, and other strange geometric shapes that just say *period products.*

Something's off, so Kai asks her mom to use her phone. We open up a private search and type in *period products.* Then we draw two more pages of period products: pads, tampons, special underwear where you don't have to wear anything, cups with so many different names. In the last one, there's a picture of the three of us in a superhero stance, how we want to look: Kai with short hair. Connie bouncing a soccer ball on her knee, wearing shoes she designed herself. Me with clear glasses and fitted white jeans. In the drawing, we're looking up, a rainstorm of "period products" falling from the sketchbook sky. At the top our title, *The Menstruators,* sits in arched letters, like a superhero group.

The more I think of it, the more I see the unfairness of it all. Why aren't period products just part of health insurance or like free or something? I make it a point to ask C.C. about that later. The bathroom passes are unfair too. I had never thought what if someone doesn't have their own period product. It's all unfair, and gives the non-menstruator pendejos a leg up in the world. Well, in school at least.

We have to channel A'niya or Lani if we're ever going to win the Speak Up competition, and if I ever want a fighting chance of getting out of going to Guatemala.

SEVEN

Sixty-eight days until freedom
disappears like Abuelita's memory,
a.k.a. Guatemala

ON THE BUS, I BREATHE hot-coffee-with-too-much-milk breath into my glasses and clean them with my shirt, but it just makes the glass smear. Our Speak Up ideas are due today, so I take out our Nerda notebook to transfer our ideas from the other night onto the Speak Up graphic organizer, except the ride to school is even bumpier than my handwriting, so I put everything back in my bag.

We're three stops away from school when Mason and Corey pretend to fall into my seat, their hands all over my sweater and bag. I flinch automatically and turn toward the window.

"My bad," they say, one after the other.

I ignore them as best I can even though their laugh, which sounds like gurgling oatmeal, lingers. I remember what A'niya said. They're just a bunch of pendejos. I stare out the window the last two stops.

In first period, Mr. Jones gives us independent work. We have to read an article about hormonal changes and respecting bodies or something and then answer questions that aren't even in the text, just so he can sit at his computer and do who knows what. I wait till he's all eyes on the screen. I reach into my bag to take out the Nerda notebook. I have thirty more minutes to finish our Speak Up graphic organizer and hopefully not get caught.

Except I reach into my bag and nothing.

My keys swish around underneath some overdue library books. I grab my glasses case. Still nothing.

I know I had it. I think back to the bus and that's when it hits me. I feel like when someone accidentally kicks your stomach instead of the ball during the soccer unit in PE. Clenching my jaw, I look up at Kai and Connie who are making fun of the blurry pictures in the article.

Corey and Mason are at the front right of the room. They are laugh-snorting into their hands as they flip through pages of something. *Our* notebook.

Mr. Jones is still all face into computer, so he doesn't see them pull out their phones. They start taking pictures of the inside pages.

I panic. The bell rings, and I watch Corey and Mason run out, and it feels like they're running out with my heart or arm or eyeball or some real important limb. That notebook is an extension of us, and it feels like a violation. I rush out with Kai and Connie.

"I . . . have to tell you something," I say, but I can't shake the quiver in my voice.

"What is it?" Connie says.

Tears stream down my face.

"What's wrong? You can tell us anything," says Kai.

"Anything?" I say.

It all spills out and I say it all without catching my breath.

"They what??"

"They took—" I say.

Kai looks desperate in a way I've never seen.

Connie starts chewing her nail.

"There's so much personal stuff in there . . . Why . . . why didn't you say anything in class?" says Kai.

I think of Monday night's The Menstruators drawing, my tía's picture—the one Mami doesn't even know I know about, or worse, took.

It's a good question. Why didn't I say anything? I couldn't. The words didn't come out. They never do.

"I have personal stuff in there—I mean, about Lani . . ."

"We all do," says Connie. "I mean, we said we were all going to get our period at a sleepover . . . at the same time. We . . . we drew period products raining from the sky, Mani!"

"I'm getting it back," Kai says, gripping her hands around her backpack straps.

"No," I say, putting my hand on her shoulder. "This is my fault. I'll get it back. You can trust me."

They walk off, and we don't even do the Nerda handshake (which is almost like leaving the house without kissing your abuelita. You just don't do that).

By English class, I see that J.J. has the Nerda notebook. We're filling out some character analysis on our Chromebooks. I open up our Nerda Google doc, the only way we can communicate without phones, since we can type and it never erases and you can see exactly who wrote what and when. There's also a chat we can communicate through, if we all have it open at the same time.

A chat pops up immediately. It's from Kai.

You get it yet?

I start to type, and then stop.

J.J. looks back at me and waves. Laughs into his stupid hand. Opens to the last page—The Menstruators—and shows it to the person next to him.

"Is there a problem, ladies and gentlemen?" says Mr. Lewis, my English teacher.

"No, sir," J.J. responds.

Mr. Lewis looks at me.

This is my chance. My chance to get it back. I can tell an adult that J.J. stole something from me. That notebook is mine. Ours. Las Nerdas. All of our personal secrets, rules, and dreams.

But I say nothing.

The Menstruators page felt so good when we made it the other night, but now? Kids are looking back at me, stupid smiles on their faces. My stomach feels like it fell out on the floor and is rolling away. I remember C.C. told me once: *Embarrassment is the enemy of women. Strive to live without it.* I don't really know what that means, but it's all I feel right now.

The bell rings and class is over, and so is my life. J.J. walks out with the notebook. My heart crumbles all over the floor. I think about all the personal stuff we've written on there, out in the open now for everyone to see. I let Las Nerdas down.

By history class, Ms. Martinez is in her usual spot outside the door, greeting everyone with things like, "Welcome, powerful ones," which sometimes we cringe at but secretly we love. She's the corn tortilla of teachers in a building full of fake flour ones. I heard C.C. say that once about someone she thought was real authentic.

Kai, Connie, and I sit at our table. Kai won't even look at me.

Ms. Martinez tells everyone to take out the Speak Up project description and graphic organizer.

"The what?" Corey yells from the back.

My teeth grind hearing his stupid voice. Our Nerdas notebook is sitting in his lap, his fingers crinkling the pages and smudging them with saliva-wet Takis stains. J.J. must have given our notebook back to Corey before class.

"The document I gave you last week, the—"

"The New York thing, stoooopid," Mason says, and slaps the back of Corey's head.

"That's not how we talk to our peers, Mason," says Ms. Martinez, and I don't know how she is so calm with so many pendejos in her class.

"My bad, my bad," says Mason.

"And let me remind all of you, that this is not just any project. Speak Up is the biggest social justice event for youth in the region, but it started small, by kids YOUR age as a way to shed light on all the social justice issues your generation is tasked with solving," she says with her perfectly lipsticked lips. I bet she got her period early.

Puchica, no pressure, right?

"OK, let's begin!" she says, with a smile that warms the room. At least my desk, and—

"I thought you were going to get it," Kai whispers between her teeth.

Now Corey is showing the The Menstruators page to his table group.

But before I can do or say anything, Ms. Martinez is already walking toward his table.

"Is there a problem?" she says, grabbing it out of his hand.

"Hey, that's my personal property," Corey says, then laughs.

"Whose is this?" Ms. Martinez says. She holds it up, violating Nerda Rule number seventeen.

WE NEVER DISPLAY THE NERDA NOTEBOOK IN PLAIN VIEW. ONLY A CHOSEN FEW CAN KNOW ABOUT ITS EXISTENCE AND THE CONTENTS OF ITS PAGES.

Ms. Martinez clearly doesn't know what's in her hands. If she did, then she would know not to hold it up, wave it like a flag, let the pages flap in the air. NERDA MANIFESTO written so big, our kiss marks and the stages of the Nerda handshake, drawn in out-of-order stages. Kai glares at me.

"You got it. We can trust you, right?" she whispers, but it sounds like an insult.

I swallow, then open my mouth. I think Ms. Martinez probably realizes it might be ours, because she quickly stops flapping it. Instead, she places it firmly on the empty desk in front of her.

"Actually, I found it on the bus, I think it's Mani's. I was just trying to get it back to her, and be a model citizen. That's all," says Corey, and then does some stupid handshake with his table mates.

"Is this yours, Manuela?" Ms. Martinez says, pronouncing it like my name is supposed to sound.

I feel Kai's and Connie's eyes lasering into me. My toes feel tingly like when you're standing in line at a big roller coaster and it's too late to turn around. I open my mouth to say something.

Then Kai's arm shoots up.

"Yes, Kai?"

"It's ours, Ms. Martinez. Corey took it without permission."

"Solved." Ms. Martinez puts it on Kai's desk.

I look at Kai, relieved it is back with us, but she just gives me a tiny nod.

"Who can remind us what Speak Up is all about?" Ms. Martinez then says to the whole class, like nothing just happened.

My words are still tangled in my throat, but I raise my hand anyways. I have to say *something*. I know how much I let Kai and Connie down just now.

"Yes, Manuela," she says.

"We have to think about a social justice thing . . . or issue . . . and create a program or campaign in our school or community, to talk . . . I mean, speak up about it." She smiles and nods, so I keep going. "We present our idea to some judges at the end of the year, and whichever group wins gets to go to New York for the annual Speak Up youth activist camp."

I sound like a robot, 'cause I took the words straight outta the brochure.

"Yes, thank you, Manuela," says Ms. Martinez. "Your group will create an action plan for a campaign, program, or *movement* that tackles a social justice issue in your school or community. You MUST think local." She adds in "movement," even though that wasn't in the brochure. Then she looks around the room. "Are you with me so far?"

A bunch of heads nod.

"You will then present your action plan and first phase of implementation to a panel of judges. The judges, from your local community, will select one winning group from each participating school, and the winning group will attend the Speak Up Youth and Activism Camp in New York for two full weeks in June. And the best part is, you'll be able to further develop your idea into something you can really implement the following school year. And I know college seems so far away, but even just participating looks really good on those applications."

I try to kick shoes under the table with Kai and Connie, but I get nothing in return. Kai forces a smile, but her hands grip the Nerda notebook, and I can tell there's something on her mind that she's not saying.

"You OK?" I ask.

"I'm fine," she says, but when she says it back that quick, I know she's mad.

"So, let's brainstorm," Ms. Martinez says. "We've spent the last few weeks talking about young people all around the world, and in the US, many young people not too much older than you, making waves in the Black Lives Matter movement, and—"

"That's racist," Corey says, loud enough for Ms. Martinez to hear.

She moves closer to Corey. "You think so, Corey? Tell me why. Let's talk about it."

But Corey says nothing; he just sits there like a pendejo. A'niya was right. Puro pendejo all day.

"I encourage you to think about it, Corey," she says. Then she turns to the class. "This goes for everyone. I hope you always feel free to speak up and share your opinions. I like being challenged! And if you can't think of something on the spot, you can always email me later."

She turns back to Corey again and gives him another chance to say something, but he doesn't take it. He just shrugs. He can't even look her in the eyes.

We spend the next ten minutes brainstorming ideas as a class while Ms. Martinez writes them down.

"Recycling!"

"A community garden on the old soccer field!"

"No homework!"

She makes a funny face at that one, but still writes it down.

"Write to Congress to let children vote."

She must like that one, 'cause she puts two checkmarks next to it.

"Remember, try to keep it local," she says.

Then a kid from the back shouts, "No police in public schools!" and Ms. Martinez puts two check marks *and* circles it a bunch of times.

She looks around the room. "Manuela?" she says, and I freeze. I think about everything we talked about with Lani. Menstruators. Bathroom passes. Learning loss. Period products in classrooms. But all I can concentrate on is the fact that Kai is real mad at me. Then my dead tía's letter pops into my brain. I think of the picture of her at a protest, with hundreds of women holding signs and singing. And I picture police "descending" on them and beating them up. I want to tell Ms. Martinez about all of it. I want to tell Kai and Connie too. Then I think about C.C. and the dress she showed me that was splattered in red paint like she dissected a big frog on it or something.

"Repro, um . . . ," I start. "I don't know . . . rights?" I say, almost like a question. I can't express everything we talked about at Kai's, Lani and her big ideas, bigger than Kai's. Almost as good as C.C.'s.

"Women's rights, or girls' rights in school, ways of reversing learning loss like free tampon dispensers, not just in the nurse's office," says Kai, not at all like a question. Not like me.

Ms. Martinez purses her lips like she's thinking. "Girls' and women's rights. Quick access to period products. Reversing learning loss. Yes. Relevant to school and beyond. I like where you're going. What would that look like, exactly? Think about it, friends, you have time. We're just jotting down ideas now."

But then Genesis, quiet gummy bear-eating Genesis, raises her hand but doesn't even wait to be called on. "Composting and reducing food waste in schools!" she says.

I scrunch my nose and squint my eyes at her like I didn't hear right. I've never heard Genesis say anything out loud in class, or maybe I've never noticed before. Definitely not anything above a whisper.

Just then I feel something soft but pointy hit my head as Ms. Martinez is writing on the board. Mason and Corey laugh. I look down and it's a paper airplane. I unfold it. There's a V written in pencil and a speech bubble that says, "Help!" On the other side, there's a gross picture of a stick figure with blood coming out.

I look behind me, and Corey is doing the gross V thing with his fingers, again, just like in first period. I want to throw my shoe at his stupid face, but before I can say anything, Ms. Martinez turns around in that I-have-eyes-in-the-back-of-my-head teacher way, puts the cap back on the dry-erase marker, and tells Corey to get out of class.

I bet no one ever bothered Ms. Martinez when she was my age. Kai waves a big exaggerated goodbye to him, while hugging our notebook with her other hand close to her chest. I start to wonder how you get a quetzal voice like C.C.'s. Like Kai's sister, Lani. Like A'niya. Like Kai right at this moment, even though she hasn't gotten her period yet. Even Genesis, who can refuse to move with just a shake of her head, and who doesn't even wait to be called on before blurting out an A+ answer. Is it something you're born with?

Corey's at the door, but right before stepping out, he turns around and mouths *Vagina girl*. But this time, Ms. Martinez doesn't see. She puts up a digital timer on the board, turns on "thinking music," which today is ChocQuibTown, a hip-hop group from Colombia.

But I can't concentrate. Pencils tap and scrape against paper. Florence at the table next to mine rubs her giant erasers against her worksheet and swipes the eraser crumbs off her desk. I watch them fall by her feet. The dry-erase marker smell starts to give me a headache.

"That was a mess. So . . . what are we going with?" says Connie.

I look up at the board, then at the margin of my paper. I don't see how we'll ever win Speak Up, and go to New York. I just know I can't go to Guatemala. I can't roll my *r*'s and I don't want to go to a place where they do things like femicide, where women get on buses and never make it back home. And I know Mami's mad at me and all, but I don't want that to happen to her either. Winning Speak Up is my only real chance.

We just have to find a way to win.

EIGHT

Sixty-three days till the most important
summer of my life stinks worse than
Takis decomposing in someone's locker

THE ATTIC IS ALREADY CREEPY, but it's even creepier when the pressure cooker and sartén aren't hissing and popping along with Abuelita's songs about Guatemala. Dad's teaching a class at the community college till five, and Mami and Tía took Abuelita to a Zumba class.

Not even C.C.'s here, but she left a note.

> *Maní—*
> *Out causing trouble*
> *Be back @ 4:30.*

She draws a raised fist, which is a reference to a song by this Guatemalan feminist rapper, Rebeca Lane, she's obsessing over these days.

I grab my dictionary, bring the ladder to my room, and lock my door, even though Mami will be real mad if she comes home and the door is locked. But whatever. Mami's already mad at me for saying porquerías in class, even though there's something in me that knows that *vulva* is not a porquería, but I don't have the words to say it, just like I don't have the words to tell her how much I can't go to Guatemala.

The tin box with volcanos and an oversized quetzal is exactly where I left it the other day. I tiptoe over even though no one's home. I pull out the second envelope. The letter is wrinkly like the first one, like it's been opened and closed a million times. It's dated three months after the first one.

Isabela,

    I hope you are getting these.

I run my finger over her words and wonder why Mami never wrote back.

    Today we covered a protest on Carretera a El Salvador.
Women blocked the road and held up signs with the name Lucía
written on them. It was so few of them that they could have
all sat around a kitchen table, but loud enough to be heard by all
who passed.
    I interviewed one of the protesters, and she told me that
Lucía had been missing for weeks, but last week, garbage collectors
found her body by a canal in the city. Police said she drowned,
but her body told a different story.
    Then, a man came to warn me and Maribel. He was in
normal clothes, but I think he was a policeman. He threatened to
grab Maribel's camera off her neck and throw it against a rock,
but the women moved and formed a circle around him. He pushed
past them, yelled, "Consider this a warning."

For the first time since covering the disappearances and killings, I felt afraid. But the women stayed to block the road.

I interviewed another woman who didn't speak Spanish, so her niece translated. She told me her daughter has been missing for two years. She has already had four policemen assigned to her case, but she's never been able to talk to any of them. She said, "I just want to know where she is. I want to know where they all are."

Then, the women started singing. They masked their protest as song and held signs with Lucía's name. They laughed and sang while they cried until they seemed louder than the honks and threats from nearby windows. I didn't know all those emotions were possible. Fear and strength together. Any uncertainty that Maribel and I felt disappeared.

It reminded me of one of the songs we used to sing, the ones you'd write for the marches. I can't wait to play my guitar again. Please keep playing it for me. Keep it alive with song until I see you again. I think this picture is one of the last protests we went to. Remember, we took two in case we ever found ourselves in different places? Well, here is yours, to keep and show your daughter, until we meet again.

Please write back.

Then she signs it like she signed the first one:

Primero una voz, y luego seremos millones.
-Beatriz

MAMI AT A PROTEST? And what picture? Why were those women singing if they were looking for missing girls? And what did someone do to Lucía? Why did they want to break Maribel's camera, and why would Tía Beatriz stay someplace where she was afraid? And WHY does Mami want to take me somewhere daughters go missing?

I wonder if daughters disappear here too. And what picture? I shake out the pages filled with my tía's words.

Nothing.

I look in the envelope again, my fingers fumbling through it, and there it is. I pull it out. But it's Tía Beatriz in a green boxy huipil shirt. The guitar is strapped around her chest; she is playing it. Her mouth is open, mid-song, or mid-yell. Behind her, protesters hold signs like in the article about femicide from last time. But the background is fuzzy and I can't read the signs. I look closer and I recognize the guitar. I realize it's not Tía Beatriz. It's Mami. But there's no way. Mami would never go to a protest. I shake the thought away.

I sneak in letters the rest of the week, and pull the picture out each time. Another article with a picture and signs that say:

No importa lo que usamos. Nada es invitación.

I want to tell C.C., but she's distracted with her own real protests and essays and meetings and other college stuff, even though it's weird she hasn't gone back to classes yet. She shows me pictures on her phone, and I realize the signs at her protests aren't that different from the signs in Tía Beatriz's pictures.

The letters start to change. My dead tía goes from being afraid to not afraid anymore. I read letters where she's happy, where she and her photographer friend, Maribel, walk through rain forests for days just to interview one person. I wonder how one person's story can be so important that you spend days in a jungle just to capture their words, from their own mouths. Another where they join a collective of other journalists also covering disappearances, some of whom themselves disappear or end up in jail. She writes about the women she meets, and I feel like I know them. She talks about the colors and sounds of birds and conversations that keep her full for days, like a big bowl of the best sopa de frijoles, and it makes me smile. It's a side of Guatemala Mami doesn't tell me about, or maybe she never knew.

I still don't tell anyone about the letters, not even C.C., and not even Kai or Connie, breaking Nerda rule number six:

NERDAS DON'T KEEP SECRETS FROM EACH OTHER.

But I wouldn't even know where to start. And plus, Kai would have all these great ideas of how to confront Mami about them and use them against her to get out of going to Guatemala . . . but this feels like something I have to figure out for myself—a secret of my own.

To my tía, Guatemala wasn't somewhere to run from; it was a magical place where people cry and sing all at the same time. Where Mami held guitars in her hands and songs in her mouth. Where nothing made her throat clench or blocked her voice like a muzzle. Where she smiled often and sang loud.

Where her songs meant something. I wonder what?

I tape the picture to the last blank page of the Nerda notebook, next to the first one, where it's safe and no one will see it. It's still my turn to hold on to it until the last week of school, even though

I almost lost it forever. There's something about the picture I want to channel, but I don't really know what. A new question swirls around my brain that feels more important than all the others: Why did Mami leave?

NINE

Sixty dinnertime lectures from Mami
about needing to be more
"decente" in Guatemala

IT'S BEEN TWO WEEKS and Mami still hasn't really said anything about Mr. Dupont or the blue paper, other than handing it back to me, except it looked like it had been all ironed out.

"Ponéte decente que vamos al mol," Mami says, towering over us at the kitchen table, and totally interrupting C.C. who's telling Tía and Abuelita that *Rosa de Guadalupe* is actually a really sexist show that perpetuates (her word, not sure what it means) stereotypes about women, and subjugates them (not sure about that one either).

That's the first full sentence Mami has really said to me since almost two weeks ago when she told me to stop talking porquerías and when Abuelita had her episode. The only way Mami would take me to the mall on a weeknight is because it's "Rebaja Thursdays."

"What do we have to get?" I ask, quiet and unsure, like it's a joke.

"You think you're going to show up to Guatemala in a couple of months wearing THAT?"

I look down. I'm wearing yesterday's baggy peach jeans and a Plaza Sésamo T-shirt I found in the lost and found at the library near where we used to live. It's so long it touches my knees. It's the perfect pajama shirt too. I think, But I'm not going. I can't.

"But there's a competition at school, and there's a youth activist camp in New—" I start. Here's my chance.

"¡Basta ya!" she says, not even letting me finish. "You just want to show everything off? You think your job is to call attention to yourself? You think you have to do more than just be a student?"

I don't know how oversized, peach-colored jeans call attention to me other than to make people think I don't know my size, or give someone the chance to say, *Yup, no butt.*

"But WHY do we have to go on my birthday? Why do I have to miss the last week, and the biggest competition of my life? Why can't I stay back with Tía Gladys? She's not going."

"That thing you told me about? Ya suficiente. We're leaving on your birthday because that's when the weather is the nicest, and the flights were cheap. There's no better time," she says, pointing upstairs, reminding me to go change.

"But I thought the weather was always nice. Abuelita says that's why it's called the Land of Eternal Spring—"

Abuelita nods my way. "Así es, chulita."

"¡Basta!"

Maybe if I finish telling her about Speak Up and how it looks good on college applications, she'll listen, but I let it go, 'cause all she's going to say is *Basta.*

There are still almost two months left and I might grow all kinds of ways by then, but it doesn't matter, 'cause I know what size she's getting me. I had begged Mami to return these pastel clothes that made me look like an Easter egg, but instead, she got a bunch of dark gray and green clothes to hide my boobs. I want clothes that can show off what little butt I have, or at the very least, jeans I won't trip on. I wasn't blessed with a body like A'niya's, or with A'niya's ability to switch back and forth so perfectly between Spanish and English, like a mango and vanilla double swirl. Not like my Spanish, some melted, nasty, old ice cream you forgot to put back in the freezer.

I beg C.C. to come with us, but she says she has to take Tía to the pharmacy to pick up medication.

"¿Para qué voy a ir?" Tía says to C.C.

Maybe 'cause Mami works in hospitals all day, C.C. looks at her in that help-me way, but Mami's barely paying attention to her, getting her purse ready, and organizing her coupons by store.

"You can't keep putting this off. Doña Marta's fish paste and tiger eyes alone won't cure your arthritis. Your arthritis is from years of standing on your feet and repetitive motion. You heard the doctor last time. Stuff like that is actually all over the news; you should get compensated," C.C. says, but stops herself and lets it go.

She once told me that even if people with hard jobs like Tía had got money as a "sorry," Tía still wouldn't get it for some reason.

"Don't waste your time on me. Don't you have to go back to school?" Tía asks C.C., but C.C. just tells her to stop changing the subject. Everyone has been asking C.C. all week about going back, but she just dodges the questions.

AT THE MALL, DAD, MAMI, and I step onto the escalators and I stand right behind Mami, hiding myself just in case I see anyone I know. There's nothing worse than running into someone you know at the mall and them seeing you with your parents.

A few girls I recognize from school pass us. Girls with tight, ripped jeans, and spaghetti straps, filming some dance on the opposite escalators on their phones. I hide my face in Mami's hair so they don't see me, even though she's mad at me. But she doesn't move. I guess I'm still her hija and there's nothing she can do about it.

We step off and into the juniors' section, and I see the white jeans with just the perfect amount of cutouts and worn pockets. But before I can even make my case of why I need those jeans, we're heading to the back, to the messy mountain of rebajas: all of last year's rejects.

Girls in crop tops slurp boba tea and pick up ugly shirts. They hold them against their chests and take selfies, then laugh. I cross my arms over my stomach, hidden by a thick T-shirt with embroidered flowers Mami made me change into right before we left. Boba tea would taste so good right now. My throat wants to scream, so I try to look the other way but each slurp makes me look the girls' direction. They finally leave after throwing the shirts on the ground.

Mami is already holding three outfits in her left hand while she picks out more with her right. Dad's making weird faces at each of them, trying to make me laugh. I want to ask Mami right then and there about the picture with her and the guitar. With her hands full of ugly rebaja clothes, she wouldn't be able to get mad at me with her hands. She'd have to use her words, and since we're in public, there's no way she'd raise her voice. But I can't bring myself to do it. She seems busy, so I slip away to the middle display of paper-white bras tangled on the hangers. Then I remember C.C.'s bra under my pillow, which I forgot about. No one's watching, so I touch one of the bras and squeeze the soft part where the boobs go. It's warm like someone's boob was just in it. I want to try it on so bad, but I'm still in a bra with no wires like I'm in fifth grade or something.

Mami's going to call me any second, but there's still no one watching. I stretch the bra closer to me. I hold it up and try to look at myself in the reflection of the metal rack. It feels—

"Hola, vagina girl," says a voice right behind me.

My body freezes in place. It's A'niya. I push the bra away and start looking around like I'm looking for something else. I want to tell her not to call me that, but each time I see A'niya, my words get jumbled up in my brain before they even get a chance to dance around in my mouth. I try to act like it's no big deal, but that's kind of hard, 'cause it is a big deal and she just saw me hold a giant bra up to my tiny boobs.

"You bra shopping or something?" she says.

"What?" I say, like I don't know what she's talking about.

"Are you looking for a bra?" she says, and snaps her own neon blue strap against her shoulder.

"Oh, me?" I say. "Oh no, whatever. My cousin, C.C.'s, in town. They're for her. She's in college."

She nods, like she 85 percent believes me.

"Plus," I say, "these are all tiny, and she has like real big boobs, you know?" I don't know why I say that. Why would A'niya know?

She laughs, but not a mean laugh. Not really. She gives me a see-you-later nod and walks away. I look around to see if she's with anyone, but no one follows her. I can't believe her mom lets her go to the mall alone and just walk around, on a *school night*.

I shove the bras far into the rack like they did something mean to me, and a few of them fall, so I immediately rearrange them because Mami told me that when they first moved here, she worked in a mall and her fingers hurt from always fixing all the clothes that got mangled on hangers. I don't want to do that to anyone.

An hour later, Mami has selected her favorite five things, most of which are loose and have flowers embroidered onto them, except for one dark green fake wool sweater that looks like the collar would probably go up to my chin or something. Plus, it looks like she got it from the men's section or something. *And* on rebaja. I look through the rest and they're all two sizes bigger than what actually fits me.

She gives them to Dad, who's following her around and holding his arms out like he's a clothing rack. I laugh a little, but Mami still has the same *cara seria* that she's had for weeks. I walk her over to the front and show her the jeans and tell her that this is the new trend.

"¿Esa cosa fea?" she asks.

"That's not ugly."

"No," she says, "and plus it's full price. And who would pay to have your jeans cut? You want to cut your jeans? Yo te los corto."

I look over at Dad, but he gives me a sorry-can't-help-you shrug. Plus, he rarely interrupts Mami when she's going on and on like this.

Mami goes on for five minutes and the more she talks, the louder she gets. I just want to bury myself under all the clothes.

"And it's different in Guatemala. My sister—your aunt—disappeared. That's what happens to girls who call attention to themsel . . ." she says, but she doesn't finish the last word. It's like her voice trails off at the very end, like she wants to take it all back. But she can't. Not really.

"Isabela—" Dad starts, but even he's at a loss for words.

I wait for her to explain, to take it back, to something. I wait for her to transform into the version of her in the picture. The one who wears colorful clothes. The one who plays guitar and sings in public, while women around her carry signs about how clothing is never an invitation. But a solid twenty seconds later, she still doesn't take it back, or explain how it was her sister's fault. I thought it was a bus crash, or—

My heart feels all achy for a tía I never met, even though I've gotten to know her a little bit through the letters. All I've ever been told is that she got on a bus and was never heard from again, but Mami never told me it's because she was calling attention to herself. And I wonder what that really means.

Disappeared. That word feels thick and heavy, like being trapped under a giant piece of metal and not being able to get out. Like how I imagined what really happened when they said Tía Beatriz's bus "didn't make it." What else am I supposed to think? No one tells me anything. I want to ask her a million things. I turn to her with my mouth open, want to force the words out, but then she picks out more of the ugliest stuff on the rack and it looks like she's forgotten everything she just said, or at least is pretending to. Uy, she won't even let me take the bus, or wear something above the knee, or wear something that fits, yet she's trying to take me somewhere where women call attention to themselves, then disappear. That's kinda messed up.

"Forget it. Las cosas son diferentes, that's all," she finally says.

I've been hearing it my whole life. *Las cosas son diferentes.* And if they're so different then why do C.C.'s pictures of the protests here look like she could have taken them in Guatemala? I'm so sick of hearing about *la violencia*, and *el polvo*, and all the millions of reasons why I can't wear those beautiful, fitted white jeans and instead have to hide behind my clothes. So I turn away from her and just start singing a Chavela Vargas song in my head about a girl who walks around the world with her own flashlight so she doesn't need the light of the moon. At least, that's what I think she's saying in Spanish.

But then Mami's eyes get watery, which makes my eyes tear up a little too, even though I don't completely know why. I want to hug her, but it's kinda awkward to go all in for a group hug by bras and last-chance-end-of-winter sweaters. Plus, Mami doesn't like llamando la atención, so we're not going to hug in public. No way. Dad's hand on my shoulder, squeezing Mami's hand with his other, is the closest we'll get to a hug right now.

In our almost-hug between the bras and rebaja sweaters, I start to think about the Speak Up competition. A'niya speaks up. C.C. speaks up. Even Genesis speaks up. Why can't I? So I do.

"Is that why you left? Because she disappeared?"

I've never asked her anything about Guatemala or why they came here, 'cause it just never felt like I had anything to do with it. Still doesn't, I guess. But I think of the letters, and the word *disappeared*, and Mami saying that it was Tía Beatriz's fault.

Mami breathes all loud, and squeezes my right hand. Her grip softens. She says nothing, but I know what it means. Her hand feels warm and safe.

I want to take my other hand and place it on top of hers, but people are starting to look at us. Plus, we're for real blocking people's paths out of the store. I look at the clothes Dad is now carrying over his shoulder, and all I can think about is how unfair it is for someone to *disappear* just 'cause of what she was wearing.

TEN

*Fifty-nine more nights listening to Mami
sing about places where people disappear
because of what they wear. No thanks.*

I STILL CAN'T GET it out of my head. How does someone die or
"disappear" because of what she was wearing? And what made her
a quetzal of a woman, like Abuelita always says?

It's Friday afternoon, a.k.a. Viernes de Canto. I've been home
over an hour now, waiting for C.C. to come back, for anyone to come
home so I don't have to face Mami alone. I couldn't find my quetzal
voice to get the Nerda notebook back that day, but today I have to
find it to confront her about what she said. But she's not her regular
self today. The guitar strums are slower and there's all this space in
between them, like she's finishing a thought in between each note.
I don't really pay attention to her songs, but I can hear that they're
sadder today.

I think about what she said yesterday, what she said and couldn't
take back. Tía Beatriz disappeared because of what she was wearing. The everything's-going-to-be-OK feeling I got from her warm
hand yesterday on mine faded and I want answers, but I also don't
want to make her cry again.

I want to ask her so many things, but I don't know where to start. I grab the Nerda notebook out of my bag, hold the picture of Tía Beatriz and Mami tightly, working up the courage to confront her. I'll tell her I found the picture when I was cleaning, or maybe that it fell from the attic door straight onto my bed. I'll expose her, make her feel bad for wanting to take me somewhere that does *femicide*, where women die because of what they wear. She'll feel so bad for wanting to put me in danger that she'll agree to let me stay, and—

"Hi, Manuela!" Dad yells from the front door. I hear the familiar tap of his mountain survival-trekking-looking backpack he uses for work hitting the floor, and I know he is bending down to pick up my shoes from the middle of the hallway.

I look at the clock on the microwave. It's 4:30 p.m. already. He does solo cooking on Fridays to give Mami more "me time" on Viernes de Canto. Doesn't even let her help. He walks to the kitchen where I am, washes his hands and then gives me a kiss on the forehead right before getting his recipe books from above the fridge. I lodge the Nerda notebook and picture under my armpit and hold it there tightly, hoping he doesn't ask me what I'm working on.

He flips through the pages of the recipe book.

The courage I was building up to confront her is gone. I'm afraid if I ask questions, I'll let it slip that I found a huge stack of letters, letters that prove Tía Beatriz didn't die before they moved here. Letters that prove that she is a liar.

"You should just go up there," he says, like he can read my mind.

But the longer I stand here, the more my courage starts to shrink smaller and smaller till I can't see it at all. Instead, it's replaced with anger. Anger that she would blame someone for what they were wearing. Anger that she wants to take me somewhere where women disappear. I take the notebook out from under my arm and put it back in my bag.

"No, I'm actually here because . . . I want to help!" I say.

"Oh, *really?*" Dad says all exaggerated like he doesn't believe me. He hands me the cutting board and knife. I hang my head down and let out a sigh, which makes him laugh.

"So, who taught you how to cook?" I ask.

"My aunt Linda!" he says, with a breath that sounds like it brings back memories from way, way back. "You remember her?"

I nod, hoping he'll keep talking. Anything to avoid Mami.

"Yes, yes, you met her once," he says.

I remember a blur of a woman with deep blue eyeliner who once built me a toy boat out of toothpicks right there in front of me. The famous architect turned food truck entrepreneur.

"You know, Manuela, if you want your mom to explain something, just go up and ask," he says.

"Wait, what she said yesterday? Oh, I already forgot about that. And that has nothing to do with me," I say, shrugging.

"You sure you feel that way?" he says, in his annoying way of answering me with a question.

Then I start to wonder what kind of family secrets Dad has.

"How come you don't talk about your family?" I say.

"Aunt Linda was my family," he says, flipping through the recipe book.

"Yeah, but what about your parents?"

"Well, they died when I was young."

"And they were from the Philippines and China?"

"No. Well, a while back. *Their* parents—my grandparents— were born there. But I never met them. My grandparents immigrated to Hawaii as teenagers with their families to work on sugarcane plantations. They actually met during the great strike of 1946 when sugarcane workers of all different backgrounds organized together," Dad says, putting down the recipe book and looking up, using the voice he uses like he's narrating a *History Channel* documentary. "You know, the sugarcane industry had tried to keep people of different races and languages apart, so they couldn't organize. Isn't that *messed up*, as the kids say?"

Ugh, of course he had to throw in a dad joke. But I'm legit interested in his story.

"Anyway, that's where they met, at these labor organizing meetings they'd go to with their parents. They didn't even speak the same language. They were just kids, really. That's all I know. It's all Aunt Linda ever told me."

I didn't know that about my great-grandparents, and how they left everything they knew to meet in a field of sugarcanes, or that a whole industry tried to keep people apart so they couldn't organize.

"People always find a way to work together," he says, winking.

I give him a half smile, wondering if he really can read my mind.

"You never talk about your background," I say.

"Well, my story starts here. But my history? That goes way back, before I was born. But I am not lucky to have people tell me about other places, and I never thought to ask my aunt Linda when she was around. She was a real storyteller. I've done some internet research to set my family's story in specific times and places, but it doesn't replace the stories straight from their mouths, you know? That's a big regret of mine, but you're stubborn when you're young." He winks again.

Suddenly I hear the guitar, even though it's been playing this whole time. There's less space between each strum. (I think of what Abuelita said once in third grade after my parents came back from a parent-teacher conference where the teacher said I ask too many questions. *Only a pendeja doesn't ask questions.*)

I grab the Nerda notebook back out of my bag. "I'll be back," I tell Dad, and walk upstairs.

"Entra!" Mami says after I knock softly.

I walk in, notebook firmly lodged under my armpit again.

When Mami sees me, I think, I haven't seen her smile like that in a while. In her hands, the guitar from the picture. This is my chance.

"Where did you get that?"

And I know I'm about to catch her in a lie.

"It was my sister's, but she was the singer. I wrote the songs."

Oh.

"You never told me it was her guitar," I say.

"Manuela, you've never asked me anything about this." She runs her hand over the body of it, like she's taking care of it, like Tía Beatriz asked her to in the letters.

Now's my chance. I'm going to tell her to take back her comment, that I know she doesn't think clothing is an invitation for anything. I'm going to tell her that I have pictures of her at a protest to prove it.

But watching her hug the guitar like that, I don't have it in me anymore.

I grind my teeth together to stop myself from saying anything.

She stops playing and motions for me to sit in the chair across from her, the one with a mess of papers, songs, notes. I don't know where to move them. She puts them in a neat stack and then lets them float down to her feet. There's no other corner in the house where Mami would just throw something on the ground. It's like there are no rules here. I wish I had a place in the house with no rules, where I could just be myself.

I grip the handles of the chair.

I wait for Mami to ask me why I'm here, why after so many times of inviting me in, I finally show up today.

"How was your day?" Mami asks me.

I shrug, and it all comes crashing down on me. How it hasn't been the same with Kai ever since I let the Nerdas down when I couldn't get our notebook back. I hear Abuelita's voice in my head: *Use your quetzal voice.*

I don't want to leave my friends this summer, I want to say. And I for real don't want to go where women just disappear.

"I had a hard day too," Mami says, pulling me back from my thoughts.

My mouth closes. Mami rarely ever tells me about her day—hospital privacy issues and all.

"I had to translate for a woman and tell her that she doesn't qualify for financial assistance because she couldn't provide a social security number. She is undocumented, and doesn't have insurance. And without this hospital assistance, the debt would kill her before her disease. The debt is worse than her condition," Mami says, in one long, heavy breath.

She doesn't tell me what the condition is, and I know not to ask.

"But I know she qualifies," she says. "I know it is just extra paperwork—sure, it's a lot extra, and she'd have to talk to other people—but the point is, it is possible. Some of this assistance money is reserved *for* people who cannot provide documentation. I just wish I had said something."

Mami's left eye starts to get a little watery, but she dabs it with her knuckle. I didn't think Mami could feel that way—wishing you could have said something but didn't.

"So why didn't they tell her?" I say.

"She's illiterate, so she also can't use the computer . . . There are just so many obstacles."

"But why didn't you help her? Why didn't you say something?" I say again.

"My job is just to interpret," she says. Her eyes don't meet mine. Her fingers are off the strings. Instead, she rubs the wood of the guitar like it's going to give her answers. "I tried to help someone once . . . do more than just interpret, and I almost lost my job. They told me my job wasn't to ask questions."

I feel myself getting mad at Mami. I thought Mami was puro quetzal, 100 percent of the time. Does that mean saying something even if she got fired? It should. I think about the woman whose bills could kill her. Who was bullied for not having a number to call or insurance card to show. Who was treated so differently because of paperwork. Or maybe she couldn't sign her name. I remember that C.C. told me once that requiring written signatures can be real elitist, that if you never learned to read or write, how can you sign your name? I had never thought of it like that. I bet C.C. would have said something, even if it meant getting fired.

"Y la doctora era Latina," she says, like an afterthought. Like a realization that changes everything. "Era Latina."

But that makes me feel even more mad. So are you, I want to say. Why didn't you help?

I want to be mad at her, but I can't be mad at Mami if I couldn't even speak up about our Nerda notebook. Mami looks real sad, and I want to tell her that sometimes, most times, I can't speak up either. But the words don't come.

"Can I listen to your song?" I ask.

This time both eyes water, but they light up again, and her smile returns.

"¡Por supuesto!" she says. She wipes her tears and shuffles through the papers she had thrown down. Hands me a new song she wrote.

I miss a lot of the song. Something about seeds you can't kill and wings you can't clip, and ideas that live on and on, and something about many voices. And then I'm lost with words I've never heard. But the more I listen, the more her songs sound like Tía Beatriz's letters, and for a moment I want to ask. I want to tell her I found them, but instead I sit there. I let the song be her hand I never grabbed back yesterday at the mall. I picture what it would be like to hear the songs in Guatemala, in one of the rainforest walks Tía Beatriz wrote about. I find myself humming, focused on the words. And I think of the women in the letters and how it's possible to be sad but also to sing.

Un día cantarán.
Un día cantarán.

One day they'll sing. It sounds familiar, and I suddenly remember the Mayan legend Abuelita told me about—how the quetzal birds used to sing beautifully before the Spanish invasion, and how 500 years later they still don't sing. How they just lost their voice and are waiting around the rainforest till they can be free again, and then and only then will they sing. For a second I wonder if she is really singing about birds, or about my Tía Beatriz.

When she's done, Mami hands me the song. She tells me to keep it, and hands me a few more.

Back in my room, I start my own pile of songs, as if these pages are her letters to me, the letters she never wrote back to Tía Beatriz. But I come back to something I can't ask her: Why did she leave?

ELEVEN

Fifty-eight more mornings left of Mami
making sure my school clothes aren't too tight
so I don't look like a "pepereca"

SATURDAY AFTERNOONS ARE MY turn to help Abuelita get ready for misa.

C.C. takes the tubos out of Abuelita's hair, 'cause she's less sloppy than me. I pick out her pañuelo for church. Abuelita's Pond's cold cream and Saturday misa hairspray dance in my nose, and it makes me happy even though it always makes my eyes water.

Mami and Tía have been asking C.C. nosy questions about her schedule and plans and *doesn't she have to return*, but she's been extra shady with her answers. Her eyes narrow in on Abuelita's gray hair, and I can tell that there's a lot going on in C.C.'s head too. Probably not as much as in my head, but still.

"¡Chuliiiiiiiitas!" Abuelita says and squeezes our faces with her hands oily and cold from her face cream. That's how we know today, at least right now, she remembers us.

Then she starts singing one of her old-timey songs; this one's about a girl who couldn't decide between two men, so she rejects both, takes her guitar, and travels the country. C.C. and I look at each other and laugh.

She grabs our cheeks again to make us smile, which makes her hair get tangled on one of the tubos. But it's hard to smile, 'cause I can't stop thinking about Mami's words. *Disappeared. Her fault.* And how I couldn't work up the courage to ask her about it. I can't stop thinking about how her voice was frozen at work, and how there was nothing I could say to make her feel better, and about all the times I can't say anything. I think about what Corey said to me on the bus two weeks ago, and of him and Mason doing the gross V thing with their fingers. It became a thing all week and more boys started doing it, especially in health class, but Mr. Jones acts like he doesn't see. I get in trouble for saying, "Vulva," out loud, but they don't get in trouble for pretending to make a vagina with their fingers. At least I know they can't get away with it in Ms. Martinez's class.

"Chuliiiiita," Abuelita says, this time to me.

Catching my face in the mirror, I stand straighter and try to force a smile. I can hear Mami downstairs setting up the pressure cooker. Great. Frijoles, again. All my life I've been hearing *Comete esos frijoles para que seas grande y fuerte.* There's nothing grande or fuerte about me. No way something so small like a black bean is going to make you big and strong. Just saying.

"Have I ever told you that in Guatemala you can hear the hiss of a thousand pressure cookers at noon?" Abuelita says, now with toothpaste in her mouth.

"No," C.C. and I say at the same time, which is a lie.

Abuelita is the only woman in this house who tells me something good about her past in Guatemala, and even though she lost her memory, I still believe her stories. I like hearing about the good things. Not even C.C. knows this, but sometimes I close my eyes and I can hear the hiss of the pressure cookers, and I feel like I'm in

Guatemala even though I've never been there. The hissing is comforting, like the sound of rain on a roof. But not enough to make me
want to go or anything. Especially not after reading my tía's letters.

"We're going to be late, let's go," Mami yells from downstairs.
Everyone is going to church and since I'm not thirteen yet, I
can't really get out of it without a real big fight. I look at C.C. for a
way out.

"I got you, Maní," C.C. says. She helps Abuelita tie her Saturday misa pañuelo and we walk her out into the hallway.

Then I hear Mami's footsteps on our creaky steps.

"Tía," C.C. starts. She starts talking in this beautiful fast Spanish that almost makes me want to make mine better. I catch most of
it. She asks Mami if I can help her with a paper she has to write, and
she adds that we'll clean the house too. Based on the way Mami lifts
an eyebrow and purses her lips, she convinced her on that last one.
Mami whispers something in C.C.'s ear, but I don't really catch it.
But then Dad gently puts his hands on her shoulders and pulls
her away.

C.C. laughs and says, "Don't worry, Tía. I won't corrupt Maní
with my feminist porquerías."

Mami narrows her eyes at C.C. I start to feel bad for Mami too.
I mean, I've never lost a sister, but I *do* know what it's like to not be
able to speak up. Then she gives us a kiss ('cause when you're Guatemalan, you always saludar and despedir no matter what. Otherwise you're a malcriada, and there's nothing worse than that. I guess
being the p-word is worse. No sé. I heard Tía Gladys and Abuelita
say that once in church, after the part where you eat the cracker
and you're supposed to be kneeling and praying, even though I just
daydream).

When the door finally closes, C.C. and I both high-five and laugh.

"I need you to help me, for real," she says.

My eyes light up. "You want *my* help?"

"Don't tell your mom, but I'm organizing this protest in a couple of weeks, and I have nothing good to wear."

I think of her suitcase exploding with clothes. I hope she hasn't noticed the missing bra.

"What are you protesting about?" I ask.

"About so much!" she screams and puts her arms up like she's holding up the sky. "Reproductive rights, access to hygiene products like pads, tampons . . . You know what's so messed up? In immigration detention centers, or cages, they don't even give people pads or tampons for when they get their periods. The centers themselves are already criminal, and then on top of that, people have to get their period and just stuff their pants with old shirts or whatever they find. Anyway, we're demanding that they have access to basic sanitation products." She finally takes a breath. "I'll be gone for like a week. We're organizing a supply drive and taking it down to one of the detention centers. Maní, I really wish I could take you."

I understand half of it, and she uses big words, but they all sound real important. Girls my age in cages? Girls get their periods, and they have to stuff their pants with old shirts? All I've wanted is my period, but I don't think I'd want it if I lived in a cage . . . I make it a point to tell Kai and Connie so we can add it to our Speak Up ideas.

"Anyway, your mom has boxes of old clothes from her feminist days," C.C. says.

"Her what?" What feminist days, I think. Mami? Feminist? Mami makes me wear clothes I practically swim in. Mami blames Tía Beatriz for what she was wearing. Mami doesn't speak up . . . I think of telling C.C. about the woman with bills that kill.

"Um . . . I think you must be talking about someone else."

C.C. smiles and grabs her backpack and the ladder from the closet. My stomach is a tight knot. Does she know about the letters? Has she been up to the attic?

She pulls me by the wrist and upstairs we go.

At first, I act like I've never been here before and I avoid all eye contact with the box of letters. C.C. goes straight for a big wooden chest at the very end of the attic, by a little window. I hadn't really noticed it before. She opens the chest and digs in like she knows exactly what she's looking for. How have I never noticed her come to the attic? I mean, it's above *my* room.

"Oh, I almost forgot," she says, and reaches into her backpack and takes out this real old iPod she's always carrying around, even though her phone plays music just as well. She scrolls through and then puts it in one of the bookshelves so it echoes. Rebeca Lane, again. This time with another artist, Audry Funk.

The beat hits every couple of syllables like a heartbeat after you run the mile in PE. I hum along quietly, considering what it means to fight for a long life. This time I look more carefully at the books in the bookshelf.

Running my fingers through the books, I find a picture stuck in between two of them. I pull it out. In the picture, a woman who looks around C.C.'s age wears a flowy red dress with a brown belt that's cinched at the waist. She's wearing a little hat, like the old kind that I've seen my abuelo wear in pictures. He died right before everyone came here. They're in a crowd, mostly women, like the newspaper cutouts and pictures I found in the first letters. It's Mami for sure—looks just like the guitar picture which I've kept in the Nerda notebook since the night I found it. She's wearing these green pants and a boxy red-and-turquoise Guatemalan shirt. I look closely, and that same guitar is strung around her. She's holding a sign, but I can barely read it. The picture's real faded like it's been stuffed and restuffed between a million different books. Her eyes are fiery, like Abuelita's when she gets stuck in the old times and starts singing and dreaming in Spanish.

"Where are they?" I ask.

"I'm telling you; your mom was a feminist activist journalist," she says. "I was young, but I remember my tías coming back all energized and glowing and then sitting down all night to put together their stories."

I knew Mami wrote stories but then she stopped when we came here, but I didn't realize . . .

"My mom wasn't really into any of this. She just did their hair and helped sew their clothes since she was in beauty school or something. But hey, I guess that still contributed to the revolution, right?" She laughs. "You know our moms aren't sisters, right? They're cousins. So we're technically second cousins, but who cares? We're *primas*."

"I know," I say, copying her smile. But my brain is still trying to figure out how Mami, revolution, and feminist can even go in the same sentence. I think back to the last picture, the one I taped to the Nerda notebook with the colorful clothes and guitar in her hand. She wasn't just singing . . . she was participating. . . .

C.C. goes back to looking through the chest full of radical clothes and picking out what she wants, and I head to the box. I look at the picture again, more closely. Mami is carrying a sign that says *We are not just somebody's daughters. We are women.* What were they protesting? Then I think of C.C. and her supply drive and how women and girls in this country could live in a cage and not be able to feel clean on their periods; I didn't think things like that could happen here.

I look over at her. "I have to tell you something," I say, hugging the box to my chest, ready to not just make this *my* secret. "I don't think Tía Beatriz died. I mean, not when they say she did."

She looks at me all confused. "What do you mean?"

"I found these letters, and they're from Tía Beatriz, and they were sent HERE, like after I was born and stuff."

"What? There's no way. She died in a bus crash or something. That's when we all came," she says, and scratches the shaved part of her head like she's thinking. "Ay, I mean I was like six, maybe I don't remember."

Then I open the box and tell her about the first few I read and show them to her. I take the pictures out of the Nerda notebook. I thought she'd be upset like I was and feel like our history is one big secret or mentira. But instead, her eyes light up with the old article clippings and pictures and Tía Beatriz's handwriting. We sit on the yellow carpet and read the next one. This time she reads it to me while I hold the article clipping it came with. It's a picture of clothing and shoes, all spray painted white, laid out along a canal, with the names of women written on pieces of cardboard. *This week, I learned to turn my rage into power*, she writes. The skin on my arms is prickly with goose bumps. C.C. and I breathe out in sync as if we've been holding the same breath all almost-thirteen years of my life. Then she hands me the letter and points to the last part.

Tell me something. How is Harold? What does Mamita say? How is Gladys? And Carolina? I still hope you can forgive me. Please tell me about the baby. What is her name? I just know it's a girl. We were meant to put more powerful girls in the world.

C.C. and I look at each other. The goose bumps on her arms prick me. I get the chills too. "Maní, this is the most amazing thing that's ever happened to us," she says.

At first I think C.C.'s just being an exagerada like Tía Gladys always says. But her words settle on my skin. And it feels good to share my secreto with someone, especially C.C.

I flip the Nerda notebook to the page after The Menstruators, and add some notes. *Rights. Pads and tampons for _all_,* and I add some Rebeca Lane lyrics in the margins. I doodle Mami's guitar and write some of her lyrics too. *Un día cantarán.*

I think of the women who were missing whose names protesters wrote on flimsy cardboard slabs. I think of the girls in cages, in *this* country. Then I think of Mami at those protests. Was Mami protesting the same thing Tía Beatriz was protesting?

The garage door opens and we feel the house shake. We quickly stuff the article and letter back in the envelope and into the tin box with the quetzales and volcanos. C.C. gathers the clothes and cuts off Rebeca Lane's and Audry Funk's voices.

I put my hand on her arm and say, "Hey, please don't tell Mami about any of this."

"I got you, Maní. I always got you."

TWELVE

Fifty-six more nights
of NOT dreaming about Guatemala
(well, maybe once)

"¡SÁBANAS! ¡QUITEN LAS sábanas!"

It's 6:30 on Monday morning and Mami is yelling at us to take our sheets off the bed. Abuelita is already up and singing about the girl from the rancho again. Tía tells her to sing quieter because the vecinos are still sleeping, but Dad is trying to sing the chorus with her, which makes Tía and Mami mad but also laugh at the same time.

I don't know why sábanas can't wait till I get back from school. Growling, I slowly get up from the bed and start pulling the sheets. I've been dreaming about Mami's radical clothes and protest sign all weekend. Before I had sat with her to watch her play last Friday, it was hard to picture her doing anything other than yelling at us about sábanas, taking care of Abuelita, and getting mad at me for every little thing I do.

I swipe the pillow off the bed, and that's when I see it.

C.C.'s green lacy bra is lying there all smooshed from the weight of my head. I quickly grab it and fluff the little boob pads out and try to straighten the wire the way it was. Except I don't remember how it was. Then I put it up to my nose and sniff it once. I bury my nose in it and smell real hard. This is what womanhood and college smells like. I can't leave it here for Mami to find.

In the bathroom, I try it on, but I can't clip it together. My arms hurt just trying to reach behind my back. I can't believe some people do this *every day.* The strap slides off my shoulder and arms and I try to clip it first and then pull it over my head, but I hear a little tear, so I stop. I slip it off and look for the tear. A few silky hilos dangle. Hopefully C.C. won't notice when I slip it back in her suitcase later.

I finally get it on and look at myself in the mirror, except I can't get a good look at myself. I stand on the toilet and lean to the left and finally find a spot where I can get a good look. The strap around my ribs is so uncomfortable and it's already making my back itch.

I put my shirt over just to see how I will look. With a real bra, they look so high like they're trying to high-five my chin. I turn to my side. Then I bounce a little, careful not to break the toilet. I smile. Now in PE my boobs won't swing around in my bra like the stupid ball in the tetherball game we have to do outside. But the more I look at myself, the more I wonder if they're big enough.

Just then Abuelita starts knocking on the bathroom door, but I feel the toilet seat crack below my weight. She knocks again. I jump off and there's a small, perfectly straight crack all down the middle. I let her in, give her a kiss on the cheek, and quickly slip out.

"Gracias, chulita," she says, and closes the door.

I slip into Abuelita's room. I look for anything to stuff the bra with. I open her drawers, but it's all rosaries, lumpy socks, and Vicks in there. I untangle a pair of socks and stuff each side with a sock. I look in her mirror, but it's all lumpy. Everyone will know they're not real. I reach in and try to smooth them out, but that doesn't work.

"¡El bus! Ten minutes!" Mami screams from downstairs.

I pull the socks out and throw them back in the drawer, looking at the tub of Vicks. I'm so desperate, I open the plastic top and dig my hand deep into the jar and scoop out a giant messy clump of it. Stuff it into the left one. Then I do the same on the right. I close it and throw it back in and slam the drawer.

I quickly run to my room and grab the only thing I can find: a purple, stringy sweater from the dirty clothes basket. It smells gross and way too much material bunches up around the armpits and shoulders, but I have no choice. I don't want Mami noticing my new boobs. Downstairs, I pull my backpack to the front of my body as I head out the door. Mami looks at me weird, but I try to act as normal as possible until I'm finally outside and walking to the stop. I switch my backpack over and stand a little straighter and taller, letting the morning sun hit my new, round, and big boobs.

I'm sitting on the bus and drawing in Las Nerdas notebook when Gonzalo gets on. He looks at me and looks down for a second and then quickly back up, but it's too late. His eyes were all over me. He noticed. My stomach feels tight and I feel happy and real embarrassed all at the same time.

But I don't have time to think 'cause that's when I feel it.

The Vicks starts burning my boobs, and I want to scream and cry like I'm four.

We have three more stops till we get to school, and I feel like I can't take it anymore. I hold my backpack to my chest and bite down on one of the straps.

We finally get to school and I run to the bathroom. Ripping a bunch of toilet paper, I wipe off what's left of the Vicks. It still burns but not as much. I put my head back against the stall and close my eyes for a minute before heading to my locker.

Kai and Connie meet me at my locker. We do our Nerda handshake, but they look down.

"Whoa," says Kai.

My hands press against my boobs.

"Yeah, whoa. You look . . . bigger," says Connie.

And I tell them everything—the bra under my pillow, the socks, the Vicks, Gonzalo noticing. Kai adjusts my shirt and sweater so the neon green strap doesn't show, 'cause Kai always knows what to do. Our eyes meet.

"Kai, I'm really sorr—"

"It's fine," she says.

"No, really. I wish I had said something that day. Sometimes what I want to say just doesn't come out, and—"

Her shoulders drop and she playfully kicks my shoe. "It happens. We got it back, and that's what's important."

You got it back, I want to say.

I go in for the biggest hug, and Connie joins us. Then I take out the Nerda notebook and show them the doodles and notes from my night in the attic with C.C.

"What's that?" they say at the same time.

"Lani was right about everything—access to period stuff is really important, and there's just so many layers of it. My cousin, C.C., is organizing supplies for girls and women stuck in immigration cages. Some of them aren't given anything if they get their periods," I say.

We all exchange glances of shock and disgust, and try to shake the cloud that hangs over us as we walk to class.

IT'S HARD TO CONCENTRATE in any of my classes. The wire feels like it'll cut me if I make one wrong move. The wide collar of my shirt keeps falling off, and I play with the bra straps. One of the straps is looser than the other, and I can't seem to get them to be the same length. I see people look at me more, but maybe it's all in my head.

Mr. Neimar changed all of our seats today, and Genesis and I are in the back this time, but on opposite corners. The back row is actually the worst place to be, 'cause if you need to use the bathroom, the walk to the back row takes longer, and everyone looks at you. And if you take longer than two minutes, they start to wonder if you went number two.

I look over at Genesis and start to think about the bus a few weeks back and wonder if she noticed that I was sitting two rows behind her that day. But she's all eyes out the window and playing with a cross—the kind Abuelita wears—around her neck. My head hangs low, and I pick at bits of eraser flakes on the desk. My stomach feels like when you're at the very top of a rollercoaster and are about to go down. I feel guilty for not speaking up for her and letting Corey rub his greasy ketchup fingers all over her hair.

"Take out your pendulum lab reflection homework," says Mr. Neimar.

I think, What? We had homework this weekend? I'm not the only one, 'cause almost everyone's looking around. A few kids take it out and try to shove it toward Mr. Neimar as he walks through the aisles.

"I didn't say give it to me," he says and starts to swat with his hands like there's a bunch of flies in the room. He walks to the white board at the front of the class above the teacher lab station and points to the top left corner.

Due Monday
Finish section 3, Pendulum Lab reflection.

Uy. That's today. I missed it. I reach into my bag to at least make it seem like I'm looking for it. Maybe then he won't call on me.

"Once again, we'll switch things up today because no one is prepared," Mr. Neimar says.

It's a little unfair for him to say *no one* because maybe about eight kids did it, but they don't say anything.

"Take your lab reports out," he says. "Whether you did it or not. We will analyze the results."

Papers rustle. I take out a random scrunched up piece of paper, 'cause it's better than having nothing. One girl knocks over her full Hydro Flask with her foot. Some kids cover their ears and there's a collective "ouch" and "ugh." It's real hard to concentrate when all I keep thinking about is my new bra.

"Find section two: results," he says. He waits for everyone to find it.

Bzzz

A kid from the middle row gets up to sharpen his pencil. It's one of those small library pencils but he keeps shoving it in the sharpener and until it looks like he's about to sharpen his fingers. He looks my way and does the gross V with his hands.

Mr. Neimar looks at him and waits. "So, in part two you are—"

Bzzzzz

"Martin, please hold off until I am finished speaking," Mr. Neimar says.

Martin takes his pencil out of the sharpener.

"So—"

Bzzzzz.

"Martin, I'm not going to say it again."

Martin blows some of the shaving dust off the pencil and watches it fall to the floor. Then looks up at Mr. Neimar.

Mr. Neimar keeps staring at him, so he takes one step away from the sharpener. "Last week, you discovered with your lab partners that—"

Bzzzzz.

More kids laugh. Mr. Neimar wipes sweat from his forehead with paper towels from his desk. He walks over to Martin like he's about to take his pencil out of his hand. Instead, he yanks the cord out of the wall. I think he's going to leave it there, but he doesn't. He picks the whole electric pencil sharpener up and throws it across the room. It hits the back wall near where Genesis is sitting. The plastic that holds all the pencil shavings cracks into tiny pieces that fall on the floor. Pencil shavings explode into the air and rain down all over Genesis's long thick braid and the yellow wool sweater she's wearing even though it's like the hottest day in April.

Martin's mouth opens. A girl from the front of the room runs out and I hear her get the teacher next door. Mr. Neimar looks like he doesn't know what just happened.

It's quiet. Real quiet, probably how he wanted it from the beginning. No one says anything and I wonder if anyone will. Not me. Genesis gets up and runs out of the door. Some kids laugh. I hear two girls make fun of her outfit. I think of getting up and going after her, but I don't really know her. But then I think of Tía Beatriz who walked through a whole jungle just to write a story about one woman, and the protests where people wrote names of those they didn't even know. But me? I wasn't even brave enough to get our Nerdas notebook back. I wasn't even brave enough to stand up for Genesis on the bus when they put ketchup in her hair. I'm not about to make that mistake again, so I get up and run after her. Mr. Neimar doesn't try to stop us.

I see the bathroom door down the hall swing shut so I run toward it. There are six stalls and the last one is closed. I can see Genesis's thick, low black heels—the kind my abuelita wears to church—and her long skirt. I can hear little cries and it sounds like an animal trapped somewhere inside.

"Genesis?" I say, but my voice cracks.

She stops crying.

"It's Mani. I'm in your science class . . . and English and history," I say. "We actually have pretty much the same schedule, even though we've never talked. Oh, and you ride my bus."

Still quiet.

She lifts one foot and pushes the stall door open, still sitting on the toilet. It's kinda awkward, but at least her skirt is still on. Her hair is in her face and her eyes are already starting to look like puffy pillows from crying so hard. She's biting the cross she wears around her neck. I guess everyone has their own weird thing they do when they're upset. (For example, I pick my toenails. At least that's better than Connie chewing her nails, because at least no one sees your toenails, unless you wear sandals, but Mami doesn't let me, 'cause sandals are for the playa, not for school.)

I can see the pencil shavings in her hair. Her hair's as dark as mine but real curly and I don't know how she's going to get those out. She starts talking superfast, so I can't really understand what she's saying. She's crying and hiccupping all at the same time. From what I can gather, Genesis's mom must be like Mami; there's no way she'd believe her version as to why there are pencil shavings laced in her hair and sweater.

I want to tell her that Mami is the same, but she starts with her crying, hiccupping, and loud snot sucking, and I can't get a word in to make her feel better. Then she puts her face in her hands. I sit on the floor. The wall outside her stall is cold against my back, but I stay and keep her company. (Abuelita once said sometimes people just need your company, not your words.)

Then I get an idea. I take off my purple sweater and I offer it to her.

"You know, just during school. You can give it back to me on the bus," I say. "And hey, maybe we can sit together?"

She smiles, takes hers off and puts it on and it doesn't swim on her. It fits her perfectly, and actually looks cute on her. Then she looks down at my shirt and she's kind of staring, which makes me feel all self-conscious. I look down and the green of the bra is the tiniest bit visible under my white T-shirt. Maybe it's 'cause Genesis is in a vulnerable place right now, but I tell her about the bra and how it's not mine.

"Are you sure you don't want your sweater?" she says. "It's just a little see-through."

"No, really. It's OK. I think it's just the lighting in here."

The lunch bell rings and I hear the roar of the hallways. Genesis's puffy, crying eyes look directly at mine.

"Hey, want to have lunch with me and my friends?" I say. "We sneak food in the library."

She nods and smiles and that makes me feel all warm and proud like when you finally don't mess up a recipe.

We fight the crowd and make it back to science class to get our stuff. Luckily, no one is there. Not even Mr. Neimar. The pencil shavings are still on the floor, but they've been kicked around by everyone's shoes.

Downstairs, everyone is crowded around the library doors with a big sign. "Library CLOSED for lunch today."

Just then, Kai and Connie get there. Kids all around us are talking, and I hear a million *Oh my God*'s and some of them are trying to look through the glass on the doors. The principal, Mr. Dupont, is in there.

"Mr. Neimar's in there too!"

I look around to see who said it, and it's not even someone from my science class.

More kids crowd around the doors and some of them step on my shoes, but then the librarian comes and covers the window with black posterboard. It seems like EVERYBODY is talking about how Mr. Neimar is going to get fired and *That is so awesome.*

Mr. Neimar's definitely not my favorite teacher, and I think it's messed up Genesis almost got hit by a flying pencil sharpener, but the thing is, sometimes I want to throw an electric pencil sharpener across the room too. Like when Corey and Mason do the V thing, or when people talk about my body like it's theirs to comment on.

"OMG is it true?" says Connie. "Did that happen in YOUR class?"

Nodding, I look over at Genesis. I introduce her even though they already kind of know who she is.

We start to walk, but Connie puts her hand on my shoulder to stop me.

"What?" I say.

"Your bra is kinda showing," Connie whispers real loud.

"I think it's cute," says Kai. "My sister wears it like that on purpose; it's like a whole style in high school. And college, I think."

I look down at my shirt. It wasn't the bathroom lighting. If you look real hard, you can see a faint green outline of a REAL grown-woman bra, but even if you don't look hard. Maybe it's 'cause I was brave enough to run out of class and help someone even if I don't know them that well, but I feel brave now, with a real bra, even though I don't have my period yet.

We head to the courtyard, but that's when we see it's pouring rain outside, and they're not letting anyone out.

"No!" Connie yells.

I just shake my head.

"Come on, Mani, the cafeteria won't be that bad," says Kai, all casual like she's forgetting Nerda rule number three:

We Avoid the Cafeteria no Matter What.

"Yeah, no one will even notice us," says Connie, trying to sound encouraging, but it doesn't work, 'cause she's the one who wrote rule number three. "No one's gonna bother us. Look how many people there are. And plus, they'll all be talking about Mr. Neimar."

I scratch below the bra strap that's rubbing against my shoulder and get a whiff of Vicks. I tighten my grip around my lunch box.

THIRTEEN

THE CAFETERIA IS MY WORST nightmare (except even in my worst nightmare, there's flan at the end).

"Eat quick, ladies," says a real nice teacher on lunch duty. "Remember we're doing a drill at some point today. Could be now," she says and shrugs.

We have emergency drills like every month at this point, and it's real confusing 'cause what we have to do if there's a threat IN the building is different than if the threat is OUTSIDE the building, and even more confusing if you're in the cafeteria or the PE fields if it happens then.

Connie counts her lunch money real quick, checking if she has enough to get french fries. Genesis reaches far down her shirt and into her bra and takes out some folded dollars. I can't help but laugh a little, but not to be mean or anything.

"My abuelita carries her money like that," I say, but I realize that probably sounded like an insult.

"My mom told me to do that so no one steals it," she says. She smooths out the dollars.

Connie grabs Genesis by the hand and they make their way to the lunch line. My face breaks into a smile thinking that my action helped Genesis make not just one new friend but three.

"Find us a good spot!" Connie yells, looking back at us.

Except there are none. Each time Kai and I see an opening, someone swings their leg and slams their tray or lunch box down. We finally find a corner of a table right next to the trash can. It smells worse than the bathroom stalls during last period. It's really only for two people, but we all squeeze in at the end of the table.

I open my lunch box. A black bean sandwich topped with crispy fried garlic between two multi-seed bread slices that are more seed than bread. Tucked underneath the sandwich wrapper is a piece of paper. One of Mami's songs that she was singing last Friday.

"What's that?" Kai says.

I quickly flatten the paper back into the bottom of my lunch box. "Nothing, just stuff my mom wants me to do when I get home," I say.

I know I'm not supposed to keep secrets from Las Nerdas, but Connie and Genesis are coming toward us and I don't even know where I would start. Some kids get hearts and *I love you* notes in their lunch box, which is still embarrassing, but I get songs about birds running the rainforest and waiting till they can sing again one day. I know Kai would have some big answer and plan for what I should do and what it all means, but like I said, this one I want to figure out for myself.

Kai's stew of chicken, carrots, and rice makes my nose all sweaty. Connie smiles at her tray of french fries, pizza, and a giant chocolate chip cookie. My stomach growls. Connie offers me a bite, but I can't 'cause pizza is her favorite.

"Look at all that food in there. Like, an entire apple. A bag of baby carrots. It's such a waste of food," Genesis says, peering into the open lid next to us.

Then I remember her Speak Up project idea, and how brave she was in class and how the words slipped right off her tongue, all confident like when C.C. talks about repro rights and stuff. She tells us about how her abuela had an organic farm back in Honduras, and how she taught women in the community to compost. She had gray water toilets, which she said are basically toilets you don't flush and that don't use water. We all agree that sounds nasty, but she says they don't smell at all.

"That farm sounds amazing," I say. "Why'd you move?"

She shrugs. "I mean, you know, la violencia and stuff," she says.

"Do you remember any of it?" Kai asks, taking the words out of my mouth. (My brain, at least.)

"Not really. I was really young when we left, but my mom's always telling me stories," she says. "She tells me to always remember where I came from, no matter where I'm forced to go. She's really dramatic sometimes," she says, and sips from her can of guanabana juice I recognize from Sabor de Mi Tierra.

We laugh, 'cause all our moms are dramatic.

"I think it was hard for them to go from living on a big farm back in Honduras, and then moving to a tiny apartment here. But check this out: My mom convinced the building owner to let us start a roof garden for all the tenants as long as they contributed and helped keep it up."

It makes sense now why Genesis got all excited and quetzal-like talking about composting and reducing food waste in Ms. Martinez's class. And I wonder how her mom's violencia makes her want to start a community garden, and *my* mom's violencia makes her scared to get on a bus, or to get me clothes that fit. (And my tía's violencia made her want to sing with random women on the sides of highways.)

"But—" she says, with hesitation in her voice, "my mom's kind of religious. OK, like really religious. I guess I am too, a little. . . ."

"My abuelita's the same," I say. "She prays the rosary like a million times a day."

She laughs in that I-know-what-you're-talking-about kind of way.

"When we first moved here, it was really hard, but my parents found a really religious church, and I guess that kind of became their community," she says. "Maybe they feel like they owe them, for helping them so much when we first got here."

I ask her if she speaks Spanish and she says she has no other option, 'cause her parents don't speak English, so they depend on her like when they sign the lease to their apartment, or go to different offices to sign up for things, even though I remember C.C. telling me that many places are required by law to provide translations, kinda like how Mami is there to translate at different hospitals and medical offices whenever someone needs it.

We ask her more about the gray water toilets and la violencia, and she's got the sparkle in her eyes that all the women in my family have. We laugh, even though we're talking about la violencia, but maybe it's kinda like my disappeared tía's letters—like joy and pain are two separate hilos that eventually come together. No sé.

Then Kai, Connie, and I look at each other in that she-could-be-a-Nerda way, even though we've never really considered anybody else.

"Hey, sorry if this is weird, but . . . have you gotten it yet?" Kai says.

"Gotten what?" asks Genesis.

"It," Connie says all mysterious and hush-hush.

"Your period," Kai says, rolling her eyes at Connie.

Genesis tightens her scrunchie and pushes around the leftover crust on her lunch tray.

"No."

"We haven't either!" Connie and I say at the same time, a little too loud, which makes us laugh. Genesis starts laughing too, and then eats her extra hard pizza crust, 'cause you know, no food waste and all.

We're still laughing when we feel drops of water. Then Genesis stops smiling and she gets all tense like when a teacher's about to call on you for an answer you don't know.

Corey, Mason, Max, and some other guys from our bus are walking over. Mason and Max poke holes in their plastic water bottles with pencils and spray the tables around them. No one tells them to stop, 'cause they're the meanest and most popular guys in school.

"Oh, it's vagina girl!" Mason practically yells. Then Corey puts down his tray of pizza and with his other hand pretends to throw his football across the cafeteria. (For one, we don't have a football team, and for two, I still don't know why he's allowed to walk around with his football if Kai isn't allowed to walk around with her ukulele.)

Then Max burps real loud in Corey's face, and throws away an unopened bag full of baby carrots. Corey fake punches him in the gut. Mason throws his almost full bottle of water out like plastic pollution in oceans and water shortages aren't a thing.

Then Corey takes a deep breath and blows into the empty bag of Takis in his hand till it inflates up like a small balloon, and with his other hand pops it real hard in someone's ear at the table next to ours.

"I bet you'd get with her," he says to Max and Mason, pointing out different girls to them. Then he squints his eyes, looks around the room and pinches his pointy nose. "Ew! Do you guys smell that?"

All I smell is the cafeteria which smells like feet, Takis, pizza crusts, and vegetables fermenting together in the trash can. Then they're standing right above me. Corey points down. He's so close, his Takis-stained finger almost touches my black bean sandwich with toasted garlic on top.

I wish Mr. Neimar had gotten all mad during lunch duty now, instead of in class, 'cause then Mason, Corey, and Max could have paid attention to the flying electric sharpener, instead of what Mami packed me for lunch. But then his finger grazes my shirt, and everything inside of me shrivels up.

"Naaaasty," says Mason and they all start laughing.

When I finally look up to meet their eyes, they're not looking at my lunch.

They're looking down at my shirt.

I look over at Genesis who's wearing my purple sweater. I want to just hide under the table. I want to jump into the trash can. No, that's gross. I rest my elbows on the table to cover my boobs.

"Hey Mani, did your boobs grow or something?" Mason says.

"Can I check?" says Corey.

I squeeze my lunch box against my chest.

"Be quiet," Kai manages to say to them, 'cause she's the bravest of all of us. She always knows what to say.

Even Connie speaks up. "Yeah, why don't you just go away," she says.

They look at me, but nothing comes out of my mouth. (It's like when you have to present in front of the class, and you feel like you're gonna barf.) Even Genesis looks at me, waiting for me to speak up. I want to stand, get in their face, talk with my hands like Mami when she's enojada or she's got something important to tell me.

What would my disappeared tía have said if she were here to defend me now? What did she say when the man tried to break Maribel's camera?

"Yeah, stop being so ignorant," is all I manage to say, except my voice is so quiet, like I've got laryngitis, or like I didn't brush my teeth and don't want anyone to smell. (No sé. Don't know what's worse. At least with laryngitis, it's, like, a medical condition or something, definitely something you can get an excused absence for.)

Then we're saved by Mr. Dupont's voice over the intercom, announcing the drill. But then his last words get muffled by the alarm itself. The idiot boys start shaking the trash can and making really weird, loud sounds. Corey throws his empty Takis bag at Max. It hits his chest and the rest of the crumbs come falling out. They leave the bag on the floor and run out toward the exit doors.

"Thank you for walking!" the lunch duty teachers yell. (This new talking in opposites thing they started doing since spring break really isn't working.)

Kai, Connie, and I head to the back door and onto the field like we were told in the first drill training, 'cause we've grown up with warnings of la violencia hanging over our heads, so it is an unspoken Nerda rule that while we fight the system, we take all drills seriously and follow instructions: If you are in the cafeteria, you run into the soccer field. Genesis follows us.

We find a spot away from trees so we can feel the sun, but I feel bad for Genesis. I bet she's toda sudando under my sweater, and I think of how hot her feet must feel in those thick black misa heels. I look down at my shirt and this stupid bra. Is this what A'niya feels like? Do guys just say stupid things about your bra and boobs all day along? Do guys still do that when you get to high school and college?

"Hey, what if we skipped the rest of the day?" I ask, partly for the adventure, and partly 'cause I don't want to go back in there with my see-through shirt and fake boobs. Back to where my voice never comes out. Not in a way that counts, anyway.

Genesis looks at me, surprised. "You guys skip class?"

"Mani's just talking," Kai says, a little too quickly.

She says it with a voice so strong and sure it sticks to the air, the kind of voice I can't seem to find in myself, ever.

"What do you mean?" I ask, even though I know what she means. Kind of.

Connie glances back and forth between us.

"Nothing. Forget it," Kai says.

But I can't forget it. My heart feels like when your bike pedal bumps up against your heel and cuts it a little. "That wasn't *nothing*. What do you mean, I'm just talking?" I say, getting closer to her but wanting to run far, far away.

Mr. Dupont starts yelling at everyone on his bullhorn to be quiet and to treat this drill like a real thing. Kai's voice gets softer and lower and there's all this space between each word.

"I'm just saying. You're not really a doer. You say a lot, but you're not a doer," she says, but her words are weak and trail off, and the last syllables get lost with the blaring bullhorn, like it hurts her mouth to say them.

AT THE BUS LOOP, Kai and Connie don't run to my line, and I don't go to theirs.

The right strap of my bra keeps getting loose and now my boobs look all lopsided. Genesis stands right next to me and tries to smile every once in a while. She even offers to give me the sweater back now instead of when we get to her stop.

"It's OK, but thanks," I say.

I put my backpack over my chest now. Having big boobs sucks. Especially when it starts to rain. All I want to do is take this bra off and go back to my usual flatness. Except I tried to go to the bathroom in between classes to take it off, but I couldn't reach the back clasp. And plus, I wore a white shirt, on a rainy day (like a tonta, even though Abuelita's always saying that in this country where you can be anything, just don't be a tonta or a pendeja, which I think are kinda the same thing).

"Take your sweater back, Mani. I'm serious. I feel bad."

But I just shake my head. I finally do something nice for Genesis and I'm not about to take it back.

"Hey, I don't want to get between you and Kai, but you gave me your sweater to help me out, even though it led to those idiots saying gross stuff and you and Kai fighting. You stood up for me. That's being a doer," says Genesis.

I force a smile in that *thanks* kind of way. I know she's just trying to make me feel better, but for a second I wonder if that is what makes a doer. And if I can never speak up for myself, at least I spoke up for someone else and well . . . does that count for something?

Our bus pulls up, and we all elbow our way on. Genesis and I sit in the third row from the front. The other glasses kids beat us to the front row, again.

"Two more minutes and we're outta here!" says Mr. Sanchez as he looks up in the mirror.

Then Max comes and sits in the empty seat in front of us. He pulls out his phone and aims it at us.

"Hey, you shouldn't film people without their permission," Genesis says to him, none of the usual softness to her voice.

"Do it, bro," he shouts above us.

Before I can look back, that's when I feel it. A sweaty, Takis-greased hand on my shoulder and SNAP!

The bra strap lifts and hits my skin so hard it burns. I hear the lace tear. The sting makes me want to cry.

Genesis jumps in her seat and puts her arm around my back and then on my shoulder. Her touch makes it sting even more, so I move away. I reach back, but my hand can't feel the back of the bra. I don't feel the lace that connects the strap to the back clasp.

"Bro, you broke her bra," Max says, hiccupping from laughing, his phone bouncing in his hand. "I got it! I got it!"

Another kid picks up the metal piece of the clasp. Only my left boob is being held up by half the bra, but it's starting to slip. A few kids point and laugh. A few girls look grossed out at the boys, but not enough to say anything. I watch Max get up and stand next to Corey, typing something and repeating, "I got it" with a stupid grin on his face. Lani's warning *Don't be in one of those videos*, rings in my ears. I think back to when I saw Corey rub ketchup on Genesis's hair and I wonder if this is what it feels like when no one speaks up for you. Then I hear Max again, "You're welcome!" and the slapping sounds of their high fives. I want to grab his phone from him and throw it out the window before he can do anything with what he just filmed.

But I can't move. I sit there, facing them, all congelada, like a tonta with nothing coming out of my mouth. The bus feels like it's spinning. Why can't I come up with something feisty to say like Abuelita? Or turn my anger into power like C.C.? Or be a doer like Kai, who obviously learned from Lani? Or get all enojada-blow-chicle-bubbles-in-your-face like A'niya?

Maybe Kai is right. I'm not a doer. And maybe that means I'll never get a quetzal voice like Abuelita tells me.

I want to transform into something more powerful. I want to raise my fist like the one C.C. draws next to her signature; the one that holds the songs of those with real quetzal voices. And so I do. Except instead of raising it up into the air, I'm standing and my right palm is on Corey's mouth. But I don't know how it got there. Or maybe I do, but my body takes over before I have a chance to stop it. And then again.

More kids start to take out their phones, and I feel dizzy. I look around for Max, worried about how much he filmed. Then I look down at my hand. I've never hit anything (not even my pillow after our old neighbor's quinceañera, when all the uncles were talking about my body, comparing boob and hip size like the girls' bodies were made up of broken pieces of a plate that you have to put together after you accidentally drop it. I decided then and there I hated quinceañeras, even though it'd be real nice to be fifteen).

A little bit of Corey's saliva is on my palm. I don't feel good about it. It was just a reaction, I think. I fight the feeling in my gut that's pushing me to say *sorry*.

The phone kids start yelling, "Fight! Fight! Fight!"

I look from my hand to Corey, who's now cupping his nose and eyes and flailing around in the back seat, even though I know I got his nasty Takis-stained mouth instead.

Mr. Sanchez's voice snaps me back.

"Hey! Stop that right now!" Then he unclicks his seat belt and I think he's going to walk over to us, but instead he gets off the bus and calls Mr. Dupont over, who's patrolling the bus loop with his bullhorn. Mr. Dupont jumps onto the bus.

"What is this I hear about inappropriate behavior on the bus!" he screams, looking at me.

I stare at my shoelaces. Then at the spider on the seat in front of me. Anything to avoid his eye contact.

"I am going to remind each and every one of you that the bus is an extension of school property," he says. "The student code of conduct applies *here*, just as much as in there." He looks directly at me again. "Young lady, you want to explain your actions?" he says, walking closer to me till he's towering above me. But it doesn't feel like a question. Not really. The whole bus waits for me to answer, and Corey flails around in his seat, all exagerado.

He snapped my bra—well, not *my* bra, but the one I'm wearing—I want to say, but for one, I don't want to say *bra* to the principal, and for two, the words are all jumbled up.

But then Corey stands, hand off his nose, and says, "I was just telling her that her bra was showing through her white shirt. I thought she'd wanna know."

His friends start laughing.

"I was trying to be nice," he adds.

"That's not true," Genesis manages to say, but I think only the people in front of us can hear her little voice, nothing like her voice when she's talking about composting and food waste. She says it a little louder, but Mr. Dupont ignores her like she's not even here.

"Physical violence is not one of the values in the student code of conduct," he says.

Neither is ripping someone's bra off their back, I think. Isn't that physical violence? My palm stings with Corey's nasty Takis mouth. I make everyone on the bus invisible, especially the phone kids Mr. Dupont hasn't even addressed. He hasn't even taken their phones away. I breathe the shake out of my voice. Maybe I am brave, I think, so I speak up.

"He snapped my bra," I finally say, even though I should've said *ripped*. "And Max filmed—"

The boys start to laugh, but Mr. Dupont doesn't say anything to them.

"It was showing, Mr. Dupont. I was just trying to fix it, I swear!" Corey says, cupping his nose again.

"Gentlemen," Mr. Dupont says. "I know our hormones are charging full force right now, but let's please keep our hands to ourselves to avoid any misunderstanding with young ladies. And how many times do I need to remind you of inappropriate phone use?"

Misunderstanding!? Genesis looks at him and then at me like she can't believe what he's saying, like it's so unfair there are no words. That's what it feels like, at least. I hate this bra, and the pointless lace and the broken strap that gave me lopsided boobs all day. I fold my arms over my chest and look away, and that's when I see

Gonzalo who's looking straight at me, but then he quickly turns and looks out the window. I can't believe I ever thought his colochos were all cute, especially now, all eyes out the window pretending nothing happened. I wish I could pretend nothing happened too.

Genesis takes off my sweater. She shakes some of the pencil shavings out that had fallen from her hair, and puts it over me. This time, I take it.

MAMI'S ALREADY GOTTEN the phone call. I know, 'cause she's washing the dishes real loud, somatando the plates like they did something to her. She must have just gotten home, 'cause her badge is still on over her work clothes.

I don't give her a hug, or a kiss on the cheek, and she doesn't turn around to say hola. I start to set the table, even though it's only 3:45 p.m., but maybe this way she'll tone down the enojo. But the more noise I make, the more noise she makes, like even our plates are mad at each other.

She turns the faucet off.

"We didn't move here so you could be one of those niñas flojas," she says, still looking at the dishes.

I think it's unfair she brings up moving to the only country I know like I had anything to do with it. And how am I a niña floja? My bra-not-my-bra was ripped off me for a cruel social media challenge, the one Lani warned us about. Maybe I shouldn't say any of this, 'cause then I'd have to tell her about the bra. But she doesn't stop.

"Your principal says you are really enjoying new attention from boys," she says. "He says it's normal for seventh grade, qué sé yo, cosa de gringo, but no señorita. Not in this house. You think attention from boys is what is going to get you to college? To a good job? To live a long life?"

I don't know why she's talking about college and good jobs and long lives, when all I'm trying to do is survive the bus ride home.

I try to picture her not as she is now, with her back turned to me leaning over the kitchen sink and angry, but like in the picture, next to clothes laid out by a canal, holding a sign that says "Our clothes did not invite your violence."

"My clothing doesn't excuse their violence," I mutter, remembering the signs from the picture.

"¿Qué dijiste?"

She turns around to face me, the kitchen gloves dripping soapy water onto the floor.

I say it again, louder this time.

"What are you talking about?"

Maybe if I tell her what really happened—that he ripped the bra off my back so hard that it hurt all just so someone could take a video and post it for the whole universe to see—maybe she'd understand, right? But then I'd have to tell her that I wore a big bra with those pillow inserts and lace, and how I stole it out of C.C.'s suitcase, and maybe that would put me in the niña floja category, and that's just one step from a pepereca, which is the worst.

So I don't. She never listens to me. And I start to doubt that the woman in the picture is really her, even though I know it is. I just go to my room and I pull what's left of the bra off. I pick up my pillow to put the bra underneath it, and punch the bra into the mattress. I never want to see it again. I imagine the torn bra in one of Tía Beatriz's pictures, tattered and staged along a canal for a picture, waiting to tell a messed-up story. Normally I'd tell Las Nerdas about what happened. I open the Nerda Google doc. Nothing since this morning. No new activity, and no one's even online. I let the screen go black on its own.

Mami barely talks to me the rest of the week (and no sé, but your own mom not talking to you is kinda like peeing in the pool. Like it shouldn't be allowed).

FOURTEEN

Forty-nine days to convince Mami
she's wrong about Guatemala

AT DINNER A WEEK LATER, I ask Mami to pass the plátanos.

She's still mad from when Mr. Dupont called her last week to tell her I've been enjoying attention from boys. Mr. Dupont had Mr. Sanchez assign me a seat at the front of the bus, but didn't assign one to Corey or his friends. One girl in the PE locker room told me she saw the video of me on that grope page Lani mentioned. She said it got a few comments, but that you couldn't really see my face with the video focused on the bra and Corey's grubby hand. *And plus,* she said, *it got lost among other videos that week that were way, way worse.* I want to tell Mr. Dupont about the disgusting page and the video of me, but the idea of anyone watching it feels like my bra being ripped off me all over again.

Dad's been trying for the past week to ask me what happened, but I don't really want to talk. Mami never asked for my side of the story. All she has said to me is, "I didn't raise you like that."

Raise me like what? I think. To defend myself?

I don't want to talk to her, but she's sitting right next to the plátanos, and if I don't get the crispy ones first, I know Abuelita will.

The edges are all burnt and crispy with cinnamon dusted on top, just like I like them.

"Can you please pass the plátanos?" I say, all muffled, kinda like when I'm singing the songs in church but I don't actually know the words.

I wait to see if she'll pass them, but she doesn't. I say it louder, except now Mami doesn't hear me for real this time 'cause Abuelita starts singing these old-timey rancheras at the top of her lungs like she's auditioning for the old *Sábado Gigante* show she's made me watch with her so many times. No one wants to ask her to stop 'cause when she starts singing, we know her mind is stuck in the olden days, and she might start crying all over again for her missing daughter like the night I told everyone I didn't know where my vulva was. So we just all talk louder, which only makes her sing louder. Dad's not here to level it all out with his calm energy, 'cause he teaches English for free one night per week at the library in our old neighborhood.

I get up and reach over Mami and Tía to serve myself. I think about what Kai said to me last week when we stopped talking. I've been avoiding them in health and history class, and in the bus loop. I stopped checking our Google doc a few days ago, even though I want to write something so bad. Her words sting like a rusty safety pin. (The kind my abuelita carries around with her at church in case anyone is looking all indecente in front of God. Like when "Juana la viuda" wore a shirt a little too low. Except instead of offering her those safety pins, Abuelita and Tía Gladys just kept calling her a pepereca while the safety pins sat snug in her purse. I don't know why someone has to dress like a nun just 'cause their husband died.)

But what do I know? When you're almost thirteen and haven't even gotten your period yet and your pimples and purple glasses are even bigger than your boobs, everyone treats you like you don't know anything worth knowing. It's not the first time I've been confused at church, or by Abuelita's feminism. I wonder if Abuelita and Tía Gladys are going to Hell for saying pepereca in church. Yeah, Kai's words hurt and confuse me worse than—

"I won't be going back to that school. Not now, but maybe not ever," says C.C.

I look up at C.C., half a plátano hanging out of my mouth.

"¿Qué?" Mami, Tía, and Abuelita all say at the same time.

I had asked C.C. for weeks when she had to go back, and she hadn't said anything. She didn't tell me first, and that stings worse than a zancudo in summertime. Maybe she tried to tell me; I've been stuck in my own problems lately.

"I got in a fight with my philosophy professor. It didn't start as a big deal, and then it just blew up. He said I couldn't write my final research paper on manspreading. He said it's not a thing. We got in a huge fight about it," she says.

"¿Qué es ese *manspreading*?" Tía Gladys asks, like it's one of those new diet fads Doña Marta is always trying to get her to try. I want to know too.

"You ever notice how on the bus and the train men take up more space? Like they just spread their legs out?" C.C. leans back in her chair, legs and feet wide apart, which is a real malcriada thing to do at the dinner table.

"No seas grosera," Tía Glady says to her, but C.C. doesn't move. She waits for someone to agree, but no one does. To be honest, when I think about it, yeah, I'm pretty sure that's how some guys sit in class.

"Ay, Carolina. You're in college to get a good job, advance in life, not . . . ," Tía Gladys starts to say, and puts her head in her hands. "I knew I shouldn't have let you go to that feminist school. Doña Marta warned me. She said they would fill your head with porquerías and you'd probably turn out to be lesbian," she says. Then she starts to cry like she just got told someone died. "¿Dime, mija, te gustan las mujeres, verdad?"

Doña Marta is a part-time tarot card reader and full-time homophobe. She has a little foldable card table next to the Sabor de Mi Tierra supermarket and Tía Gladys always stops to see her. I guess it's fine and all to go to a tarot card reader until they make you do something stupid. (Like once, she told Tía Gladys to stand in a fountain barefoot at midnight and "Tu vida se llenará de hombres." But instead of a life full of men, all it got her was a nasty fungus on her toe. I don't know why she still goes.)

Mami is staring directly at C.C. like she's lost in some deep thought.

"Stop talking about that vieja homophobe," C.C. says. "This is real. The way men take up space affects women's bodies; it makes us shrink, and walk around public spaces like we don't belong in them. It's a public health issue. It's a type of violence."

When we used to live in the apartment, we took the bus to go get groceries. Mami would sit me on her lap to make space for others, like she was making us more compact than we already were, for the rest of the world. For men. I think about that time Tía Gladys took me to her citizenship class at the library 'cause no one else could watch me that day and I couldn't stay home alone, and the immigration officer who came to give a talk walked around like we were in trouble, and he kept putting his hand on his gun, and how Tía Gladys flinched each time he did it, and she never went back, and—

"Then he started mansplaining stuff about how that's not how women feel or walk around and other garbage like that, and basically trying to tell me how I experience the world, and then he got weird asking me if I thought he did that—"

Abuelita stops singing and C.C. realizes how loud she's speaking over her, so she lowers her voice.

"Chulita," Abuelita says. "How do you ever expect to start a family with all those feminist thoughts?"

It's like against the law or something to get mad at your abuelita. But just then I get so upset with her and wish she would switch to the part of her brain that thinks the world is all unfair and we should all be feminists and know where our vulva is.

"Carolina, that's not why we came here," Tía Gladys says. "We didn't sacrifice for you to just quit." She rubs her temples and sighs all loud like C.C. just squashed her American dream.

Sounds like what Mami told me a few days ago. All I hear about is all the reasons why they *didn't* come here, but not one of them tells me why they *did*.

"That's not a reason to leave school, C.C. If you didn't agree with your professor, you should have just challenged him, in a productive way," says Mami.

Challenge!? Why didn't Mami tell me to challenge Mr. Dupont? All Mami ever tells me to be is obedient.

"We can talk about this later," Mami says, then looks at me. I hate it when she changes the subject right in front of me like I'm not mature enough to hear what they're talking about.

"Manuela, how was school today?" Mami says, and I can't believe she has the nerve to make *me* the center of attention.

There's a lot I could say.

"In history, we're working on a project . . . the Speak Up competition that happens every year . . . if we win, we get invited to New York for a social justice camp thing just for people my age. Kai, Connie, and I picked our topic. The final presentation is on my birthday, so I have to—"

"¡Ya basta con eso, Manuela!" Mami says. "We're going to Guatemala. We have to leave that day. We have something the next day. Es complicado. We just have to, understand?"

I throw down the other plátano I've been picking at, like it did something mean to me. I'm tired of her shady answers, and her shady history that has nothing to do with me but that she still makes me feel guilty about.

"Going there doesn't mean anything to me anyway!" I say, way louder than I've ever spoken to Mami.

That's when she says it.

"Sometimes I don't even know how you came from me," she says. She puts her hands on the table and looks down, and it looks like it hurt her to say it.

Her words cut me worse than like five paper cuts in a row when you're trying to organize your binder. It makes Kai calling me not-a-doer not that bad. My eyes burn. The tears start to fall down my face, and they taste all nasty and salty in my mouth, not like sweet, burnt sticky plátano stuck to my teeth. I push my chair back.

"Maní, wait," I hear C.C. say.

But then I hear my Abuelita say, "Dejala, chulita. Crying is good for you. Tightens the skin."

I run upstairs and bury my face in my pillow. The tears streaming down my face and into my ears muffle their voices downstairs.

I WAIT FOR C.C. OR MAMI TO come upstairs, but they don't. Instead, from my room I hear the creaky door to the porch, and I know they're heading outside, where I can always hear conversations right below my window. They'll probably be out there for a while like always, so I go grab the ladder and bring it back to my room and lock the door.

I climb to the attic and go to the tin box with the stack of letters and pull the next letter from the pile. It's dated six months after the last one. Behind it is an article. "Women's Protests Grow in Numbers." Below are pictures from Maribel. I see her name in tiny print at the bottom of the pictures. A woman in a traditional bright turquoise and yellow boxy shirt and long red skirt holds a bullhorn and a sign that reads, "¿Dónde estan?" A woman next to her in a green shirt holds a sign that says, "Ya no tenemos miedo."

There's a handwritten note on a small piece of paper taped to the article. In the note, Tía Beatriz says that with the collective of journalists they started documenting groups of women who are looking for their daughters and challenging the police, led by a woman whose daughter was "disappeared" by her police boyfriend. She writes something about the instruments they carry and the songs they sing, and how the air is filled with both laughter and pain.

Then I open the letter clipped to the article and find several more pictures.

Dear Isabela,

I screamed when I received your letter!

Mami wrote back!? I reread the words over and over again like maybe I got it wrong.

Please don't apologize. There is nothing to forgive. I understand what you did. I might have done the same if I were you. And look at her. Manuela is beautiful. Thank you for sending me her picture. I keep it with me while we're working. She keeps me safe and brave.

Forgive her for what?

I hear the patio door close and it scares me so much I drop the letter and accidentally step all over the stack. My ear is pressed against the attic door, and I hear C.C.'s voice. They've moved to the kitchen table, where the voices echo up into my room:

"Worse, he put his hand on my back and started rubbing it and said he could help me figure out other topics." She had a quiver in her voice that made my heart kind of sting.

I hear her start crying, and then hers, Mami's, and Tía's Spanglish turns to a little more Spanish, so between that and the crying, I don't really catch much of it. Their voices get all high-pitched and they're all talking at the same time. Kai told me once that her sister stopped piano classes 'cause the teacher would always touch her knee while she was playing. Eventually it was her thigh, and then more. She kind of sucked at the piano after that and then started hating it. Maybe that's when she broke Kai's finger. But Kai's sister is tough and almost as cool as C.C., and there's no way something like that would happen to them, right?

And then I think about what Tía Gladys told C.C.

That's not why we came here.

My whole life I've been hearing that they came here because bad things happen in Guatemala. But C.C. just quit school because her professor was trying to touch her.

Now I know that in this house we keep secrets and only say them out loud when squeezed like limón. I know what happened to C.C. isn't as bad as like getting on a bus and disappearing like Tía Beatriz, but it still seems messed up.

Then they switch completely to Spanish, which feels like opening the horno after everyone told you *not yet* and feeling like your eyeballs are getting burned off. And I start to hate Spanish all over again, like that time Mami's cousin's uncle stayed with us and when I was alone with him in the kitchen, he made a comment about how my boobs looked like little lemons, except the Spanish word he used for boobs sounded all nasty and gropey and I decided then and there with my little lemon boobs that I hated Spanish. And I did until C.C. got me excited about it with her books and ideas and stories. But I decide here and now that Spanish is a language of hurt and secrets kept in dusty attics.

I lie down but that's when I remember that C.C.'s bra is under the pillow. I pull it out and put it on again—even though it's ripped and won't close. I put my hands against the bra, in the safety of my own room where no one will rip it or touch me when I don't want to be touched. There's a lot I can't get out of my head. I think about what it's like to be the sad C.C., the C.C. who lost her quetzal voice when someone tried to rip her wings. It seems like all this bad stuff people are doing against girls and women is happening all around me. Not just in Guatemala.

And I never realized until today. The rest of the week, I think about how somewhere, somehow, a tía I never met turned rage into power.

FIFTEEN

*Forty-five days till I'm forced to sit next to Mami
on an airplane and practice my pronunciation
so I don't embarrass her*

By Friday, fourth-period English stinks more than normal. And normal is already bad. Today it smells like fresh farts and Sharpie markers trapped in a plastic bag on a warm day.

"Does anyone else smell that?" I say to everyone and no one.

Jordyn turns her head to the right and looks at me like I didn't even say it in English. I shouldn't be surprised. Her brain is all small when she's mean. (Like once, she asked me if they have Taco Bell in Mexico like I would know, and then asked if I'm better at speaking Spanish or Asian. Like she couldn't even pick one dumb thing to say.) J.J.'s desk is right in front of mine. He sucks the orange powdered cheese off his fingers while he eats Doritos. Florence to my left has every color highlighter, and she color codes all the different parts of speeches on last night's story. I can't concentrate or write when all I hear is *click pop* and then the smooth streak of highlighter on paper. Genesis is sneaking Takis from the pocket of her hoodie. I want to get her attention to ask her for one, but—

"Clear your desks, pencils out!" Mr. Lewis shouts, walking between all the desks. He bumps into my desk real hard causing my body to shake a little from the impact. J.J. turns around and looks straight at my shirt and says, "Ew," and I feel all gross and exposed (worse than that time someone walked in on me helping my abuelita in the bathroom at Pollo Campero). I should have put C.C.'s bra on this morning, rips and all. Then my chest wouldn't have bounced and squished all over the place. Kai would know what to say to J.J. Except ever since she told me I wasn't a doer, it's only been awkward nods between us; we haven't even had our normal library lunches. Genesis and I have just sat in Ms. Martinez's room to eat lunch. And there's still no sign of activity on our shared Google doc. I checked this morning. Kai was on it for a second, but immediately got off when she saw me.

Mr. Lewis sits on top of his desk. He swings one leg up to rest it over some papers, probably our essays from last month that he says he graded but hasn't given back. His foot knocks over a bunch of pencils, which makes me all mad 'cause I asked him if I could borrow one at the beginning of class, and he said no. I wish C.C.—or even Mami and Tía Gladys—was here to see it. Mr. Lewis is manspreading all over the classroom.

"Wake up, people!" Mr. Lewis yells after only about half of the students clear their desks.

J.J. always sits in the front even though he's the tallest boy in school and is always blocking everyone's view. I know being tall is not his fault or anything, kind of like having a tiny butt and no boobs and no period aren't my fault, but like today it really bothers me. He sits right in front of me and blocks the board and he's never once offered to switch seats so that I can see better. Not only that, but he stretches like every five seconds, and he sits with his knees way wide apart and his left leg all the way stretched out, like he's sitting at home all alone in his underwear playing video games.

All the manspreading everywhere is overwhelming me, worse than the polvo that falls off the ceiling fans on Limpieza days.

"I said, clear your desks, pencils out!"

Uy. Pop quiz. Everyone grunts. I'd be all mad about it too except when I clear my desk I see *Corey Wuz Here* written in fresh pencil. Gross. I share a desk with Corey who's in here a different class period, and he's always writing stupid stuff on it. Every day there's less and less blank space. Plus, the surface is all sticky, and I can picture it now: Corey twirling his gum around his finger and then drumming the desk like he's any good at drumming. I think the tamales from Panadería Guate that have been in my freezer since last Christmas can play the drums better than him. I roll my eyes hard, but that's when I see it, and my face must look like one of the characters on my abuelita's Thursday night telenovelas. Ever since the bra and video incident, it's like I can't get away from him.

Help Mani #wheresmyvulva is written in fresh blue sharpie. The whole desk is filled with barf-inducing hashtags. Then I look closer, and it gets worse. There're gross things written about girls, calling girls sluts and pencil drawings of different body parts being groped.

My stomach feels empty and gets butterflies all at the same time.

"You have ten minutes to complete both prompts. First, write a letter to your future self. Second, analyze how the main character feels at the end of the chapter you read last night. If you did your homework, this should be easy. If you didn't, it sucks to suck," Mr. Lewis says.

A few of the guys laugh when he says "suck." But I'm only half listening. I look back at Genesis. She's got her scrunched-nose thinking face on. Maybe it's the way she's holding her pencil, but something's off about her today.

"One minute down!"

I put pencil to paper but I can't think of the words. So I start to doodle on the remaining blank space of my desk. Mr. Lewis circles around the class, though he doesn't really focus on anyone in particular. He finds an empty desk next to Hector, who's been getting over a cold since like fifth grade. Mr. Lewis sits on it and lets out a big yawn.

"Remember, you're answering both prompts," he says.

Then J.J. turns his ugly face to the left and asks Hector if he's going to be a house painter like his dad, and I want to punch his ugly face and send his braces across the room. I wouldn't mind if they hit Mr. Lewis on the way. I've known Hector since we were little. Hector's dad was the maintenance guy in the apartments we used to live in, and then when we moved, my parents hired him to paint the outside of our house. Hector's mom died when he was two, so his dad used to bring Hector to work. I'm always mad at Hector for not defending himself. But then I get all this guilt and I wonder if being mad at Hector instead of J.J. is just as bad as making fun of someone's dad's job.

The writing warm-up is the longest ten minutes of my life. How can I think about my future self when my chest feels like it is about to explode with all the things I can't do. I want to get to high school already and be a woman. All I want to think about is winning Speak Up, taking away C.C.'s pain, finding out what Tía Beatriz forgave Mami for, and the fact that somewhere along the way Mami abandoned her supposed "feminism" and I'm the one paying for it. All I want is for Mami to listen to me and think of my life and feelings, for once.

Five minutes left. My eyes scan the desk. What feels like barf rises in me, but I do my best to keep it inside. All of it, right in front of me. The gross drawings. The gross social media pages that never get shut down. The girls they draw . . . that could be Genesis. That could be C.C. That could be me. And that's when I realize, it could be any of us at any moment. It doesn't matter if you're strong like C.C., or walk-through-a-jungle-for-days-activist-journalist Tía Beatriz, or if you're like, well . . . me. I think of the signs in my tía's newspaper clipping pictures—*clothing is not an invitation*—and how that is still relevant today, so many years later and miles away. *Here.*

"Two minutes left!"

My paper is blank. I push it aside and put the tip of my pencil against the desk. I begin to sketch around their violent drawings and stupid hashtags. I decide to turn my pain into power. I sketch my tía, and next to her, Mami, in a world where I *do* come from her. I picture knowing her not as Mami, but as the woman who made signs—the one C.C. called a feminist. Then I draw stick figure me at a protest, the kind Tía Beatriz and Mami went to, the kind C.C. goes to. In the picture, I'm wearing these white jeans that actually fit me, and holding a sign. I don't stop there. What would my sign say?

My bra is not an invitation.

Then I give the original stick figure girls their own signs.

Respect my body.

I can't stop. I don't stop until Corey's stick figure grope scene turns into a protest scene, and—

"Genesis, wake up! Please share what you wrote."

I jump at Mr. Lewis's voice calling on Genesis. I look back at her, but she's all heads on desk holding her stomach like she ate expired cheese. She lets out a groan, but Mr. Lewis gets up and walks away from her before she gets a chance to say anything.

He looks around the room, and our eyes lock.

"Manuayla, what are you doing?"

I rest my elbows on the desk and frantically try to write something—anything—on the paper.

But it's too late. He snatches the paper from my hand like it's his to grab. His long fingernails scratch my knuckles as he lifts it up to take a better look. Then he looks down at my desk.

"Why are you drawing on your desk instead of completing the assignment?"

All I manage to do is shrug.

"What's that?" Mr. Lewis says again, standing so close to me his spit lands on my forehead and I can feel the heat of his breath on the tops of my eyelids. I don't know why he can't just let it go. He's just trying to make me feel embarrassed, like that time I got pantsed on the bus in second grade. (When I told the secretary in the front office when I got off the bus, I felt like I was being brave, but she just said, *Oh, boys will be boys, dear. Just sit in the front of the bus next time.* All my warm, brave feelings went away like pieces of a popped balloon flailing away in the sky. Just like now.) I feel all . . . What would C.C. say?

Violated. I feel all violated right now 'cause Mr. Lewis starts waving my blank paper, then tapping his fingers onto my desk, and manspreading all over MY space.

"What are you, in kindergarten? Stop vandalizing my desks," he says.

But all these desks have drawings. I look up and over at J.J.'s desk. His has drawings too—the gross kind—and I've never heard Mr. Lewis say anything.

"Erase it now," he says. "*All* of it."

Reluctantly, I begin erasing.

I look over at J.J. who is laughing at me.

Something in my stomach flutters, but all the while I stare back at Mr. Lewis ('cause like Abuelita told me once, *When your enemy stares you right in the face, you stare right back at it and wish it diarrhea.* I know she said that during one of her episodes, but still, lucid or not it seemed like solid life advice.)

The rest of English class feels longer than the time we waited for the results after Connie took a pregnancy test she found in her mom's bathroom, because she kissed Lester on the staircase right before PE. (I think she peed on the wrong end of it, but I'm also like a gazillion percent times sure that you can't get pregnant from kissing someone. And there's the period issue. Everybody knows nothing happens if you don't have your period yet. Connie is always taking things too far.)

The room spins for the rest of class as Mr. Lewis moves through the lesson, and worksheet after worksheet. I look back at Genesis who's still all head-on-desk and wrapping her arms around her stomach. I toss a piece of my broken eraser at her head to try and get her attention. She looks up, but just rolls her one open eye and puts her head back down. I told her the blue Takis make your stomach hurt.

"OK, get ready to turn in your reading comprehension guides!" Mr. Lewis says.

Genesis gets up before anyone else, almost trips on her long yellow skirt. She looks dizzy. For real, she's still holding her stomach as she walks up, all hunched over. Her skirt is caught in her butt and she starts digging it out. Some kids look up from their papers and laugh. And that's when I see it. A bright brown-red smeared spot on the seat, like jalea de fresa on toast. I start to put it together. Her stomach hurts. She looks all pale. Blood on her seat. Puchica.

Genesis? There's no way . . .

How does Genesis get her period before me?

But I push my envy down to the very depths of me 'cause I know I need to be a good friend. I dig through my backpack and find the purple sweater I loaned her last week. It smells worse than the locker rooms on Friday afternoons, but it's better than nothing. I run to Genesis, who's about to turn in her paper in the class bin.

"Wrap this around your butt NOW!" I say in her ear.

She's confused at first. Her eyes get all wide. She looks over my shoulder at her seat.

"Just do it," I say between my teeth, pushing the sweater into her hands.

I motion for her to wrap the sweater around her waist. I just hope she doesn't get blood all over my sweater, 'cause I don't know what I'd tell Mami.

But some boys in the back are already laughing and pointing at the red smear on the seat. Some girls purse their lips in sympathy, but it's not enough to help, or wipe off the seat so no one else notices.

"Oh my God, what do I do, Mani?" Genesis says. And for real, she's waiting for me to tell her.

"I don't know," I say, 'cause I don't. Not really. "Maybe go to the nurse?"

"Maybe we should ask Mr. Lewis," she says. "He'd know what to do."

But that's like one of the dumbest things I've heard. I can't believe Genesis just became a woman in front of my eyes but she's talking like a little kid. (Thinking an old man teacher knows anything about periods is like when you're little and you think rain means the sky is peeing, you know? You just can't think that when you become a woman.)

"Man-u-ay-la, please leave your hardworking classmate be," says Mr. Lewis. "Unless you are done with your reflection paper, which I doubt it, you don't need to be talking."

"Can we please go to the bathroom?" I ask Mr. Lewis.

He leans back and sits on top of his desk and folds his arms. "If I remember correctly, you already used your three passes for the quarter," he says.

But then a girl from the way back of the class looks up. "What? We only get three passes per quarter?" she says like we didn't have a whole town hall about the new bathroom pass system in the beginning of the quarter. "Like, what if we have lady problems?"

Wait, that's it. *Lady problems.* If we have lady problems, we can break the three-pass rule. Like, legally, right? Air fills my lungs again. I'm feeling bold. Bolder than when I hit Corey on the bus after he snapped my bra so hard it ripped.

"We have an emergency lady problem situation," I say.

He slides around on his desk and looks at us. Maybe he doesn't know what that means. "Ms. Semilla," he says, 'cause I think trying to say my first name makes his mouth hurt. "Do you know how many girls have said that to try and get out of doing classwork?"

Genesis sniffles a little, and a yelp rips through the air. In my head, we're back at Kai's kitchen table, listening to Lani explain the chain of events from period to loss of education, and Connie putting it all together. This is exactly what Lani was trying to get us to see. I look at Genesis's skirt, then back to her seat. "I can feel it," she mumbles, sucking in boogers. She reaches behind her to feel the back of her skirt while I'm covering her. She starts to turn toward her seat, but I grab her arm. There's no way I am going to let her sit back down in her dirty skirt and have blood gushing out of her like she's a volcano or something. I look around the room. There are old Chromebook chargers that don't fit the new computers we got at the beginning of the year. There's a bucket of TI-83 calculators (even though it's not math class and I definitely asked to borrow one in math one day when I forgot mine, and my math teacher went on her rampage about the county schools building new football fields but can't buy enough calculators for each math classroom). But what's not in the room? Period stuff, so Genesis doesn't have to walk all the way to the nurse and miss classtime.

I get mad. Like getting-your-bra-ripped-off-your-back mad.

"Are you calling us liars? Is it 'cause I'm a girl? No one believes women! Stop manspreading all over your classroom and listen to us!"

Some kids laugh. A boy from the front pretends to slam dunk on Mr. Lewis.

Mr. Lewis stands and points to the door. His eyes narrow. "Get out."

I grab Genesis by the arm and run out into the hallway with her. She tries to tighten the purple sweater around her waist and starts to cry more as we run toward the nurse's office. A teacher I've never seen tries to stop us and ask us where our hall passes are, but I say, "It's that time of the month!" and we keep running. She doesn't follow us.

Genesis starts hiccupping like the first time I saw her crying. "Can you please stop telling everyone that? It hurts to run."

Mrs. Orellana-Roberts, the school nurse, is wearing these big turquoise earrings that are longer than her hair. (She changed her name and added the hyphen when she got married last year, so she lost a few feminist points for me. I told C.C. that once, but she pointed to her "This is what a feminist looks like" shirt and told me that feminists come in all forms. Then she gave me my own shirt to match hers, and I stopped being so judgy and thought, Maybe it's kinda cool to have two names.)

Mrs. Orellana-Roberts is wearing this flowery shirt and jeans and she has a bright yellow wrap around her short hair.

She puts down the stacks of folders she was just organizing and gives us her full attention. "What can I do for you, my friends?" she says with a smile.

Genesis is still crying. She tries to talk, but then she starts hiccupping again, so between the cries and hiccups she can't get any words out. So, I speak up. "This is Genesis. I think she got her period. She was bleeding all over English class."

Mrs. Orellana-Roberts puts her hands up in the air and I can't tell if that's a good thing or a bad thing.

"Ah, welcome to womanhood," she says. Then she winks and gently puts a hand on Genesis's shoulder, motioning us over to a drawer at the end of the room.

"You ladies are always welcome to this drawer," she says, and I get goose bumps 'cause she called me lady, which is like one step away from being called a woman.

She opens the drawer and there are rows of tubes wrapped in plastic and paper. They almost look like candy. She takes one out. "These are our most popular. They're flexible. You can do PE, run around, no problem. They're the most comfortable. You just insert it and forget it's there."

Comfortable? What is comfortable about sticking a whole tube of cotton up there?

I look at Genesis and she has a look of terror on her face, like she just accidentally walked in on her abuelo naked or something. She holds on to the cross on her neck. "I've never seen those so close," she says.

"Oh Genesis, honey, is this your first period? We also have other options like—"

"The pastor's wife talked to my girls' group at church. She said the devil makes tampons."

Ms. Orellana-Roberts and I look at each other. I want to touch Genesis's forehead. I wonder if she is feeling OK in the head. I look at the brand: Flexi Active. I want to tell the pastor's wife that I'm pretty sure a big company made these, and not the devil.

"If you wear one of those," Genesis says, "you lose your virginity, and that is something you can't EVER get back."

Whaaaaaat?

Before Ms. Orellana-Roberts can say anything, I grab Genesis by the shoulders and say, "Genesis, the church is mansplaining your vagina to you! I know I don't know anything about virginity and losing it and periods, but like I am 99.999999 percent sure that is NOT TRUE!"

Ms. Orellana-Roberts puts her hand on my arm to loosen my grip on Genesis. "Sweetie, I want to respect your beliefs and I don't want to do anything that would go against the values of you and your family. We also have pads. Those are just linings you put on your underwear. Nothing goes inside your body."

How is she not mad? How is she not agreeing with me? How is she not telling Genesis that her church is wrong? How does she not call out Genesis's church right then and there?

She opens the drawer right next to it. There are different sized pads. "Grab whatever you think you need."

Genesis grabs three of the biggest pads, the MAXI ones. (They look thicker than the diaper at my Tía Gladys's friend's party when all the women told me to change a baby's diaper and I thought it was so unfair and sexist because there were like five boys at the same party and no one asked them. They just got to keep playing their video games and picking their noses like God made the world just for them. Jerks.)

"Genesis, I don't think that's—"

I swear I think she's shaking. Mrs. Orellana-Roberts gives me the let-it-go look. I look at the clock above her door. English class already ended. I think of Lani. No period products in class + shady bathroom pass system = a lifetime of learning loss for menstruators. Does Mrs. Orellana-Roberts know? I can't let it go. If I let it go, I'm not a doer, like Kai said. I think of Mami and how she told me I didn't come from her. And it burns me like when you touch a really hot sartén. But if I don't let it go, maybe I'll get in trouble again, and Mami will tell me something even meaner.

But for real, what kind of world is this where women disappear 'cause of what they wear, where tampons make you lose your virginity, where asking about your vulva gets you sent to the principal's office, and where getting your bra violently snapped is your fault, 'cause boys and their hormones just can't help themselves? What kind of world is it where groups of kids grope and hurt someone just to film it? And where these companies never take the videos down and profit off of them? All the rage swells in my brain, and I don't know how to solve any of it.

I know there's only one thing to do. I can't take down all the videos from that awful site that the school itself hasn't figured out how to shut down. I can't go back in time and defend C.C. from her gropey professor, Lani from her piano teacher . . . but I can help Genesis right here, right now, feel better about her body. And that's got to count for something, right? I have to prove to Genesis that tampons don't make you lose your virginity, 'cause I'm a doer. Tía Beatriz was a doer too, and I bet that is how she would turn her rage into power if she were here.

SIXTEEN

*Forty-three more jokes about how horrible
my Spanish will be in Guatemala
just 'cause I can't roll my r's*

I SPEND ALL WEEKEND THINKING about ways to help Genesis and in general regain control over the information women and girls get about our bodies. (I heard C.C. say that last part once.) By Sunday, I haven't come up with anything brilliant.

"Ouch!" I yell when Mami hands me a steaming chunk of pollo that she just pulled out of boiling water with her bare hands. No sé, but I think you have to be real Guatemalan to hold hot things in the kitchen like that, not a half Guatemalan like me who can't roll her r's.

I drop it on the plate in front of me.

"Niña, you couldn't have worked the first job I had when we first got here," says Tía Gladys.

That's easy for her to say, sitting at the table peeling the papas.

Apparently, Tía worked some job where she stood all day and pulled raw chicken on a moving conveyer belt, and if she did it too slow, her bosses would yell at her. I think that's why she uses the brace on her arm and wrist. And she almost never got to use the bathroom. And when she did, she was timed and if she went over some really short time frame, they'd take it out of her pay. Once, she stood for seven hours straight and fainted. She had to stay in the hospital a couple of days, and when she came back, she didn't have her job anymore.

I kind of feel bad, but not as bad as they make me feel for not being Guatemalan enough, or not coming from Mami. (She still hasn't really apologized.) But, for one, this chicken is burning hot— hot enough to melt the uñas off my fingers. And for two, they moved here for a better life and blah blah blah so why are they insulting me for not being able to do the things they had to do as new immigrants? What do I have to do with that?

Whatever. At least they never had to worry about cell phones and someone filming their bras getting ripped off their backs and the video being on the internet for all eternity. (Well, till the end of internet.) For days behind closed doors when she thinks I can't hear her, Mami's been going on and on with Dad about how girls don't go to school to get boys' attention. But she's also been leaving papers with parts of new song lyrics in my lunch box. Maybe that's her way of apologizing? I just want her to be there for me, the way I'm trying to be there for Genesis. Dad tried to talk to me about everything a while back, but I was too embarrassed to tell him what happened, even though I know he'd listen. Just not ready to say "lace," "bra," "boobs," and "rip" in the same sentence, you know? Plus, ever since C.C. told them about her professor, Dad's been helping her file some sort of report at her school, so they've been busy. Maybe if I told him the truth . . . and about the video . . . he could help me file a report. I let the thought float away.

Once all the chicken is *bien disminuido* so it's easy for Abuelita to chew, Mami puts it back into the soup. "Ya regreso," she says, and heads upstairs. It's sábana day this week, even though it's Sunday. Mami has to go to work extra early tomorrow morning, so sábana day got moved up. I forgot she told us yesterday, so I didn't take my sheets off the bed this morning like she had asked. I hear the doors open and the windy sounds of sábanas being pulled off beds.

C.C. and Dad walk in through the front door. C.C. is finishing a sing-songy Spanglish conversation on her phone. Then she walks around the room, saludando Abuelita and Tía Gladys, but stops in front of me. I can feel her gaze, and the longer she stares, the more it warms me and I want to break down and tell her everything. I could really use her advice right now. I'm angry, but I know I shouldn't be. I guess I just thought she'd tell me first about her gross professor trying to touch her and how it made her give up school and everything. I thought she was the only person who treated me like I could handle tough information, so it hurts.

"Maní?" she says.

My shoulders drop. I want to be a good listener the way she is a good listener to me, the way I'm trying to be to Genesis, and the way Tía Beatriz was to women she barely even knew.

"Want to go on a walk with me?"

I'm about to say yes, but then Mami's voice rips through the walls like a relámpago.

"¿Qué es esta porquería?" Mami's voice booms from the middle of the staircase.

She's holding up C.C.'s green lacy bra by the one good strap, the feathery threads of their ripped silkiness dangling.

She throws it down the stairs. She must have found it under my pillow as she was pulling the sheets off. Everyone is looking at me and I want the floor below to open real wide and tragarme whole, purple glasses and all.

C.C.'s eyes are fixed on me, but I can't look back at her. She picks up the bra from the bottom of the staircase and sits back down next to me at the table.

"It's just a bra, Tía," says C.C. "I let Maní borrow it. Her body's changing. She needs to get out of those training bras."

"Tú callate," Mami says to her. "You've done enough."

C.C. looks real hurt, and she gets quiet.

"Do you know what happens to girls who dress like this?" Mami says.

Yeah, I know, I think. They get their bra snapped and ripped.

"Isabela—" Dad says, and walks up the stairs to try to calm her down.

"Clothing is not an invitation," I say, just like the signs she held in an alternate galaxy where she was once supposedly a feminist.

She looks caught off guard, but only for a second.

"You don't know what you're talking about," she says back, slicing my words into pieces on the floor.

Maybe it's the ripped bra that she dangled in front for everyone to see before throwing it down, but something in me boils up like it did back on the bus.

"Well, you're not perfect either! You didn't help that woman, and her bill probably killed her by now!"

Mami stares at me, soul to soul, still from the staircase. Her eyes start to water, and I instantly want to take it back. I don't think this is what Tía Beatriz meant when she said *turn rage to power*. (Definitely not what Abuelita means when she tells me to find my quetzal voice. I once asked her how I'll know when I get it, and she just said, *When you have it, you'll* know. Well, this isn't it.)

"What are you talking about, Mani?" asks Dad.

Suddenly all the enojo that was there seconds before disappears and it's replaced with just . . . sadness.

Tía and C.C. look at each other, then at Mami. Did Mami only tell me? My stomach feels empty, like when you're forced to run a mile even though you didn't eat enough for breakfast.

Then I wait. I wait for her to keep talking, to scold me in English and Spanish. We all wait. But she doesn't. Mami starts crying, and she has no words left. Instead, she walks down the stairs and goes outside to sit on the porch. Only Dad follows her out.

I run upstairs and C.C. follows me. I turn to her in my room and start to apologize but she stops me.

"Don't even worry about it. I stole that from my roommate. It wasn't her size anyways," C.C. says, smiling.

Then I tell her all of it—the bus, Mason and Corey, and how it stung real bad, and how somewhere (everywhere) on the internet, there is a video of it for all to see.

She's mad. She's riled up, and talking about safety and fairness and assault, and how she can't believe the kids filming it didn't get in trouble. Her face is twisted in disgust as she looks for the site on her phone. My stomach's in a tight knot, until she says there're so many videos she can't even find mine.

"But I want you to remember something, Maní," she says. "It's not about what happens to us. It's about what we do with it."

And I wonder if she says that for herself as much as for me. I nod anyways, but I still don't know what I do with all of this. How

I turn rage into power. Then she points up to the attic with her finger. We grab the ladder and head up.

We sit extra close this time, and I rest my head on her shoulder. After a while I finally get the courage to say it.

"I heard what you told Mami and Tía outside. I guess I just thought you'd tell me first." But saying it out loud makes it sound silly all of sudden, 'cause it wasn't about me . . . "Sorry—"

"Don't say sorry," she says and scratches my head.

"I guess I just didn't think that things like that happen to people like you," I say.

She laughs, but not the condescending laugh that other adults have. More like a laugh that has a million words, just none of them get said out loud. She doesn't say anything else, but she doesn't have to. Sometimes you just need to blurt it out loud to the universe and let the wind take it away, y ya.

I get up to grab the box of letters and sit back down. I pull out the next letter and this time, she reads it out loud.

Dear Isabela,

Today we covered the biggest protest yet, held outside of the police station. Sara, a woman who worked at the first ever domestic violence center in the city, was murdered by her husband, a police officer. There was no investigation. When Maribel and I got to the protest, there were about twenty women, and even a few men. They held pictures of the woman and signs that read "Justice for Sara" and "Hold the police accountable." Several other journalists from the collective were there too.

Police officers came out and began threatening the women. I was trying to interview both police officers and the protesters. As the police got more physical, the women began to put down their signs and to link arms, creating a human chain, a sort of armor to protect them. But the police grew more aggressive. Maribel was taking pictures and one of them hit her head.

My notebook and recorder, my idea of what it meant to be a journalist and follow the rules, felt more like a barrier between me and the women, so I did something I never thought I'd do. I dropped everything and joined them. I walked up to the women on the end of the growing human chain, and I linked arms with them. It felt exhilarating. Women around me smiled, and we felt joy even amid the screaming and threats. Maribel put her camera down and followed me. The line grew and grew.

I couldn't just stand there. I couldn't be just a journalist. And sometimes you have to do the unpopular thing. I've thought a lot about what it means to be not just an activist journalist, but an activist, period. Which walls do you break down, and at what point? Sometimes a woman just reaches a limit, and there's little left to do.

Primero una voz, y luego seremos millones.
Beatriz.

C.C. and I sit there for a long time.

I wish I could be as brave and bold as the tía I never met. Start a collective and turn everyone's rage into power. Sitting here, I'm overwhelmed with the feeling of wanting to go to Guatemala, to hear those sounds and feel like maybe they are a part of my story too. To get to know the side of Guatemala Mami knew—the one from the pictures—the side she won't tell me about.

C.C. and I talk about the collective as C.C. scrolls through her phone trying to look them up; she says she wants to do a research paper on them. We talk about the power of coming together, even if you are not directly affected by something. We read more letters. The letters sound happier and happier after this one. Some talk about traveling the country with Maribel and the joy my tía found everywhere, about meeting the other journalists from the collective, and about how she could never leave her beautiful country. She wrote about women leading peace and justice efforts, that maybe one day people will learn from the incredible work women are doing there. *A blueprint for women's protests everywhere*, she writes. She wrote about meetings filled with laughter and the beautiful sounds of birds outside, so much that I could almost hear them.

I think of the word *collective*. Las Nerdas is a collective. What's our mission? Lani gave us an idea, so I think harder about our mission—at least for the Speak Up. Our mission is period products in every bathroom. What would Tía Beatriz think of that? Is that something she would fight for, or is that nothing compared to the kind of stuff she dealt with? Would she fight against the cruel videos? What would Mami think of that? (Not the un-feminist Mami who makes me wear baggy clothes and doesn't ask me my side of the story when I fight with boys on the bus, but the guitar- and sign-holding, protest-going Mami from the secret pictures.)

I'm left with the overwhelming feeling of wanting to do something. Anything.

SEVENTEEN

Forty-two days till my dreams
of womanhood burn up as they
blast into the stratosphere

THE MEAN KIDS FROM English told what seems like the whole school about Genesis getting her period in class last week (which is probably worse than getting your period in church, or even at the mall).

In history class, Kai and Connie pass notes back and forth to just each other; it's been awkward nods and short *hellos* for weeks. Still is. Kai leans over to Genesis. "Don't worry about those idiots," she says, and gives me a half smile. I give it back.

I look at Genesis. The maxi pad pokes out of the back of her black skirt. It might have been better to just stuff a whole wad of toilet paper in her underwear. She's squishing around in her chair and pulling at her skirt. She still hasn't gotten used to it. She sees me looking at her and smiles. I force a smile back, but there's a tiny part of my heart exploding with envy. OK, my whole heart. Because, you know, Genesis got her period before me. Like, c'mon, seriously?

"Manuela," Ms. Martinez says, and it feels good to hear my name pronounced the way it should be. "Do you mind passing out the final Speak Up guidelines?"

I pass out each paper and get to Gonzalo's desk. I glare at him, but I guess he didn't actually *do* anything when Corey ripped my bra. Maybe that's just the problem; he *didn't* do anything. I lick my fingers and try to separate the papers to pass out, but it doesn't work for me like it does when Ms. Martinez does it.

"OMG, hurry up. Just put a stack at each table and let people distribute them," says Joel, who is the most stuck-up kid I know.

Kai turns around so fast I think she's going to break her neck. "Shut up, Joel!"

I smile and my heart starts to feel a little better.

"That is not how we talk to our peers," Ms. Martinez says. Then she looks at me and says, "Almost done there, Manuela? Do you need help?"

"I'm almost done," I say, and catch myself before saying "sorry" because Ms. Martinez is always telling the girls to stop saying sorry, so they don't become women who say sorry all the time. Apparently, that's, like, a thing. Well, definitely not in my house. I don't think Mami will ever apologize for telling me she didn't know how I came from her, which is basically like telling me I didn't come from her, like I don't belong there. At least that's how it feels.

We have five minutes to read over the Speak Up guidelines and write down at least two questions we have. I look at my paper, then up at the board, and back at the clock that's been at 2 p.m. since it stopped working at the beginning of the year. I look anywhere but in front of me, 'cause I haven't been able to look Kai straight in her eyes since she told me I'm not a doer.

But then Connie's rainbow Converse shoes slide under the desk and kick my foot. I look down and there's a little piece of paper she's sliding toward me, even though it would have been easier to just hand it to me since we're sitting at the same table. I bend down to grab it. I shake off the caked dirt and hair it's picked up from the floor.

That's when I realize what they were passing back and forth was for me.

I unfold the piece of paper. It's a drawing of me: a stick figure wearing big purple glasses, and those white pants I want so bad. In the picture, I'm wearing a super Nerda cape—which is just a Superwoman cape with "Nerda" written on it—and punching a stick figure kid on the bus. Kai, Connie, and Genesis stick figures are in the background breaking phones. I hadn't told them about the bra ripping incident, but Genesis had. I'm not gonna lie. When they didn't reach out to me, it hurt, but this apology note is better than any phone call from Kai's mom's phone to Mami's phone.

There's a little scribble to the right that says: "I'm sorry. Do you forgive me? Circle Sí or No."

Looking up at Kai, I smile, fighting back happy tears. I feel all warm inside, like when you eat pan dulce straight out of the oven at Panadería Guate, and it sits at the bottom of your stomach and makes you glow and smile, like the sun rises and sets in your body or something. Kai reaches under the table. We squeeze hands and do our Nerda handshake, minus the tooth flicking part.

Ms. Martinez goes over today's agenda. Today we have to finalize ideas for Speak Up, plus also research activists so that we can get inspired. "Just for today, I will be merging some groups and individuals, because I don't have enough copies of the sheets on the activists you will read about. Copy machine problems, story of my life, gente! Today, we'll read about real-life examples of people not too much older than you and the incredible things they did. I hope you find inspiration and ideas in these examples."

Ms. Martinez always gives us the best projects. She turns to the giant dry-erase board and starts to write down the group names. "Remember, today I want you to investigate a current activist. I want you to notice that's not their job title. I want you to see how you can be an activist while you are a doctor, a mechanic, a gardener, a janitor, a lawyer . . . a student," she says and on that last word she turns around and it feels like she is looking at each one of us.

She reminds us that our final action plan will be judged by a panel of real people who do real things outside of school. I picture people in suits and shiny glasses who shake our hands even though we're not real adults yet.

She finally writes out the last group: us. *Kai, Connie, Genesis, Manuela, Gonzalo.* Gonzalo!? All I can think about are his headphones in his ears and eyes out the bus window. Kai and Connie side-eye me. They know how I felt about him weeks ago, but that was like a gazillion years ago at this point.

"OK, I asked you to write two questions you have," says Ms. Martinez. "Let's hear some of them."

Mason doesn't even raise his hand, 'cause he obviously thinks he's too good to follow Ms. Martinez's rules. "So, like, how's this going to help us in real life?" he blurts out.

"It's 40 percent of your grade. That's real life," says Ms. Martinez, smiling at her own joke. We giggle as he sinks in his seat. "The winner of the project with the most promise, as judged by our panel, will be invited to attend Speak Up, a social justice and activism youth camp in New York this summer, and will develop their idea into real, actionable steps they can implement the next school year."

"Don't worry, Mani. We're going to make sure you don't have to go to Guatemala," Kai whispers.

I force a smile, even though a warm feeling fills me from head to toe, that I have friends who are always thinking of me.

"If we actually win, you definitely won't have to go to Guatemala this summer, right? I mean, your mom wouldn't stunt your growth like that?" she says.

"Yeah, plus, she's always telling you to do things that would look good for applying to college," says Connie. "Even though we're only twelve and college is like a million years from now.

"Um . . . yeah," I say. I try my best to look happy, because I don't want to go, right . . . ? It's just that I do want to feel the joy that Tía Beatriz described in her letters when she talks about Guatemala. Even if just for a moment. I don't want to see the dead women or anything, but I want to feel all the good things, you know? But I push the thought down real deep in my stomach to where not even the champurradas make it. There's no way Mami can know that the tiniest part of me wants to go. She can't win.

After today's groups are announced, we sit in our corner, down the hall by big windows and the bathrooms. It's our favorite spot to work, even though it's nasty having to hear the toilet flush like every five minutes. A white poster paper is sprawled out in front of us. We stare at it like it's going to talk to us at any moment. Genesis folds and unfolds her legs, pulling at her skirt and looking real uncomfortable at first. I can hear the sticky plastic of her pad crinkling as she tries to get comfortable. (She told me on the bus this morning that she found out the first period lasts the longest.) Everyone looks at each other. I rustle the folder around to mask the sound of her pad, but that makes it more obvious.

"OK," says Kai, breaking the awkwardness. "Ms. Martinez wants us to read the article together, get some new ideas for our final projects, and then in our own groups write down what our final project actually is, right?"

"Yeah, we have to work like a collective," I say, smiling.

"Totally," says Connie, slapping the envelope in the middle of our circle. We all stare at each other in that who's-gonna-open-it kind of way.

Genesis reaches over and grabs the envelope. "I'll open it!"

But then she gets real quiet again when a bunch of the phone jerks from our bus walk by, clearly skipping class. Seeing their phones out, ready to film something, makes my fingers curl up inside my palm.

"Don't worry about them, Genesis," Gonzalo says. "They're jerks to everyone."

Then he looks at me, but quickly looks back down. That's nice, I guess. But whatever. Too late, you know? He could have said something on the bus a few weeks ago, instead of looking away while Corey snapped my bra so hard it ripped.

We wait for them to turn the corner. Genesis opens the envelope and unfolds the paper. Her eyes light up for the first time in days. "Whoa, I know that name! She's from Honduras. I remember hearing about her. I've NEVER read anything about anyone from Honduras in school before."

Kai grabs it and reads out loud. "Berta Cáceres. Honduras. Environmental and Indigenous Rights activist. Some believe she was killed by her own government."

Killed. By the government. Sounds like something out of Tía Beatriz's letters.

We open our school computers and everyone types Berta Cáceres's name into a Google search.

Indigenous activist . . . environmental activist . . . neighbors report that
a group of men entered her house . . . found shot. . . .

At first, we're reading what we find out loud, but then we get all quiet the more we read. She tried to stop a dam from being built, 'cause she wanted to protect her community's access to clean water and their livelihood, which no sé, but I think means their ability to keep living or something like that. Tía Beatriz and her photographer friend, Maribel, come to mind, how they dropped their notebooks and cameras and joined a human chain to protect each other. The women in her letters who were found dead pop into my mind, and I think about how Berta Cáceres could have been one of them.

My stomach starts to hurt and I ache all over for the women I've never met but somehow feel connected to, like there's an invisible hilo holding us all together. And I can't control it, but then C.C. comes to mind, how her professor was all gropey with her and made her quit school even though she's real smart and head of her university's Centro Comunitaria (spelled wrong on purpose). Then Kai's sister, who got real mean and hated music after her piano teacher touched her, but how Kai or her family have never used the word *harassment*, but that's exactly what it is. And me.

Mason and Corey and the boys on the bus and how they can do the gross V thing and tear my bra, film it, and get away with it. No one's calling it assault, but I feel like that's what it is. I know it's not the same as what happened to the women in Guatemala, or Berta Cáceres in Honduras, so I try to get them out of my head, but it feels connected, like it's one long hilo that goes for miles and miles and Berta's story and C.C.'s or Lani's story is on either end.

Because the more I think about it, the more I realize it has to do with our bodies feeling safe, and fighting against the things preventing girls from living a long life, what Rebeca Lane and Audry Funk sing about. And I think about that line in one of their songs . . . that she'd rather be a weed than a flower . . . but she should feel free to be anything without fearing something will happen to her body, right?

Everyone's still reading. Connie's looking up YouTube videos about her. My brain goes to the woman my tía talked about in her letter, the woman she made a sign for and blocked the road for. *Say her name*, she had said. Even though I never met my tía, I can imagine her voice, and I think of all the posters I've seen that said the same things, *say her name*, except there were so many women's names I couldn't count.

"I know, guys," I say, interrupting everyone's reading. "Let's make signs for our campaign. We can still do something on rights, or anti-bullying, or access to period products, like we talked about before. But signs should definitely be a part of it. Like *say her name*, or something like that."

"Yeah, like the one that my sister made at the BLM protest last year! My parents wouldn't let me go, but I helped her make the sign," says Kai.

Gonzalo shakes something out of his hair and looks over at me. "I think that's a great idea."

I want to say thank you, 'cause it's the nice thing to say. "Yeah, it's whatever," I say, shrugging.

"It's so messed up what happens to women," says Kai.

"Well, there have been activist men that—" Gonzalo starts.

No, he didn't. Gonzalo didn't just do that. We all jump on him. Well not literally, but almost.

"Look, if Berta was Berto, she probably wouldn't have been killed," I say, 'cause it sounds like something C.C. would say.

"I'm just saying I know a lot of bad stuff is happening to women, but I think the focus here is that she was an activist, and there's violence against AC-TI-VISTS." He says it all loud and annoying and separates all the syllables like when some people try to talk to Mami when they assume she doesn't speak English.

But before I can say anything, A'niya is walking down the hallway toward us saying, "Hey hey heyyy."

I freeze. The last time we were so close, we were in the mall, and I was feeling up the bras on the rusty hangers. Please don't bring that up, please don't bring that up, I think. Genesis is adjusting her skirt again, and her eyes look all teary, and I think there is NO WAY her period blood got through the maxi pads she's been wearing for days now.

A'niya stands over us, arms crossed. "Hey, vulva girl," she says to me, and then walks toward the bathroom door right across from where we're sitting in the hallway. I turn to look up at her, and I swear I see the outline of a tampon bulging out of the back pocket of her white jeans, with the tip of the colorful plastic wrap poking out. Even I know you don't wear white when you're on your period.

No sé, I guess when you're all mujer like A'niya, you just don't care.

A'niya opens the bathroom door and disappears. I wonder how long it takes to be all confident like that after you get your period, and I realize it's what I want so bad for Genesis. Knowing I'm not envious of Genesis, that I just want her to be confident, kind of makes me glow inside. I guess I just kinda wanted Genesis to shine like

A'niya does, the way all girls should shine when they become women, you know?

But just then, the idiot boys with their phones are back in the hallway, laughing about how they just got kicked out of class again. When they pass by us, one of them gives Genesis a dirty look, and they all start to laugh.

"You guys, I feel weird saying this, but I'm scared of being one of the kids on those videos. Enough people saw what happened in class last week . . . I just feel like more people know who I am and I'm like a target or something. I mean, it was awful what happened to Mani, and the worst was feeling like I couldn't stop it," Genesis says.

"They're so gross," Kai says, grinding her teeth.

"We're going to make sure to stick together," says Connie.

I didn't know Genesis felt so awful she couldn't stop it. I didn't know she wished she could have done something. I know how that feels. And I don't know what to do about everything going on and the stupid phone kids, or about making sure nothing like that happens to Genesis.

I think of my abuelita, who told me and C.C. last weekend that it's important for women to know their bodies. I didn't know exactly what she meant by that or how literal I should take it, but I knew it was true.

"Genesis, someone at your church told you that tampons make you lose your virginity," I start.

Genesis's eyes bulge out wide.

"And that has you feeling all kinds of ways about your body, and . . . and the information about *our* bodies."

Uy, it's not coming out how it sounded in my head.

"Guys," I say, turning to Kai, Connie, and Gonzalo (pues, just 'cause he's there). "Genesis's church is giving girls backwards information about our bodies. We need to help. We can't have Nerdas walking around here not knowing their bodies."

Everyone turns to look at Genesis, who just buries her face in her hands.

"Genesis, if God didn't want girls to lose their virginity, none of us would be here right now," Connie says.

That doesn't even make sense, but I know Connie is just trying to help.

"OK, how? What do we do?" says Kai.

Here's my chance. I have to be a doer. I come from a tía who was a doer supreme. It's got to be something that's inherited, right? Tía Beatriz would want Genesis to feel better . . . to not be scared . . . to be confident, right? To feel some sense of control? What would she do about this?

I take a deep breath. "We have to find a tampon. A used tampon. We have to prove that tampons don't make you lose your virginity. Otherwise, Genesis is going to keep having to wear that diaper for the rest of her life and she's going to keep feeling bad about her body 'cause of some lies her church made up!"

"Gross!" yells Connie, so loud that Ms. Martinez pops her head out of the doorway. We all smile at her.

"Mani, you've gone too far this time," whispers Kai. "And plus, where would we get that?" says Kai.

I push my glasses back far to the bridge of my nose in that I'm-thinking sort of way.

Just then, A'niya swings open the bathroom door, walking out and past us like we're not even there. I wait till her white pants are down the history hallway and finally out of sight. Then, I lower my voice.

"You know how the bathroom has the little boxes for pads and tampons, or like other stuff like that?" I look at everyone, including Gonzalo.

"No . . . why would I know that?" he says

"'Cause, it's like in every bathroom," I say.

"Why would it be in the guys' bathroom?"

Now that I think of it, that is kinda stupid, but I don't admit it, 'cause like my abuelita always says, *You're only a tonta if you look like a tonta.* So I just sit straighter and look him right in the eyes until he looks away, and good thing he does, 'cause my eyes were starting to burn from not blinking.

Then we all jump as Ms. Martinez pops her head out and shouts, "Five more minutes till the bell! If you're on a roll, I suggest you get together after school!" Then she looks back. "Oh, but I definitely need your final project ideas," she says.

"Our final projects!" Connie says, biting her nail. "We need to finalize a topic, now! Something specific and actionable, and write how Berta Cáceres inspires us," she says, quoting Ms. Martinez.

Gonzalo takes out his own worksheet.

Maybe because I'm the one with the crazy tampon idea, but everyone else looks at me for an answer. I can't let them down again. I won't. "I guess . . . free period products in every girl's bathroom. That is specific and actionable. And we are inspired by Berta the activist because we will make signs about the connection between barriers to period product access and educational loss . . ."

My words aren't as smooth as Lani's, but we can always change it later.

Kai quickly writes it down and gets up to go turn it in.

Gonzalo writes down his own topic, but covers it with his hand like he's in third grade or something. Then he looks up at us. "What if you guys do something that might benefit all students," but soon as he says it, even HE looks like he wants to take it back.

I start to get riled up again. "Whatever. If men got their periods, pads and tampons would be falling from the sky."

"Yeah," says Connie. "I bet even birthday piñatas would be stuffed with that stuff."

Kai's writing all of it down like if she doesn't, we might forget it.

"Men would be manspreading all over the place with their period products," I say, folding my arms and shaking my head. "We can't just let Genesis drown in these backwards ideas that have been mansplained to her and are making her feel like her body isn't hers. Information is power!"

"One more minute! Start to pack up!" Ms. Martinez yells from the doorway.

Everyone's looking at me like I'm important and got important stuff to say, and it feels so good. I can't do anything to make C.C. confront her professor. I can't do anything to change what happened to Kai's sister so she can feel better and stop being mean to Kai, and I can't change the people who do bad things to women just because of what they wear . . . but I can help Genesis.

"Please trust me," I say, but my stomach flutters like there are quetzal wings trapped in there.

"OK, Mani. I still don't get it, but I trust you," Kai says.

"Yeah," says Connie. "And like you said, we're a collective."

Watching A'niya leave the bathroom gave me an idea.

I don't know if it'll work, but I need to prove that I'm a doer. To myself. And right now, this is my only chance. I want to be a doer like the people in the protest pictures when we Google searched Berta Cáceres . . . like the people in the pictures of the newspaper clippings from Guatemala. I don't want to be the girl who does nothing.

EIGHTEEN

ALL BATHROOMS ARE NASTY, but *middle school* bathrooms are nastier than the diaper I had to change with two other girls at my old neighbor's little brother's bautizo.

The door slams shut behind us and we all jump. Genesis is the last one in, and when the door hits her, she leaps forward with her arms stretched out wide and goes flying into Gonzalo. Now, I don't know anything about periods or being a woman or anything like that, so maybe it's 'cause she's a woman now, but puchica, Genesis is so dramatic. It's like a domino effect. Gonzalo pushes into Connie, who pushes into Kai, who tries to stand straight, but she bumps right into me and I have to catch myself as my face hits the stall door.

"Uy!" I shout. "Why does this stall door smell like hot dogs and ketchup?" I wipe my face with my palms and then wipe my palms on my pants.

The smell in the bathroom is overwhelming. Worse than the locker room after running the mile. I put my hand back on the stall door and look back.

"OMG, open it already," grunts Kai, who reaches her hand over my face to try and push the door.

"OK!" I yell. "We don't even know if this is the one." I open it. There's a little shiny metal box attached to the wall.

"Whoa, I never noticed those before," says Connie.

"It looks like an envelope. But like a metal one, not a real one," says Gonzalo, all quiet like he's scared. It *does* look like an envelope, except it's like smaller than an envelope, like a toy envelope in a weird envelope museum. They expect every kid's pad and tampon to fit in *that*? What if everyone is on their period at the same time? I mean, it's smaller than my lunch box. Not even my little leftover plátano container would fit in there.

"Genesis," I whisper. "There's, like, no way that your maxi pad diaper thing is going to fit into one of these little things." I know that sounds harsh and I'm not trying to be mean to Genesis, but now that she's, you know, a woman, she's got to toughen up a little bit.

"OK, we should leave soon," says Gonzalo.

"Why are you whispering? We're the only ones here," I say.

I don't really even know why he's here if he's going to get all scared. Plus, all he's doing is awkwardly standing in between two sinks and sweating like a liar. (At least that's what my abuelita says: You know who the *mentirosos* are at church based on how much they sweat. *The guilt of their dirty mentiras is what makes them sweat, chulita,* she always says. But I'm like, what if it's just hot in there?)

I open the first metal box. Nothing. I look back at Las Nerdas and Gonzalo and shake my head.

Genesis looks defeated. "What if she's already flushed it down the toilet?"

"No, that's against the rules," I say. "Remember when the toilet backed up—"

"That was from a roll of toilet paper," says Kai. "One of those dumb social media challenges last year."

"Actually, it was a Lunchable, or, like, a tamal or something," says Connie.

"OK, for one, those are two very different things, and for two, outside of us right here, maybe, like, six other people in this school even know what a tamal is," I say.

Genesis looks confused. The rest of us all roll our eyes at each other, which I guess cancels out all the eye rolling and it's like rolling your eyes at no one.

We go to the second stall. The stall door creaks so loud, worse than the first one, when I push it open. I tip open the silver box. It's just as small. Nada.

"See, she flushed it. I knew it," says Genesis. And I swear I think I see her eyes get all watery.

"What's wrong?" I ask.

"It's just that . . . we're never going to find out," she says, and picks at her skirt again.

I can't let Genesis down. We check the third stall and still nada.

"Let's just go," says Genesis, breaking Nerda code, rule number six:

WE DON'T BACK OUT
(UNLESS IT WOULD GET US IN TROUBLE WITH OUR MOMS!)

We see almost everything through to the end, no matter how stupid, and this is like the complete opposite of stupid. Our future as women depends on it. I grab Genesis by the shoulders and get real close.

"Genesis, do you want to understand your womanhood and stuff? Do you want to feel control over your body?"

"Maybe?" she says.

Before I can say anything else, we hear footsteps right outside the main bathroom door. I panic. I shove Genesis into a stall. Gonzalo runs over to us into the same stall, and he looks like he's about to cry. Kai grabs Connie and they hoist Genesis onto the toilet seat, and they get up there too. We all hold our breath as if we'll suck up all the sound in the process.

The bathroom intruder walks in. It can't get worse than this, I think, but then I look down. We picked the one stall with the unflushed toilet.

"Whatever you do. Do. Not. Look. Down," I whisper.

Except they all look down at the same time.

I try to reach up and put my hand over Connie's mouth, but before I can reach, she gasps as if someone just stepped on her new shoes. Finally, Kai puts her hand over Connie's mouth. We hold our breath again and just wait.

Then we jump, 'cause we hear a SLAM! I peek under the stall door and see the intruder's shoes a few stalls down, at the first one. She's humming a song, so she must have headphones in.

Genesis starts to lose her balance even though she is sandwiched right in between Kai and Connie. She teeters over the unflushed toilet.

I press my finger to my lips and make the *shhh* motion. Connie tips her head over the stall to see who it is, but Kai hits her. Connie starts to wobble, like real dramatic. Gonzalo steadies her. I look at Gonzalo who still looks like he's about to start crying any second.

"I really shouldn't be here," he whispers, and I can hear the fear in his voice.

"Mani," Connie whispers.

"What?" I whisper back.

"I have to pee."

Uy. "You couldn't have picked a worse time!" I say.

Gonzalo leans in. "What if they don't leave soon?"

"They have to eventually, right?" I whisper.

That's when I look at the silver box on the wall. The only one we didn't check. I tip the lid open. It squeaks ever so quiet and then—

"Score!" I shout.

Genesis slips off the toilet seat and her bulky shoes go right in the toilet bowl. Water splashes up and out, spraying all of us. Connie's face is wet, and she looks like she just saw La Llorona.

Finally, the intruder leaves. We wait. I think I'm going to hear the sink, but nothing. She doesn't wash her hands? Like, for real, that's gross. Kai and Connie rush out, they don't even help Genesis, who is silently crying now, probably wondering if this is really what it's like to be a woman or how any of this is going to help. She walks out of the stall, and we can hear her feet and socks squishing around in her soggy shoes, and maybe it's the sound, but that's when she finally starts crying for real.

"Genesis, I know what just happened is bad, but we are so close. This is about YOUR womanhood and YOUR body and your right to feel safe and confident in it. And we're not letting anyone make you believe something about your body that's not true, so you need to woman up NOW!" I say.

Uy, that was harsh. But it works. Genesis takes a deep breath and stands a little straighter.

I reach down to grab what I know has to be A'niya's tampon, but before I reach any farther, I say, "You guys! There are two!"

"Score!" Kai shouts. "But still gross."

"Yuck," says Connie. "This is the nastiest thing we've ever done."

"It's really not. It's natural. It's just our bodies," I say, holding my breath and trying to believe my own words.

Genesis starts to cry again, for real now, like a baby. I think she says, "How do you know which one to get?"

"It doesn't matter," I say. "We have TWO used tampons. That probably makes this experiment even more reliable." My smile is about to burst off my face, 'cause I know I sound real smart right now.

Reaching my hand down farther, I freeze.

"You going to do it, or what?" Kai asks.

But they're all staring at me like they think I might not do it.

I pull a bunch of toilet paper and roll it around my hand and fingers. Deep breath. My face squishes together and I close my eyes as I reach in and feel around for a tampon. I start to pull it out by its long, dried-out, bloody string. I'm a doer. I'm a—

"Uhh, what is the string supposed to do?" says Connie.

I suck my teeth at her. "Obviously, just in case you go to put in a tampon and you accidentally forget you already had one in there." I swear, I thought Connie knew stuff with her mom being a nurse and all.

"I don't think—" Kai starts.

"I'm so hungry," says Connie.

Who can be hungry after what we've just been through? Genesis looks down on the ground and starts to talk all quiet and soft like she didn't already become a woman. "This doesn't tell me anything."

We hear the toilet water swish around her shoe as she shifts her weight from one leg to the other. "Of course it doesn't, we need to look at it under better light!" I say.

They all look confused at, like, exactly the same time.

Kai looks out the main door first to make sure no one is coming then waves us all out. Gonzalo's face steams with sweat, so we push him out first. Connie runs out after him. Genesis looks down at her wet, smelly shoes, but she takes a deep breath and walks out. I follow her.

We all check Gonzalo's phone for the time. There're only fifteen minutes left of math class. Kai and Connie are missing orchestra.

Gonzalo slips away and disappears through the doors. I want to stick my tongue out at him, but he can't see, so I guess there's no point.

"What are we going to do?" says Connie.

That's when I search my bag for paper—I find an index card. I don't even think about it. I start writing.

Please allow Mani, Kai, Connie, and Genesis
into the library during class. They are finishing a project.
Ms. Martinez.

"But history class was last period," Connie says.

"Ms. Nesbit doesn't have our schedules memorized. Plus, this looks like a legit note!" I say.

"Mani, are you feeling OK? You've never forged a note," says Kai.

"Trust me, it'll work," I say.

"But isn't forging someone's signature fraud or something? I can't go to jail right now," says Connie.

"Connie, it's not that serious," I say, but for a second I get nervous.

Kai smiles and nods. For once, everyone is listening to me and my ideas. I'm taking charge.

Our regular table with the beanbag chairs is open. I look around, slowly creep my arm around, and set the tampons in the center of the table.

Everyone backs away like it's alive and it's going to eat us.

"Calmate, you guys," I say. "It's just a tampon. Well, two tampons."

"Yeah, used ones with, like, blood on them," says Connie. "We should be wearing gloves," she continues, like all of a sudden she knows everything. "My mom wears gloves at the hospital. She said you should always wear gloves when handling blood."

"Hospitals are for sick people," I say. "This is about womanhood, control over the information about our bodies, and confidence. Not sickness."

"This doesn't tell me anything!" Genesis says again, this time louder and with a little anger in her voice. I guess I'd be mad too if my foot was swimming in pee water.

"Shhhhhhh!" Ms. Nesbit hisses from behind the stack of books on her desk.

But everyone's looking at me like I have all the answers. I mean, I guess it was my idea. It sounded like a good idea, but sitting in the library right now, skipping class for the first time, with A'niya's— maybe-not-A'niya's—used tampons in the center of the table where we eat and read and write, all I can think about is how I am going to get into so much trouble. I look at the two tampons, all deep red-brown and shriveled, and I get an idea.

"Yup, totally still a virgin. Yup. Tampons do NOT make you lose your virginity," I finally say. Silence. Like they're waiting for me to say more. "It's hard to explain. It's an anatomy thing. I read it in an article once," I say.

I'm always hearing C.C. talk about how she *read it in an article*, so I think that sounds real smart.

"Ohhhhhhh," says Connie.

"Yeah, makes sense," says Kai.

Then a collective "Yeahhhhh" from everyone at the same time.

Then a familiar voice rips through the air, and I freeze at the sound of my name mangled in someone's mouth.

"Young ladies. What in God's name?"

And maybe it's that I have someone's period blood on my toilet-papered hands or that I retrieved something so powerful and mysterious that I feel powerful and mysterious, but I stand and am face-to-face with Mr. Dupont. OK, more like face-to-elbow, since he's way taller than me. Something rumbles in my stomach and I hope it's my quetzal voice.

"Someone told Genesis that tampons make her *do it* even though she's never done it before, and it's not healthy to think that badly about your body. It's time we take control, because our bodies and sense of worth and safety are under attack at this school," I say, and stare him right in the eyes like Abuelita told me to do whenever you talk to a man.

But the more I look at him the more I want a meteor to come and hit this table and take the tampons far, far away from here.

NINETEEN

Thirty-nine more reminders
that everyone is a woman now but me

C.C.'s GOING ON AND ON ABOUT how Dad's the best and helped her file a complaint with the "Office of Equity and Inclusion" so there's a paper trail of what happened to her with Professor Nastygrabs, as we nicknamed him, and how she won't lose this whole semester and her scholarship will be reinstated next year.

But I'm only half listening. I can't help but wonder why *my* school doesn't have an office like that. C.C. can tell I'm not really listening, and I feel all kinds of bad about it, 'cause Abuelita's always telling me not to be *egoísta*, which means selfish but I think it's even worse in Spanish.

"I'll work on getting back into it in the fall," she says. "So . . . that means I get to hang out with you all summer—take you to New York, because you're totally going to win that competition thing and convince your mom to let you go." She winks and gives me a nudge while I'm half-slumped over on the kitchen table.

I unpack my bag and lunch box—more of Mami's songs stuffed in between sandwich sleeves and containers with fruit. I fold them up and put them in my pocket. It's 4:30 p.m. and we have a good hour and a half before everyone gets back home. Abuelita's always telling us that when life gets hard you have to be a pan in the horno. Seeing C.C. full of life and energy again talking about solutions and rising above stuff—all pan rising in the horno—makes me want to stop moping and talk to her about everything.

So I do. From the vulva mess, to everyone calling me vagina girl, to the fact that the grope videos have gotten so big that Genesis walks around scared at school, thinking it's going to happen to her. I talk about more letters, to new ideas for the Speak Up project, how I don't want to go to Guatemala, to Genesis thinking tampons are the devil trying to take control of her body, to stealing the tampon to prove it's not true and Mr. Dupont promising me that we could *expect a phone call tonight*. Except that was days ago, so I'm still waiting.

C.C. laughs, which makes my blood boil at first. "Maní, you took a used tampon out of a trash can? Why? That is so disgusting!" she says and then I start to laugh with her. Then we can't stop.

Finally, she says, "Look, if he was going to call, he would have already done it. Plus, ten years from now, when we're on a girls' trip causing trouble and changing the world, you won't even remember that phone call, IF it happens."

Normally I hate it when adults say that, when they talk about how I'll feel or won't feel in ten years, but when she says it, it's different. I smile and hope it's true. Then I get an idea.

"Hey," I say. "Can you help me on a project?"

I take out my school computer and the research prompt about the woman in Honduras and how I'm supposed to get inspired by her activism or something. I tell her all about the pads and tampons ideas for our Speak Up project, but how seeing all the pics online of Berta Cáceres's signs made me want to make signs too, and make the project about something bigger.

"OhmyGoddess, you got Berta Cáceres?" she says.

"Yeah, you know who she is?" I ask

"Are you kidding? The Central American Student Union held HUGE protests when she was killed. They even staged a sit-in right outside the Honduran consulate! There are pictures of it all over the student union building."

All I think is, I can't wait to be in college, where you can wear all kinds of lacy bras and you can go into offices called Equity and Inclusion, and do sit-ins in front of important places with groups called the Central American Student Union. She tells me things about Berta that I didn't know. Like, she had a daughter who has carried on Berta's activism. I even take notes in the margins of our Las Nerdas notebook. She shows me pictures on colorful "leftist" and "feminist" websites, and in every picture of Berta Cáceres, she's always in a protest or something, always yelling, kind of like Mami and Tía Beatriz in the pictures, but at people who are trying to pollute her water. I'm even more inspired to make signs for our project now.

But in between pictures and articles about Berta Cáceres, I keep thinking about A'niya and how I took something from her that I wasn't meant to take. It feels like I did something wrong and I try to think about how A'niya would feel, even though she'll never know. I shake off the thoughts, trying to focus.

"Wait," I say. "This one looks like it could be one of Tía Beatriz's pictures."

Then we start talking about the letters and how they go from happy to sad, to laughing to violent, and I didn't know you could have all of those things in one person.

"I don't understand how she seems happy, but she's also talking about dead women. Adults are so weird." I look at C.C. like I'm waiting for her to explain. I guess I kind of am.

C.C. laughs. "That's life, Maní. Un poquito de todo. And that's what these posters and signs reflect. They're not just sad. It's people turning their sadness and rage into power."

I nod, trying to understand.

"And stealing a used tampon . . . is not turning anything into power."

We both laugh, as I bury my face into my hands.

"Speaking of . . . your project posters aren't going to make themselves."

The white poster paper in my room is still in its plastic wrapping, but C.C. tells me she has a better idea. She takes a box out of the hallway closet. It's filled with like seven trophies of stuff Mami used to do back in Guatemala.

"In real life, protests aren't projects," she says. "No one goes and buys materials. You use what you have." She gets an X-Acto knife from a shelf in the closet and carefully trims the flaps and cuts a perfect square out of the box for me. "Think about it. You think Berta went to Craft World and bought poster paper for her signs? You think the women your mom and Tía Beatriz interviewed in the streets hit up the local craft store for fancy poster paper? You won't always have a store to buy stuff, but you can almost always find a cardboard box or something you can write on," she says.

Markers of every color are before me, but I think about what C.C. said about stores and using what you have, so I pass on the bright purples reds and oranges and grab a pencil and a black marker.

"For the first assignment, I have to replicate an artifact from a day in that person's life," I say. Sometimes I get confused, 'cause Ms. Martinez's assignments use big words and ideas you can't really touch.

"Think of it as something you can hold, something that's present in your day-to-day life," C.C. explains. "Like if someone were to think of an artifact from you, me, Tía, Mami, Abuelita . . . what would they think of?"

"Santa Ana statues," I say.

"Your mom's guitar."

"Vicks."

We laugh. Berta Cáceres was an environmental activist, among many things. So I sketch thick, wavy lines for rivers, and write *¡No a polusion! Empower! Protect!* I draw a speech bubble coming out of the river that says *¡No me toques!* And although we're talking about the environment, I can't help but think how we're also talking about our bodies.

C.C. looks over my shoulder as I make the poster and adds accent marks and changes my *s* to a *c*. She's always correcting my Spanish but it doesn't bother me when C.C. does it. I smile at our drawings.

"Look at you getting your homework done early! Your teacher will really like it," she says.

"I want to make signs like these for my Speak Up project too, even if it's still a few weeks away." I say. I tell her the ideas that have been floating in my head for days since I first learned about Berta.

"I think that's an awesome idea," says C.C. She opens her phone and puts on Rebeca Lane and Audry Funk. They're rapping about wanting to be alive and how all girls deserve to live a long time without fear. C.C. sings along, and she knows all the words. The lyrics play over and over in my head. I know no one's dying around me . . . but we deserve to feel safe.

I wonder what A'niya's doing and how she's feeling, and I get sad just thinking about taking something from her. We sing and write and draw. C.C. puts accents on my words, and I shade hers in with a pencil. And everything I've been carrying on my shoulders falls to the floor along with the bits of eraser from our pencils. Maybe it's the song pulsing through my blood and fingers, but our signs start to change. She draws a woman with a fist raised. *NO al femicidio, NO al acoso*, she writes.

I remember the word femicide from my tía's article, and I feel smart knowing what everything means. *Hasta que regresan las desaparecidas*, I write. *No more assault. Groping is assault. We will stand up! Let's form a collective!*

I turn the cardboard over and draw a bra with a big X over it. *Hands off! ¡No me toques! You are just as guilty if you stand by and film!* I write. Then I draw a phone with an X through it. We look at each other. "This is not just about getting tampons anymore," I realize.

C.C. winks, but then I hear the keys on the door. I tense up, hold my breath.

"It's OK, Maní, it's a homework assignment," C.C. says.

I take a deep breath and nod, but still turn my poster over to the side about pads and tampons.

Mami walks in first and gives us both a kiss on the cheek but doesn't say much more than a faint hola. I don't mention the songs.

Dad, Abuelita, and Tía Gladys follow and drop their things on the table.

Mami looks down at my poster, and then at C.C.

My palms rest firm on the poster. My spit is stuck in my throat as I try to swallow. She yanks the poster and flips it over, causing it to tear on one of the edges. We're both waiting for her to say something, but C.C. looks way more sure of herself than I do.

"¿Qué es esta porquería?" she asks.

I feel her eyeballs over my head.

"¿Qué es esta porquería?" she repeats, this time looking at C.C. "You're going to let her take this to school?"

"We're not in Guatemala, Tía," says C.C. "This is a totally acceptable school project on people's access to free period products."

"Don't tell me about this country or Guatemala. I've lived here just as long as you have. I've been an adult in two places, don't forget that," Mami says, and I know her words are meant to hurt. Then she goes on and on in real fast Spanish about how they came here so we could be safe and get an education and move freely without something bad happening to us, but all I keep thinking about is how I couldn't move freely on the bus or school. C.C. couldn't move freely in college without getting groped, girls at my own school don't feel safe, and we're a bunch of lakes and skies and hours and quetzal birds away from Guatemala. I want to speak up, but the words don't come.

Now it sounds like they're fighting over something way bigger than my class project.

C.C. steps up to Mami and doesn't let her words trample her into quiet. She switches to English and I wonder if it's for me. "Tía, activism is in our blood! Instead of being so scared of it, help Maní develop it. She needs y—"

"Ya bast—" Mami screams.

Tía Gladys rises from the chair to put her hands on their shoulders, and Dad follows after her, but they start talking over each other and don't back down.

"Tía, you're such a hypocrite!" C.C. says. "You just hide behind revolutionary songs but you're afraid of real action."

My mouth is open. I'm looking between C.C. and Mami, wondering what Mami will say next. That, and I don't know how a bunch of songs about birds singing one day is revolutionary, but there's a lot of stuff I don't understand in this house.

Then the phone rings. But before any of them can get to it, Abuelita elbows her way between C.C. and Mami and picks it up, even though they always tell her not to, 'cause she usually starts singing, or inviting telemarketers over for dinner.

"Mamita, danos el teléfono. ¿Quién es?" Tía says.

Abuelita starts singing. Mami and Tía gently struggle for the phone, but then Abuelita presses the speaker button.

I freeze. Mr. Dupont's unwelcomed voice rips through the wall, and my feet are cemented to the uneven kitchen floor. His voice in my house feels like salt in horchata, like it just doesn't belong.

"Ay, you want to speak with Manuelita? Of course!" says Abuelita.

I shake my head real hard.

"No, no. Bu-ainas tardeis. Es posible hablar con Senora Semilla? This is Mr. Dupont. Soy el principal de escuela," Mr. Dupont says in Spanish worse than mine.

Mami narrows her eyes at me, and grabs the phone from Abuelita's hand, but then Dad grabs the phone and takes it off speaker.

"Hello, Principal Dupont," I hear him say. "This is Harold Semilla. Manuela has a father too. You can ask for me anytime." I hear Mr. Dupont struggle through his next words like he didn't expect me to have a dad or something. I want to fist-bump my dad.

"Your dad's a freakin' feminist, Maní," C.C. says all quiet, and I smile.

I never thought of a guy as a feminist. And Dad? Mami tries to listen in and grab the phone from him, but he gently holds his hand out. He nods, but he doesn't look at me. I start biting my nails, which is something Connie would do. I'm praying to all the saints they talk about in misa and the ones I hear Abuelita talk to before every meal. I'm praying to Santa Ana, the saint of mothers and daughters. (I'm praying to San Nicolas even though he helps you find things you lost, like your hairbrush or something. I'm—)

"Man-u-haila seemed to be the leader of this little group that was skipping class."

I jump at the sound of his voice filling the room again. Mami had pressed the speaker back on, and with the look she's giving my dad, he knows not to turn it off.

"And they had a, a . . . ," he stutters. "A female sanitary napkin product just there on the table like they were about to play a prank with it or something."

I want to jump into the pot of frijoles that Mami left soaking in water since this morning and disappear forever. But then C.C. can't help it; she starts laughing. And I don't want to, but I start laughing too. I can't stop. And then Abuelita starts laughing, which makes us laugh even more. Mami takes the speaker off and holds the phone to her ear.

"Chulita, when I was your age, we had to use cloth, and then wash it by hand. We were environmentally friendly," Abuelita says, in a moment of lucidity before going back to her song.

I can't imagine just getting my period all over a towel and then having to wash it by hand. If it's anything like Rosa de Jamaica juice, that stain never gets out. No gracias.

"I will talk to her, thank you, Mr. Dupont," Mami says real tranquila and soft-spoken, the way she does when she talks to gringos, and hangs up. "¡Qué barbaridad! I'm sick of this!" she yells. "¿Qué te pasa, Manuela?"

Maybe it's the protest signs, but I feel bold, like maybe I have a tiny speck of quetzal voice buried deep inside me that can grow if I just let it out a little bit.

"My new friend Genesis got her period, and . . . and her church is making her feel bad, and making her wear giant pads 'cause they said tampons make you lose your virginity, and I just wanted to show her that's not true, and she thinks she's a target because boys in school have been touching girls, and——" I start to trip on my words and get so mad that I grab the signs in my hands just to hold on to something. "And I don't know why he had to call! We were just looking at it, and we threw it away right after! He's the worst!"

"¡No seas mentirosa, Manuela!" Mami yells. "You're going to school to learn, not to skip class and to be a mentirosa."

C.C. steps in between us and says, "Mentirosa? She's not lying! You lied to Maní. We found the letters!"

My jaw drops. The room spins and my toes dig into the floor, 'cause otherwise I might fly away.

"Calmate, hija," Tía says to C.C.

She promised me she wouldn't say anything about the letters. For the first time ever, I just want C.C. to stop talking.

But she doesn't stop. "We know Tía Beatriz didn't die before we moved here." Her last words are quiet, and her voice doesn't sound too quetzal anymore. She takes a deep breath and swallows. "Why don't you tell her the truth? This is her history too. And mine."

I look at C.C. and she looks back. I'm all rage and feelings pulsing through my body and thinking about her words, *I've got you, Maní.* And now Mami's going to superglue that attic door shut and I'll never get to read more and find out what happened, or get to feel closer to the tía I never met.

And then a silencio this house has never heard. Tía just looks at Mami. Dad looks down, like he's thinking of what to say. Mami looks everywhere but at me. Abuelita stops singing. It's worse than yelling. C.C. just stomped all over my heart. She promised she wouldn't say anything. Her fake words ring in my ear. *I got you, Maní.* I look at C.C., water in her eyes. She knows she hurt me. Her eyes say it all. But she can't take it back.

"Let's all go sit down and talk about it," Dad says.

But no one moves.

"Your boobs are growing, chulita. You are changing. Now you have to be more careful with what you say and do," Abuelita says. "Es la injusticia de la vida como mujer."

It's the injustice of a life as a woman.

But I'm not even a woman yet, and if this is what it's like, maybe I don't ever want to be a woman. Not in Guatemala. Not here.

I can't stand this non-feminist Abuelita, who loses her memory and says backward stuff. I want to talk to the Abuelita who thinks girls should know things. I want the world she sings about, where women choose friends over men, where they pick up their guitars and travel the world alone, singing, and safe. Where their boobs can be as big as they want and it doesn't change a thing.

'Cause in this world, feminist cousins betray you and ex-feminist moms keep secrets in attics.

C.C. reaches for my hand, but I pull away.

"You're the worst!" I finally yell, but I don't know who I'm yelling it at. Girls at school say that to teachers and talk about saying that to their moms, but it's not something I ever thought I'd say. It would have gotten me limpieza-grounded for days. But Mami says nothing. I push the posters across the table and they slide and fall off.

After running upstairs to my room, I slam and lock the door. Mami told me that door slamming is what gringas malcriadas do, but right now I don't care. And I guess she doesn't either, 'cause she doesn't run after me.

TWENTY

Thirty-two more mornings
wondering if I'll be the only woman
without a quetzal voice in Guatemala

IT'S TWO IN THE MORNING and I'm wide awake.

No one can sleep, 'cause Abuelita's singing "Mi Rancho Lindo," a song about a girl who leaves for the city but cries for her big house in the countryside. Each time she sings that song I want to ask her why the girl doesn't just move back if she misses it so much, but then they'll just tell me what adults always say: that I'll understand when I'm older. I think that's what adults say when they don't know what else to say.

I take out the papers with Mami's pieces of songs on them—almost ten of them. One line sticks out from all of them:

Y un día cantarán. One day they'll sing again.

I grab the old iPod C.C. gave me, and put the headphones in my ears. I click on Rebeca Lane's "Este Cuerpo es Mío." Today I just don't want to hear Abuelita sing. Except I find myself singing Mami's lyrics to Rebeca Lane's beat. I squeeze my eyes tight and try to get it out of my head.

I haven't talked to C.C. since she betrayed me last week, and Mami has been quiet; she hasn't said anything about the letters, and neither have I. Ever since stealing the tampons, I've been dreaming of them. Last night, I dreamed of a pad opening up real slow, like *slow motion* slow, and making that crackling sound, like when you first put milk in your Rice Krispies.

Abuelita's singing so loud, I can hear her over my headphones. It feels like the windows are about to shake. It's not the first time it's happened, and most of our neighbors know that Abuelita lives in and out of memories, but it's like sometimes they forget. From my window, I see Mrs. Williams from across the street come out in her robe. Her hands are on her hips and she's glaring at our house like her stare alone will quiet Abuelita down. It's not like when we lived in the apartments, where Abuelita's songs were one of many, where other abuelitas sang other songs of other places. Where you could smell everyone's comida and no one complained of the noise. In this neighborhood, it's like we have to be more quiet. I guess that was the sacrifice for me to finally get my own room.

Then Mr. Lazarte, who lives next to Mrs. Williams, opens his window and yells, "It's late! Be quiet!"

But Abuelita keeps singing. "Isn't that nice, chulitas?" she yells loud enough that we can all hear through the walls. "They like my song."

I take my headphones out. I flip my pillow over and punch and fluff it and lie back down.

It would be fine and all, I guess, except then she starts crying, and I don't think that's part of the song anymore. I hear Mami and Tía get up and rush out of their rooms, Tía's plastic overnight hair curling tubos clinking against each other as she speed walks. They're talking to Abuelita, but it's all in this quiet Spanish, like it wasn't meant for me to hear. Between the tears, and the whispering, and the secret Spanish, I barely understand a thing except for "Estás aquí. Estamos aquí." I know that means *You are here. We are here.* I can't explain it, but it even made me feel a little better, like when your toes are all cold at night and someone puts a colcha over them.

I try to go back to sleep, but there's no point. I tiptoe across my room. When I open the door, I jump and almost scream 'cause C.C. is at the top of the steps.

"Shhhhh!" she says as I open my mouth. "It's me. I couldn't sleep. What are you doing?"

"I couldn't sleep either," I whisper back. It feels good to hear her voice, even though I'm still mad at her. At least, I want to be.

We sit on the edge of my bed and she says she has good news. She enrolled at the local community college just ten minutes away. She'll get some of her requirements out of the way this summer till she's ready to go back to her actual school in the fall. I can't help it. I give her a big hug. She hugs me back real hard and says sorry, but I stop her.

"Women shouldn't say sorry so much, right?" I say. "You know, I've been thinking . . . Tía Beatriz talked about the wall you have to break down to do the thing you were meant to do, or to truly step into your power, right?"

"Yeah?"

"Well, I think these letters are like the wall my mom and I have between us," I say.

C.C. breathes out hard. "She hasn't tried to talk to you about them?"

I shake my head.

We quietly grab the ladder and head up to the attic. I grab the dictionary out of habit, but I won't need it as much this time because she can help me with words I don't know. She takes out her phone and finds the Rebeca Lane radio.

"Oh, this one's my favorite!" she says, and starts singing along, something about wanting to fight and not be a statistic. It's like the words and the letters come to life and I'm surrounded by Spanish that's not a secret, like it was meant for me to find all this time. We read the next letter together, out loud.

Please stop saying sorry. You had to leave. You did it for your daughter. You made a choice for her future. And look what you have now. Thank you for sending me pictures of Manuela. One day I will meet her and I'll tell her about her feminist mother.

I look up from the crinkly lined paper. "My *feminist* mother?" Now it's not just C.C. saying it, but Tía Beatriz too. I want to believe it. And maybe she was, but not anymore. "Mami is like the opposite of feminist," I say. "AND, you saw how she reacted to the posters."

C.C. puts her arms on my shoulder. "Feminism doesn't look the same everywhere. For our moms and Tía Beatriz, in Guatemala, it wasn't about what they were allowed to wear or not to wear. For them, at that time, in the work they were doing and what they were covering, it was about being able to make it somewhere in one piece, without harassment or violence, you know what I mean?"

Rebeca Lane's song comes on again. Then I think of her other songs when she says we deserve to live a long life. I think of Mami's songs. What am I and Las Nerdas fighting for right now? Suddenly it clicks. What do I want for Lani? For C.C.? For Genesis? For me?

I want our bodies to be respected, and information not to be used against them.

The girls I know aren't facing death or being found on the sides of roads, but . . .

"You know, it's not that different from here, *sometimes*," I say.

C.C. puts her hand on my foot, which is enough. We keep reading.

Consuelo, the secretary of the local church who's been searching for her daughter, has been holding meetings in the office at church. The police aren't doing anything about all the violence against women, so Consuelo started creating a database of all incidents, on the church computer. The priest has been telling any police who ask that Consuelo is running a computer literacy workshop for wives so that they can help their husbands' businesses. There is something about a group of women that really scares men. What do you think it is?

We're keeping a database of women who have been dis-appeared, harassed, even the things some people would consider small or common, like grabbing on the street. Beyond that, it will also help hold people accountable so that they don't keep getting away with this.

One lady goes into the capital Monday-Saturday to work as a maid and nanny for a British family and said the husband puts his hand down her shirt often. He never gave back any of her identification paperwork from when she first started working. He told her that now she can never leave. In between tears, she said she stays because it pays more than any other job and that she could at least be with her own children on Sundays. At least four

different women told similar stories. Women talk about sending
their daughters to the United States and Canada where they
won't have to deal with that.

I want to scream at the letter: But they DO deal with that here! What was Mami telling her? I want so badly to read what Mami wrote to her, but maybe I'll never know. I picture those letters floating off the side of the mountain where her bus supposedly fell, or disappeared, or maybe they were ripped apart by a giant rock someone threw at her window. Or maybe she buried them under a floorboard at church during her secret meetings.

"I don't know, Maní, I think your mom kept these above *your* room for a reason. It's part of your story."

I consider it. My story and my history. I never thought of either of them forming in Guatemala, a place I've never even been. I think of what Dad says about himself: that his story starts here in the U.S., but that his history goes way back. C.C. starts yawning. She looks at her phone.

"I'm sorry, Maní," C.C. says. "I'm so tired."

"Yeah, no problem. I'm just going to stay up here a bit more, OK?"

C.C. gives me a hug and heads down the ladder. I decide to do something different tonight, instead of just sit here. I decide to write back to Tía Beatriz, even though it won't actually reach her.

Dear Tía Beatriz,

I know you never met me in person, but I am your niece, Manuela. My close friends call me Maní, and C.C., your other niece, calls me Maní, like a peanut, because she says peanuts can surprise you and be hard enough to break your tooth if they wanted. I've never broken my tooth on a peanut, but I bet it hurts worse than a papercut, or falling out of a tree. I like to think of myself like a strong peanut, especially on days when I feel stupid, or weak, or like there is so much going on around me and I can't do anything about it. Did you ever feel that way? I have learned a lot about you through these letters, more than Mami has ever told me. I have so much to say and ask, but today something is burning in my chest like when you light a match, and someone dares you to put your finger to it. Did you ever do that? No, you didn't have time for stupid things like that. Your friends were doing more important things.

Anyway, I want to tell you that bad things DO happen to women and girls here, even though a lot of people come here looking for a better life. It might be better in some ways, but that doesn't mean bad stuff can't happen. My best friend Kai's sister was assaulted by her piano teacher. Her family has never used that word, but I now know that's exactly what it was. And instead of telling someone, she kept it rolling around inside of her for a really long time, like a really hot marble burning around in your stomach or something. She even broke Kai's finger once. (I know Kai shouldn't take that personally, but don't you think it's hard not to?) Or C.C. She's real smart, but she quit school for a while because her advisor was being creepy and manipulative and trying to touch her. And me, I haven't told Mami this, but a boy ripped my bra off of me, and several people filmed it. Somewhere, someone is watching the video and laughing. I know all of this doesn't sound as bad as what happened to the woman you made the sign for, or the woman who has to work as a nanny for that

creepo British guy, but it's affecting our future, opportunities,
confidence, and our right to live in a world where our bodies are
respected, so like, isn't that considered a type of violence too? If
it's not, it definitely should be.

Love,

Maní, your niece.

Oh and P.S. Primero una voz, y luego seremos millones.

I fold the letter and hold it in the palm of my hand. I wish I could put my hand out the window and let the wind carry it to Guatemala. I imagine my tía alive, reading it in a colorful kitchen, with birds singing outside her window, while she makes a protest sign on recycled cardboard. I imagine the stories of so many women written in her journalist notebook, their voices recorded on her voice recorder, each story fueling her every move, her own story beginning to weave into theirs.

I smile, 'cause in spite of everything, the women Tía Beatriz wrote about smiled too.

TWENTY-ONE

Twenty-one more mornings
of mansplaining by Mr. Dupont
over the school intercom

IN THE SCHOOL HALLWAY, Mr. Lewis is telling us to hurry up and get to first period even though we have seven whole minutes till the warning bell. My disappeared tía's words about how girls in the United States don't deal with things swirl in my head. I've kept low for over a week (which in middle school can feel longer than that part in church when everyone gives each other la señal de la paz and it's all besos for days, and you know there are only a few songs left before you get to leave, but they're the longest ones).

I walk past Corey's locker, but I take a deep breath, roll my fists up tight.

A plastic water bottle falls out of his locker and he kicks it my way as I walk past him to my locker. I know we're supposed to be the generation who saves the world and reverses climate change and stuff like that, but walking through the seventh-grade hallway, you wouldn't really think it. A boy to my left finally slams his locker, and that's when I catch a glimpse of A'niya at her locker at the end of the hall. She's surrounded by a group of girls. They give each other those fake air kisses on the cheek and I hear echoes of "Bye, chica" and "Later, girls."

Soon as her friends leave, that's when I see them: those beautiful white pants again that she never stains no matter what—period, cafeteria, bus loop benches. Nothing.

I close my locker, and twist the lock a few times to the right. Two of Corey's friends crowd around him and start to take their phones out. I roll my eyes at them and start to walk to class. A'niya's still at her locker, and I'll have to pass her. Maybe I'll say hi. No sé. In my head I play out what I could say. Hey. Sup. ¿Qué onda? Hey, chica.

No, definitely not the last one.

I'm several lockers away from her, but I don't get a chance to say anything even if I was brave enough, 'cause Mason and Corey come running down the hallway, slamming into a few kids on the way.

SLAP!

Corey slaps A'niya's butt so hard the sound rings in my ears from like six feet away. Mason pulls her hair and they both make some really gross sounds. Like *gross* gross. Corey pinches her boob, like right in the middle where it hurts. Pain shoots through my body. I wince like it was me.

It all happens too fast and I'm just standing there, mouth open like an idiota.

"Hey!" is all I can manage to say, after it already happened. Then they run off. With all the commotion, other kids in the hall start to take their phones out.

"Tell me you got that!" Mason yells back to one of the phone boys, while slapping Corey on the back.

Phone boy stomps his foot on the ground. "I didn't press record!" he says, walking past A'niya like she's not even there. Like she's not even a person.

A'niya hasn't moved her head at all. Her eyes are fixed on the mirror inside the door of her locker. Suddenly, she doesn't look like a sunflower anymore. She's just staring like her locker mirror's gonna give her answers.

"A'niya?" I manage to squeak out.

Why doesn't she say anything? A'niya ALWAYS says something. That's what makes A'niya . . . well, A'niya.

I clear my throat. "A'niya," I say, louder.

The hallway starts to clear out more, and it's just me and her. Her eyes get puffy like when they fill up with water but you don't want anyone to see you cry, but I see it. She slams the locker shut.

"We need to report that," I say, surprising myself.

"We?" She looks at me like I'm chicle stuck on the bottom of her shoe or something. "Report what? They've been doing that to girls all year and filming it. They're all over that page on Instagram. There's nothing to report."

"I know . . . someone told me I was on it?" I say.

"Whatever. It's not the first time. Kinda just embarrassing with all these people around, being all metidos, that's all," she says, and from her look, it's obvio I'm the metida.

"At least it sounds like they were too stupid to figure out how to press record," she says, trying to make a joke, but her voice cracks.

I point to her butt. "Hello? They slapped you. And made gross sounds. And then grabbed your boob. That's harassment, and assault. Or both, but either way, it's not right."

"Mani, *you. Are. So. Dramatic.* I don't need a play-by-play, OK? And do you even know what assault means?" She does that thing adults do—treating me like I don't know anything worth knowing.

But for real, there's also a sadness in her voice that I can't shake, and in PE last quarter we did this empathy lesson so I've got mad empathy for days. I want to tell her that yes, I do know what that means . . . that I know what it means in Guatemala and here, and that we need to call it what it is.

"That shouldn't happen here, or anywhere. They shouldn't keep getting away with that. And everyone who films it or even tries to film it should get in trouble . . . They should be held accountable. It's assault . . . it's sexual harassment. I'll go with you to report it," I say, even though I wonder if that will hurt more than help, since I'm kind of in trouble with Mr. Dupont and the vice principal, Mr. Robertson, after putting used tampons on the library tables. Even though it was for a good cause.

She looks down, which is weird 'cause A'niya's the kind of girl who always looks up, straight in your eyes.

But then she nods. Except I don't have a plan of what I'll say or do there. Not really.

We make it to the main office, and none of the secretaries look at us. Mr. Dupont is holding the intercom phone up to his head and finishing saying the Pledge of Allegiance, and it's weird to hear it in person instead of blasting through the intercom.

He doesn't acknowledge us either, so we go to the vice principal's office. Mr. Robertson is always on the intercom saying, *Come on by, my door is always open!* and it is. It's wide open, so we walk up to it.

I knock on the door, even though it's open. He looks up and then sets down the coffee mug it looks like he was just about to drink from.

"Come in, *young ladies*," he says, probably 'cause he doesn't know our names even though he's the seventh-grade administrator.

A'niya's mouth is shut. She barely moves, so I do all the talking. I tell him about what I saw, even though the words feel uncomfortable at first. He nods, picks up a pen and scribbles something on a notepad. Then he takes a sip of his coffee with his other hand and asks me what hallway, where, and what time, like the first thing I did was look at the clock or something. What kind of question is that? But I'm trying to be bold like Abuelita's always telling me to be, like a quetzal that's been waiting to use its voice for a long, long time. She tells me to be directa. Tell people what you want, and you'll get it. Except all we get now are crickets.

"So, we'd like to file a sexual harassment report," I say.

Mr. Robertson almost chokes on his coffee.

"Now hold on, young lady. Not too fast. Our sexual harassment report is saved for extreme cases and involves a thorough investigation. We have a bullying report, but it has to happen repeatedly for it to be a pattern of bullying."

I think about my bra getting ripped off me on the bus. A'niya looks like she's sleepwalking. I want to shake her a little, but I turn to Mr. Robertson. "But, that's not fai—"

"I tell you what, ladies. I will have security check the cameras. Or even better, how about I go check them myself."

He looks all proud of his idea, and he's looking at his watch and then at the door, obviously waiting for us to leave. But no sé, doesn't sound like a good deal to me. I plant my feet real deep into the carpet of his floor.

"No," I say.

A'niya turns to look at me.

"No." I dig my heels in even more. "We're not leaving. This needs to be solved," I say, but I don't know where it comes from. Or maybe I do. No sé, but it's coming out strong.

"It's—it's been happening all year," I say, and look at A'niya for support.

Nothing.

"And instead of stopping it or trying to help, kids tried to film it. When are you going to do something? And can't the school help shut these sites down?"

Mr. Robertson stands. Abuelita says any time a man feels the need to be taller than you in an argument, it's 'cause he feels threatened. So I stay exactly where I am, and so does A'niya, even though she's giving off puro zombie vibes right now.

And that's when his tone changes night and day.

"I'm going to give you some advice, ladies. I have granddaughters your age, and I'd give them the same advice." He taps the pen against the notepad he had scribbled like three things on. "You've got to protect yourself these days. When you wear tight or revealing clothes . . . well, you've got to think about what message you are sending out . . . and . . . and sometimes you get unwanted att—"

"What do clothes have to do with it?" I blurt out before he can finish.

A'niya was just putting her backpack away, probably about to check her eyelashes in her little locker mirror, no sé, but like minding her business for real. I'm so mad and I can't hide it from my face. I don't want to.

But then A'niya comes back from zombie mundo and starts laughing. What's wrong with her? This isn't funny. Mr. Robertson and I both look at A'niya, but I quickly look back at him like there's nothing wrong here.

"I'll tell you what," says Mr. Robertson. "I'll go talk to these boys myself. Right now, in fact. They see a pretty girl and they don't know what to do," he adds, waiting for us to get out.

They don't know what to do? "Pretty girl? So it's A'niya's fault? If she wasn't pretty this wouldn't happen?" I say.

That's when he puts down his coffee real hard, and clicks the pen a few times. "Point is, ladies, it technically has to be a repeated offense to the same person to count as bullying."

"But we don't want it to happen again!" I say, feeling the veins pop on my fists. "Why do we have to wait for it to happen again for this school to do something about it?" My voice feels like it grew long green-and-red quetzal wings in this dusty cinderblock building.

I keep going. "We want accountability so that it sends the message that harassment is not accepted in school."

Mr. Robertson wipes his forehead with the paper towel his coffee was just resting on. "I wouldn't want you ladies being any later to class. We will check out the cameras and talk to those boys. After we talk to them, we can get you all together and talk it out in a circle." He writes us passes to class. Everything in my gut tells me to stay where I'm standing and not let him get away with doing nothing, but A'niya finally snaps out of her weird daydream and gives me the back-down-now look.

We shuffle out with our heads down but stop at his voice.

"To avoid any situations like this in the future, I suggest you wear things a little more school appropriate," he says, eyeing A'niya's shirt. "You can head down to the gym locker room. They'll have something for you there."

Before I can say anything, he closes the door, and puts up the "In a Meeting" sign, obviously in no rush to check the cameras or go talk to the boys, and find all the ones who tried to film.

My fists ball up in frustration. "Why were you so quiet? You ALWAYS have something to say," I tell A'niya. But what I really want to ask her is how she can just shut off her light like that.

"Because, Mani. I knew they wouldn't do nothing. Did they do anything about your bra video? It's still on there."

I wince at the thought. "I shouldn't have listened to you. That was so embarrassing." With vida back in her body, she walks away from me toward class.

"A'niya?"

She stops, and looks back at me. "I don't want to talk about this again, OK? And don't tell anyone. For real, Mani. No one."

And I feel like when someone tells you an awful secret, and you don't know how you're going to keep it tucked away, 'cause it burns real bad.

TWENTY-TWO

Ten more days watching boys
get away with everything

EVEN THOUGH IT'S JUNE, it's cold and rainy.

This morning, I grabbed the only clean sweater I had left and I'm full of clothing regret. It's the puke, or "rainforest" green, itchy wooly sweater Mami got me on rebaja last time we went to the mall. Except the color's not even the worst. Seeing it on makes me realize she definitely got it from the MEN'S clearance section, and it's even bigger on me than I remembered.

Starting first period with health class is always bad, but today it's worse than eating mushy plátanos. A'niya's secret has been burning in my chest for a whole week and a half, and I'm only twelve (almost thirteen) so that's like a significant percentage of my life.

When Mr. Jones starts to shout the Pledge of Allegiance in sync with Mr. Dupont's voice over the intercom, I'm scratching where the sweater collar scrapes up against my neck and under my arm so hard I think I cut my skin with my nails. Mason and Corey and a couple of other boys stand tall and shout it just as loud as Mr. Jones. I feel the sweater making my back all itchy, so I reach my hand around

and under my shirt. I just feel my skin and the elastic of my training bra. Uy, I was so tired this morning that I never put on a shirt
underneath. I see Mason looking this way, so I quickly put my hand
down.

"And to the republic—" Mr. Jones shouts.

"Did you hear?" J.J. says. He's flicking his finger against his
thumb, which obviously means he's flicking a booger. With everyone turned toward the front of the room, he picks his nose so hard
it looks like his finger is going to break off all up in his stupid, sexist, manspreading bully nose.

I kind of want to know what he's talking about, but I also kind
of don't, 'cause J.J.'s brain is smaller than the booger he just launched
across the room. He once tried to start a petition to fire his Spanish
teacher just because she had an accent when she spoke English, and
it was hard for him to understand. For one, she was like the best
teacher in school other than Ms. Martinez, and for two, she spoke
like five different languages. That's four and a half more than J.J.

"Did you hear?" he says again, when someone else from the back
row says, "Did you see what she wrote?"

Then there's more whispering. I try to tune them out. I look up
at the empty seat where A'niya should be. I start rapping a Rebeca
Lane song under my breath, "Siempre Viva," the one about being a
weed no one can destroy. I never heard a song where a woman
wanted to be a weed instead of a flower, but I get it, especially now.
For real. Except, I think of A'niya and how she should be able to be
a flower if she wants to, without getting groped.

After we talked to Mr. Robertson almost two weeks ago, A'niya's
locker was moved to the basement level, so she wouldn't have to run

into Corey or Mason. They changed *her* schedule so that she wouldn't have any classes with them other than first period health, which they couldn't change. That was Mr. Robertson's big solution. But that's not even the worst of it. They gave her a map of the school so she could figure out different routes to avoid running into the boys. Actually, the real, *real* worst part is that they did NOTHING to Corey or Mason. They got a "warning" that they'd be taken off the lacrosse team if they pull anything else. They get to walk the same way they've been walking. They get to use the same bathrooms. They get to keep their same lockers. They get to pick on whoever, whenever, like what they did wasn't even wrong. They didn't get a map of the moldy school.

The Pledge ends and Mr. Jones turns to write on the board and everyone starts whispering again. A'niya's words, *For real, Mani. No one*, swirl around in my brain.

There's a big empty space in the front row where A'niya should be sitting. I haven't seen her in the library or hallways either. The only time she ever misses school is when she and her parents go to El Salvador, but I always know when that is because her friends decorate her locker with balloons and "We'll Miss You" signs with annoying crying emojis. I picture A'niya decorating her basement locker next to the spooky abandoned storage closet all alone, and it makes me sad. Or worse, not decorating it at all. The more I think of it, the more my blood boils.

And that's when I realize that all the whispering going on is about A'niya.

"A'niya took down her Instagram and Twitter," says Mason. "Because of US!" he adds, and he high-fives Corey.

"Yeah, but first she wrote, *Choose your friends wisely. #truefriends-dontstayquiet*," says Corey. "That's something my grandma would say. She's like a grandma, and a slut. A slutty grandma."

The minute he says *slutty* and *grandma* in the same sentence, about three different boys lean in to high-five him, but they bump into each other and all miss.

"Dude, nah. It's granslutma," says J.J. They all laugh.

"Yeah, I heard the principal told her mom to tell her to stop dressing like a slut," says another boy in the back row.

"I heard her parents are making her move back to Mexico and live with her grandma, or she's, like, transferring to another school," says another.

"Slut school," another says. Their hyena laughs pierce the air, again.

"I can't believe you idiots didn't film it," says Mason.

I want to say something so bad, but it's like I have cement in my throat. Abuelita once told me during one of her not-feminist episodes: *Calladita más bonita.* But I don't want to be quiet and pretty. If I'm quiet, nothing changes. If I'm pretty, which I'm not really, I'm just a girl who can be an A'niya to them. I'm not even paying attention to Mr. Jones. All I hear is the boys in the back making fun of A'niya for her fitted white pants and having a body that's . . .

I want to shout at them and tell them what I think. I mean, I'm a doer, right? Like my Tía Beatriz. She was a doer. A big doer. And what she faced was like so much bigger than a bunch of stupid seventh-grade boys. But the words get all caught and then melt away all bitter in my mouth like when you put a Sour Patch Kid on your tongue and just let it sit there till it melts away on its own.

Am I just as bad as they are if I don't say anything? Am I like Gonzalo who didn't speak up for me as my bra got ripped off me and filmed for all to see?

LATER, IN ENGLISH CLASS, Mr. Lewis passes out all the writing warm-ups. Florence's markers go *click pop swish click pop swish* like always as she's highlighting the directions. Hector's hiccupping, Jordyn's laying out her assortment of fruity-smelling ChapSticks, tiny mirrors, and makeup on her desk. J.J.'s manspreading all over his seat and his pencil is scraping on the desk as he writes all over the surface with stupid hashtags.

I just can't focus. I start to doodle and write *don't tell anyone* on the margins of the warm-up sheet.

I can't stop thinking about those idiot guys in health class. What they were saying, how they were all laughing and high-fiving. And I think about Tía Beatriz's letter when she said she couldn't just stand back and watch. She was a part of it. She demanded accountability.

And I was there and said nothing. I just—

"How do you think the young woman feels at the end of 'The First Job'?" Mr. Lewis asks, holding up Sandra Cisneros's *The House on Mango Street*.

My school got like a F+ or E− when it came to "promoting diverse voices and intercultural understanding" or something like that. Anyway, it's cool 'cause now I actually get to read stories I like. We started reading the short story "The First Job" which is only three pages. I didn't know you could write a story that's only three pages long, but she makes it work.

"Three pages people. Three pages. I will repeat. How. Does. The. Young. Lady. Feel. At. The. End. Of. The. Story," he says.

Only a few hands go up, but Mr. Lewis glazes over them. It's quieter than my living room when Dad is listening to the lottery numbers, even though he always loses. I asked him once if he ever gets sad about losing. He smiled. *You can't get sad over something you never had.*

Not getting sad over what you don't have—but A'niya was sad when those boys grabbed her in the hall. What did she have that they took from her?

Mr. Lewis asks the question again, but with different words. Teachers are always doing that. "What is going through her head at the end, when the coworker kisses her but she thought he was just being nice?" he says, clearly embarrassed when he says "kisses."

Some kids start to pick up the story now that they know there's kissing.

"I'll wait," says Mr. Lewis.

Pages flip and rustle. I raise my hand. Today, I don't want to be quiet. Mr. Lewis nods at me in that go-ahead type way.

"I think . . . she didn't want to be touched. She was just trying to go to her job. She didn't ask for it," I say in a voice so shaky I should have just kept it in.

"She didn't NOT ask for it," says J.J.

A bunch of kids start laughing.

I want to say it again, louder, even though I wonder if Mr. Lewis hears me. Even if he does, he pretends not to. I think again about my abuelita and Mami and how they want me to be quiet and unseen. Then how A'niya is always being seen but not wanting attention like that.

Mr. Lewis looks around the room. At Jimmy Torres yawning. At Melody R. texting under her desk. At everyone just . . . like me.

Saying nothing, or saying it so quiet it might as well not have been said. He finally gives up and tells everyone that laying off the video games would do us some good.

"Turn to page fifty-six," he says. "Melody, put your phone away."

I write on the edge of my paper. *I don't know exactly what it means, but I know she didn't want to be kissed in the break room, even if she didn't say no.*

I crumple it up and throw it in the blue recycling bin on my way out.

It's finally history class, and Ms. Martinez's voice makes me happy, like when my parents let me stay home with Abuelita and she lets me drink black coffee with no milk. She's laughing at something Hector tells her, and no sé, but her laugh is like water—like it's good for you, you know?

"Listen up, mi gente," she says.

"This isn't Spanish class," Mason mutters from the back, but Ms. Martinez pretends she doesn't hear him.

"Unfortunately, we only get ten minutes to work on our projects today because Mr. Dupont and your seventh-grade administrator, Mr. Robertson, have called an emergency town hall for seventh grade," she says, pursing her lips 'cause ten minutes isn't a long time when the Speak Up event with all those fancy judges is happening in exactly ten days. We only have town halls at the very beginning of the quarter, or unless something real bad has happened.

"Then I'm just gonna chill for the next ten."

It's Corey. Corey-Can't-Keep-His-Octopus-Hands-Off-Girls Corey. Ew. I glare at him.

"That's what your grades said!" says Kai.

Connie and I put our hands to our mouths to stifle laughter. Kai's been real mad ever since I told Las Nerdas about A'niya. No sé, maybe she's thinking about her sister.

Ms. Martinez puts a slide on the board: *Five-minute café chat: Look below for your assignment partner. Sit with your partner. Tell your partner about your Speak Up campaign/project and how it will benefit your school and community.*

OK, that's fun. I start to think about all my ideas that Kai, Connie, Genesis, and I have been working on the last few weeks. Free period products, and how we already got the school to place a free box in the bathroom next to the locker room, with the support of some initiative from the school district. We want it expanded to every bathroom in the school, and even talked about asking the county school board to put it in a packet for girls when they start middle school, kinda like a welcome-to-middle-school-and-periodhood packet. That's a little much, but Las Nerdas dream hard.

But there's a thought I can't get rid of, like an itch on your back you can't reach. Ever since what happened to A'niya, I've been thinking about how hard they made it to fill out a sexual harassment report, if a real one even exists, and A'niya's words: Tell no one. How many girls are walking around "telling no one"? I need to know. I think this is bigger than A'niya. But then I have to blink like a million times to make sure I am seeing things correctly.

Corey is my café chat partner.

He leans back in his chair. Both feet are wide out on the floor. He bites his nails. Then spits a piece of nail out. "I'm not movin'," he says.

And in that moment, I think Corey is worse than when you throw up so hard it comes out of your nose. Corey is legit worse than even nose vomit.

I take a deep breath. This is my chance to confront him, since Mr. Dupont AND Mr. Robertson won't. I walk toward him. His foot is blocking the front of the desk I'm supposed to sit in. "Can you please move your leg?" I say.

He laughs. "What's the password?"

Before I can say anything, Ms. Martinez sternly says from her desk, "Corey, if you don't move your legs and start this activity, you'll get a zero for this."

"Whatever, my dad will complain and sue you," he murmurs and looks around to see if anyone smiles or air dabs him.

"What was that, Corey?" Ms. Martinez asks.

"Nothing," he says. 'Cause he's too weak to actually say it loud enough for her to hear.

He looks at me. "I guess I'll go. Normally I'd say ladies first, but I don't see any ladies."

I look over my shoulder for a save from Ms. Martinez, but she's helping another group.

"Pfff, I don't know," Corey says. "I'd do a campaign for better stuff in the vending machines. Also, higher prices on the vending machine stuff so that not just anyone can get stuff and then it's not empty by the end of the day. Oh, and I'd make them allow phones in school. Like not just during lunch. Like *all* day, in class. I told my dad when Ms. Martinez took my phone for texting him back, he was so mad because having a phone is a safety issue. She's lucky she still works here."

The rule doesn't stop him from filming horrible stuff . . . and it doesn't make Mr. Dupont take any of their phones away.

"So . . . you want vending machines to be for rich people and free access to cell phones?"

He looks at me like I for real just farted. Before it's my turn, he leans to the left of his desk and tries to get Mason's attention.

Then we're all saved by Mr. Dupont on the intercom calling all seventh-grade classes to town hall.

I'm burning up in this green men's clearance sweater I can't take off. It's going to feel even hotter in the gym, 'cause that's where all the town halls are. But then I start to think that maybe this random town hall might be about him. This whole time I thought how unfair it was that they haven't even talked to Corey and Mason. Maybe they're going to call them out in front of everyone.

I start to get mariposas in my stomach like in PE when you're the last person left on your dodgeball team and you think you might still have a chance.

TWENTY-THREE

IN THE GYM, NO ONE's taking the front row bleachers, 'cause you can't get away with using your phone when you're in the front. Las Nerdas don't really do any of that, but still, we look for a row at the top. I want to be able to see everyone's reaction when they call out all the assaults and video recording.

The school band is playing as kids file in, but uy, it's so hot. I can feel drops of sweat from my armpit on my bulky, itchy men's clearance sweater. I keep scratching at the neck, careful not to let anyone see that all I have underneath is this stupid training bra.

Genesis's hair is twice as big as it normally is, and she's having fun seeing how many pencils she can hold in it, oblivious to the fact that all her fears about being targeted for one of these stupid videos are about to be squashed. Matt Zelaya lifts his armpit to another girl's nose and that starts a bunch of kids doing it, like it's a thing.

We wave at Connie who is next to the band behind the giant screen, doing tech last minute, like a jefa, 'cause this town hall is so last minute. The teachers are yelling at the kids to put their phones away, but no one's listening. Then Mr. Dupont and Mr. Robertson threaten parent phone calls and after-school detention. Phones are stashed fast and people get all quiet, 'cause they call parents so fast it's like they're going to *collect what's owed to them.* That's what Abuelita says in Spanish. I can't wait for Mr. Dupont and Mr. Robertson to collect the phone of each kid who ever filmed and uploaded one of these assaults.

The gym smells worse than that time Doña Marta told Tía Gladys to soak her feet in apple cider vinegar to cure heartache. And I never understood that people's hearts can actually hurt, until now. I think about how sad A'niya looked and it pinches my heart and makes it hurt all kinds of ways. But everything's going to change now. That's why they're calling this town hall.

"Look," says Kai.

Then I see her.

A'niya walks into the gym, and the tightness I was holding in my hands softens. I didn't recognize her at first, with her hoodie up and covering part of her face. She's not wearing any makeup, which is weird for her, but she looks beautiful. Like for real. I smile real big and wave at her, wondering if we're in the friend zone, but she doesn't see me.

"Is this thing on?" Mr. Dupont says, fumbling with the extra-long cord he almost trips on. "Ladies and gentlemen! Clap twice if you can hear me!"

About half the gym gives two claps. Everyone else is clapping nonstop. It's about to happen. This is when he's going to call out Corey and Mason. He'll throw in Max and J.J. while he's at it, 'cause they're Nasty Jr. He'll call out the boys on my bus who throw things down girls' shirts, and the ones who film . . . even the social media sites, and the adults who pay kids to upload these videos. I hold on to the edge of the bleachers.

"They're for real going to call them out, right?" I say to Kai.

"Of course, why else would they have this?" she says.

We do the Nerda handshake low by our knees and my heart feels full and ready to sing.

The whispering dies down and we all wait for Mr. Dupont to keep talking.

"In a few months you will be eighth graders . . ."

Whistles erupt. "I'll . . . I'll wait," he says.

Everyone quiets down again, for the most part.

"You'll be the leaders of the school . . . and so you need to start setting good examples."

He pulls at the long and heavy cord. (Don't know why the school can't buy cordless.)

A few sections of the bleachers are still talking.

"I'll wait," he says, firmly this time, and dead-eye looking at those kids. They stop.

OK, OK. Good intro. But I'm ready for why we're here. They don't even know what's coming.

"We're here today to talk about dress code, language, and having respect for your own body, and making good choices. Gentlemen, I've heard a lot of language that is NOT representative of who we are as seventh graders or as a community," he says. "Language that is not . . . gentlemanly, to be quite frank. And ladies—we need to start dressing in a way that sends out the message that you respect your own body. Because if you don't respect your own body, no one else will."

WHAT.

The room is spinning. *I'm* spinning. The sticky, nasty Takis crumb floor feels like it's shaking underneath our feet. Kai and I look at each other. Our mouths are open in shock (like the first time I saw my abuelita pull her teeth straight out of her mouth and I realized her teeth weren't real). I search for the right words in my head. It's unfair? Unjust? Injusto? That sounds closer. Manjustice, which is like the opposite of justice? No sé, sounds weird.

"We have a couple of weeks to correct this before the end of the school year. It's never too late," says Mr. Dupont. "Gentlemen: pants up and hoods down. And control yourselves."

Some boys laugh. I wait for it—what's supposed to come next.

What about the gropings? The assaults? The videos stuck on the internet where they'll stay forever? People making money off the videos? Something stings in my throat, my stomach, the void where a quetzal voice could be, if only, just only, it would ever decide to come out, to be given the chance.

"Ladies," Mr. Dupont continues. "Belly buttons aren't meant to be shown. Pants do not need to be that tight. Let's be honest. Seventh grade is a time of change, and hormones are raging, and people might say or do something you don't like if you're sending the wrong messages."

WHAT? Some *Boos* come from the bleachers.

I look around. Ms. Martinez stands by the doors. Uy, she has a look on her face that could cause arrugas. She's all angry texting too. A couple of girls roll their eyes so hard I think they might see estrellas or something, but not enough to start a *revolt* or anything. Ms. Martinez uses that word a lot when she teaches us history, and I like it.

I look around the bleachers. A few people look as disgusted as I am. But most aren't even listening.

"And if we hear about phones being used inappropriately, trust me. They will be confiscated."

More *boos*, but I don't know if they are for the fact that phones are being used to film what is happening, or because they might be confiscated.

Then I see Corey and Mason. They're just sitting on the side, breaking a pencil into tiny pieces and putting it down the shirts of everyone in the row in front of them.

My head starts to hurt. My eyes sting. My hands ache from squeezing into fists.

I think of my disappeared tía, and then about A'niya, who's been sitting head down in the front row. What happened to A'niya isn't like what happened to the women my tía would meet in her secret church meetings. But I think about C.C. and Kai's sister and A'niya who was just at her locker, the random girls I don't know who were just walking home from school and were targeted for these stupid social media challenges, and all the women I don't know anything about: the woman in my tía's letters who kept working for a guy who groped her just 'cause it's the only job that would give a day off and he stole her papers. And I'm pretty sure that's what's called human trafficking 'cause Dad always makes me read news around the world and when I asked him why people get trafficked in other countries, he told me actually a lot of people get trafficked in the US.

It just feels like . . . the common thread holding it all together is boys and men getting away with . . . pues, todo. It's kind of like Rebeca Lane's song "Nos Queremos Vivas." Women just trying to live a long life and do stuff. Women who just want their bodies respected. *Our* bodies respected. Women I know.

I don't know what, but *something* needs to be done.

"Can you believe he said that?" I say to Kai.

"Well, yeah, I can," says Kai, "but it's still messed up."

Then Mr. Robertson tries to project a video against the wall behind him, but it doesn't work.

A'niya's head is still low, hoodie over her head and hands in pockets. She's just looking down at her shoes. None of her usual friends are around her. She's just there. Alone.

Something has to be done. I look at Kai. "Las Nerdas forever, right?" I say.

"Yeah . . . ?"

"I'll be right back," I say.

I walk down the narrow steps of the bleachers. Even though I've asked Mami before if she can get me a skirt, it's good I'm not wearing one now ('cause then everyone would see my days-of-the-week underwear, which is so elementary school, but ever since washing my own clothes became one of my chores at the beginning of the year, I've lost track of them, and I'm definitely wearing Sunday's even though it's Friday).

"C-an I please use the bathroom?" I manage when I reach a teacher at the bottom of the bleachers.

"Make it quick," she says, and gives me a half smile. "You don't want to miss this really important stuff," she adds, and I can't help but think that even some of the teachers see how unfair this is.

I slip out the main gym door, but it makes this loud SLAM behind me. Looking both ways, I see there's no one in the hall. Just pencils, an empty Doritos bag, a really thin pad in its wrapper, and one locker with balloons and decorations all over it for someone's birthday.

I walk around to the other entrance behind where the school band is. I take a deep breath except I choke on air, if that's even possible, so I have to cough it out. I try again and open the door. The band kids are talking. About half of them notice and look back at me, as I try to let the door close softly behind me. Mr. Dupont is standing right in front of the bleachers, with his back to me, but he left his mic on a chair by the band. Connie and the other tech kids are trying get whatever video he had planned to actually play. Mr. Robertson stands over them, not helpful at all.

My heart races, like when you put too much sugar in the horchata mix. Mr. Dupont starts to pace. The bleacher crowds get restless so he tries to use the time to make announcements he would have said at the end of the day. Then he tells Connie and the other tech kids to hurry up and get the video working. He's sweating hard now and takes his jacket off all fast and flustered, and throws it on an empty spot in the front row of the bleachers.

I take a step forward, but I stop, 'cause I see it.

The worst thing I could ever see.

Mr. Dupont is wearing the *same puke green sweater as I am.*

I freeze. (Like, tamales-in-the-freezer-for-three-years-congelado, you know?) A few of the band kids look back at me. Kids from the bleachers start to notice and point. Some of them start to laugh, and slowly more and more people notice.

The only thing worse than being one of the only girls to not get your period is twinning with your principal right before you're about to steal his mic.

I run for the mic anyway. I pick it up and notice how heavy the cord is.

I tap the top of it twice, 'cause that's what people do. "Um . . . Hi."

I'm surprised by how loud it is. Connie gives me wide eyes as Mr. Dupont looks up and notices me. I clear my throat, but it's all loud through the mic and a bunch of kids say, "Ouch!" and cover their ears.

"Sorry. Many of you know me as vagina girl . . . even though it was actually *vulva*." Uy, where am I going with this? That was *so* two months ago.

Some girls take their phones out, and a few kids laugh. Then, silence. They're waiting for me to say more. Mr. Dupont and Mr. Robertson are heading toward me, but not before telling Connie to cut the mic, but she fumbles all over the soundboard like she doesn't know how to use it. I think of my tía's words. *Sometimes it's all a woman has left to do.*

Mr. Dupont walks faster and he's coming for the mic.

"I just want to say . . ." Dizzy, I start to sweat and trip on my words all at the same time. But looking up and seeing Kai's giant grin from the bleachers steadies me.

What do I want to say? Uy, nothing is coming out right. Abuelita is always telling me to speak up. *No seas tonta*, she says. And this isn't the moment to start thinking about this, but how is it that the same person who tells you to be quiet and pretty is the same person who tells you that staying silent makes you look like a *tonta*?

"I just want to say that boys are getting away with too much in school . . . and . . . and it's not girls' faults," I say.

I hear a few whistles and claps. More people look up at me. Mr. Dupont is getting closer, and Mr. Robertson is walking toward Connie and the soundboard. I know I suck at math and all, but I've calculated I've got a solid fifteen seconds before I have to start moving.

"Over a week ago, Corey and Mason ran up to A'niya and slapped her butt real hard. Like so hard it hurt my ears, so I bet it hurt. Instead of stopping them, their friends tried to film it, but it didn't work. They did other stuff too, and, like, she didn't ask for that. She was just at her locker, putting her stuff away, like all of us do every morning. They did other gross stuff too, and . . . and that's, like, a violation. No, that's actually, technically assault."

Mr. Robertson is angry-talking at Connie and telling her to cut the mic, but she just keeps saying, "I don't know how," even though she definitely does.

Mr. Dupont swipes at my hand to grab the mic.

I dodge his reach.

I look at A'niya. She puts her hoodie up even farther over her head, and then buries her face in her palms. Oh no, she told me not to say anything. I didn't mean to say her name. It just came out. I should have said "someone" but it's too late. She must feel like I felt when C.C. betrayed my secret.

Mr. Dupont gets closer and reaches for the mic, but I speed walk around the band, the heavy mic cord following me. Some kids are trying to high-five me as I walk around them, but I just don't have the time to high-five back, 'cause Mr. Dupont is walking real fast, so I start to walk faster as I speak into the mic.

"And . . . and they never got in trouble. Nothing happened to them! But A'niya got her locker moved! To the basement. And . . .

her whole schedule got changed. And listen to the message today: Girls, cover up. Like if we don't, we're asking for what boys like Corey and Mason do. But did you hear anyone address boys' behavior?"

I hear a few kids say, "No!" until a whole section of the left bleachers is yelling, "No, we didn't hear that!"

"They just have to *control* themselves like it's normal behavior," I say.

Now there are *boos* from every section of bleachers.

"And they do know about the phones being used and nothing has been done. There's been no accountability for the kids who film these planned attacks and who profit off of the videos."

"Grab her!" Mr. Dupont yells to Ms. Martinez, but she doesn't budge.

I'm running now, and the mic cord is so long, it wraps around the band's feet. I have to catch my breath, 'cause I'm not used to running and talking. And the next part comes out of my mouth without even thinking.

"I know that's not the only example of assault, so I just want to invite anyone who has experienced something like that, when nothing was done about it, to come talk to me. I am going to . . ."

I have no idea what I'm going to do. Not really.

I'm running, like PE class running, with the mic. Sweat runs down my back. The entire gym is listening. Phones out, feet stomping. And I don't have a plan. Doers have plans. Doers have—

Kai stands. Connie stands.

Then a few others stand. Gonzalo stands. Gonzalo? I'll have to give him a nod on the bus, if I make it out of here viva.

"Man-u-ella," Mr. Dupont says all mangled as I squeeze in with the band. His shoes squeak to a stop on the gym floor. I'm out of breath, but I put the mic back up to my mouth.

"I'm going to start a database," I say. "You know, like a Google doc or Excel sheet, you know, and write all of it down. We need to keep records of things like this. Maybe send it to the school board . . . start a petition . . . no more sexual harassment in school."

Pues, I don't know what the school board does, but when we had to watch student government videos, they all talk about the school board, so I assume they're important.

"No more basement lockers!" I shout.

It echoes and falls away.

That was not what I thought was going to happen. For real, like where was that movie moment thing that was supposed to happen? I yank the mic cord—

CRASH! The mic extension cord tips over a bunch of guitar stands and they all come down, sending loud screeching feedback through the speakers.

Everyone covers their ears and crouches.

A'niya runs out of the gym. Mr. Dupont stumbles his way through the band kids and broken guitars, to me, and grabs the mic right out of my hands.

I look at his sweater. He looks at mine. "My office," he says.

I feel sick. Not 'cause of being in the biggest trouble ever, but 'cause I want to run after A'niya and I can't. Mr. Robertson cuts the mic off and he's blocking the side entrance, Mr. Dupont is standing right in front of the main doors. I promised her I wouldn't say anything. I wish I knew how to turn on my quetzal voice in a way that didn't cause hurt. I wish a big, ugly meteor would come and destroy today—and this stupid, sexist town hall.

But then I hear a voice. A voice I've never heard. It comes from the left.

"Yeah, stop letting boys get away with everything!"

And then another "yeah!" Then a girl in the top middle row starts stomping real hard and yells, "Hell yeah, no more basement lockers!" and I wonder if she'll get in trouble for swearing. And then the sound of other feet joining in on the bleachers. Mr. Dupont and Mr. Robertson try to tell everyone to be quiet, but the mic is off. There's all this noise from the bleachers, and I think I'm being booed but when I listen closer—people are cheering.

And for a few seconds all I can hear is the sounds of rising voices and feet on the bleachers and the mix of anger and joy. It feels like I just grabbed on to a big balloon, and I am floating up and up.

They are cheering for me. For what I said.

TWENTY-FOUR

I'VE BEEN SITTING IN THE principal's office for so long, it feels longer than that day in fourth grade when Elvin Navidad spit his gum out on the bus and it landed right in my fresh-cut hair.

(It was picture day too. When I got home that day, Mami, Tía and, Abuelita all worked hard to get it out. I wanted so bad for Mami to storm into Elvin's house and yell at him and his mom, but she never did anything, except make my hair smell like vinagre and peanut butter for days after. She just told me to find a better seat on the bus. Yeah, I've been in here definitely longer than that.)

I just wish A'niya could have stayed to hear the claps, to hear me talk about the database. Maybe then she wouldn't hate me. My mind is racing. I wonder if what I did is just like what Corey and Mason did, or worse. Peor. Did I mess up so bad that I'm no better than those gropers and filmers?

Mr. Dupont gave me the student code of conduct to read, and since he makes me wait FOREVER, I actually read it. For one, there's nothing about NOT standing up for justice and demanding that something be done to protect students against harassment. (And for two, it's more boring than the user manual for the new smoothie blender Dad got, which Abuelita made me read to her 'cause she really wanted to make some special Guatemalan fruit juice for Christmas. Except it was August. And I didn't have the heart to tell her 'cause she woke me up that morning with the biggest smile, singing "El Burrito Sabanero," her hair curling tubos wrapped in the weekend newspaper and stuffed in little gift bags, for ME.)

It's getting real hot in Mr. Dupont's office, especially in this stupid green sweater that HE'S also wearing. I fan myself with the student code of conduct, and that's when I hear it. Ms. Martinez's earrings dangle as she pokes her head in. They sound like wind chimes and make me smile. Except she's not smiling.

"Hey, just checking in on you," she says, hands on hips.

Uy, I'm in trouble. "My mom's going to be so mad at me," I say. "I've never gotten in trouble so many times in my life than I have this year. I'm not trying to be *that* girl, it's just—"

"Manuela," Ms. Martinez says. And my ears perk up at the sound of my name all bright with the vowels hitting all the right notes, like a song in a room with the ceiling all high. "Manuela," she says again. "A veces . . . you just gotta be that girl." Then she smiles.

I smile so hard I think my face is going to burst.

"Now I'm not saying you did everything perfectly . . ." Her smile disappears. Then she checks her watch and I know she has to run to teach her next class. "Manuela, there's no going back. This is your chance to articulate what you want to do. You brought up really important stuff. You asked people to confide in you with sensitive information, and if they do, what do you plan to do with that information? That's a question you have to answer for yourself."

Uy, I guess I hadn't really thought of that. I consider it, not just 'cause Ms. Martinez uses fancy words like "articulate," but because she's right.

Then she winks at me and puts her hand on my shoulder. "But there is something you need to make right."

My mind instantly goes to A'niya. I look at Ms. Martinez like I don't know what she's talking about, but she gives me that look that Mami does, where her eyes speak what her mouth doesn't say.

"Dios mío, I'm glad I'm not you right now," she says.

"But I was doing it for her!" I say.

As soon as I say it, I have to admit that that's the part I could have handled differently.

"Do you think she sees it that way?"

I look down. It's not a question I'm supposed to answer out loud.

"Manuela, when I was your age, something similar happened to me. I wish I had had a friend like you to stand up for really unfair stuff going on," she says.

Her words soak into my skin as she turns to leave. They reach in real deep and shake me up. The sound of her earrings hitting her neck fades away.

Then Rebeca Lane's song is in my head again, the one about not wanting to be a statistic, yet the number of women I know start to stack in my head.

But then I hear *it*, and it's not good.

I'd be able to hear it from a bazillion miles away. I know that sound so well, the pelos on my arm stand straight. Like a meteor about to hit earth, but it's worse.

It's Mami and her clunky, leather, polish-paste, smelly heels, the ones reserved for days when she has to go to the bank, or school meetings. The heels smack against the booger-, spit-, sweat-crusted school floors with each step.

Then it's quiet. Her feet reach the carpet in front of the secretary, Ms. Wiznitzer's desk. I look through the crack of the door. She's standing in line behind two moms with perfect English. I know 'cause I recognize them from all the PTA events the school does in the middle of the day, when Kai's mom, Connie's mom, and Mami are usually at work.

I bet she's rehearsing what she'll say and praying to San Sebastian, 'cause that's who my abuelita tells us to pray to when we need strength and courage. But today, she's probably even praying to San Antonio, the saint you pray to when you lose things like your llaves, or hairbrush, the one-third measuring cup, your favorite pencil, or the jar of Vicks Abuelita just opened but can't find anywhere. He gets called on a day like today, when you have to walk into school and say you're here because your hija malcriada (who never got in trouble before this year) stole the mic and broke guitars in the process. (I didn't mean to do the last part.) Or peor, defied authority. I don't know why Mami is so scared of defying authority. But it's like my disappeared tía said: *Sometimes it's all a woman has left to do.*

I move closer to the door to hear and get a better look through the crack, but I only see Ms. Wiznitzer's white fluff of hair. I brace myself for what comes next. Mami is a terremoto when she's mad . . . (worse, she's the grumble before the terremoto, when the earth is still thinking about what to do).

"How can I help you?" asks Ms. Wiznitzer, without even looking up.

"Good afternoon. I'm here to meet with the director," Mami says. Her voice is calm, like when the sugar melts in the flan pot, right before you forget to lower the temperature and it explodes on your stupid purple glasses. (It happened once.)

"You mean the principal?" Ms. Wiznitzer says.

Like, obvio! What a stupid question, I think.

"Yes, excuse me, the principal. My daughter is Manuela Se—"

"I'm sorry, can you please repeat that?" Ms. Wiznitzer says all loud. I swear she needs to get her ears checked, 'cause I heard Mami just fine.

"My daughter is Manuela Semilla. I have a meeting with the director . . . principal of the school," Mami says, real slow and careful his time.

I get so mad when people act like they can't understand Mami. They look at her and assume she doesn't speak English, so when she does, they act like someone next to them is eating nachos all loud in their ear with their mouth open and they can't hear.

"My daughter is Manuela, Mani. I have—"

"I heard you. Please take a seat." Ms. Wiznitzer says. "*Principal* Dupont will be with you shortly."

Except there's no seat, 'cause the PTA moms already took them, and they're probably discussing fundraisers, or how to stop us from reading library books about racial diversity, or about our periods, or standing up for our rights. Mami tried to join the PTA, but couldn't keep going to the meetings, 'cause a lot of the unofficial meetings (where the important decisions are made) were mostly during the day, and Mami started working as a medical interpreter three years ago, and, like, that's important.

I think about how loud and strong Mami is at home, but when she comes here, she has to be all quiet and careful, and choose her words exactly and say them like they're wrinkly shirts that need to be ironed out perfectly, or else no one will even notice her, even though she's actually really good at English. But when you have an accent, you're judged more harshly. Or people will assume she doesn't know anything. I wonder if that's what she feels like at work too, why she can't speak up for a lady whose bills will kill her.

And now she's embarrassed by me.

She stands by the corner of the door while the other two moms keep talking, occasionally looking at her up and down. Finally, Ms. Wiznitzer says, "You can wait in the office with your daughter if you would like." She motions her to the door.

Uy, no.

Mami opens it, and we're face-to-face.

I start to panic.

Mami pulls out the chair right in front of mine. I'm not going to apologize to her. I turn my head and think about A'niya instead. I don't want her to switch schools, and hate me forever. I want to run and find her.

Mami sits. I'm still looking away at pictures of Mr. Dupont's Cancun vacation. I hear her cross her arms, ('cause Guatemalan crossing your arms is like its own sound) and it's loud. I put my hands in my giant sweater pockets. I look up, down, away, until finally, there's nowhere left to look. I look at Mami.

Our eyes meet, but she's definitely smiling.

What?! I am so confused but before either of us can say anything, Dad comes in through the door, with the car keys still in his hands.

"Dad?" I say.

"Parking was difficult! Must be a lot of kids in trouble and their parents are coming to pick them up," he says, smiling, and takes a seat in one of the empty chairs.

I cringe at his dad joke, but smile for real.

Before we can say anything else, Mr. Dupont walks in. "Mrs. Semilla, thank you so much for coming in for this meeting."

Mami nods, looking at his sweater, and then at mine. She looks a little embarrassed. My elbows are on the table and then she glares at me in that no-seas-malcriada kind of way, so I put them down.

"Mr. Semilla, I wasn't expecting you! We really appreciate you coming as well," he says, looking Dad up and down.

"Why wouldn't I? I am her father!" He smiles at Mr. Dupont, putting his hand on my shoulder.

"Manu-ay-la, I told your mom at little bit about what happened, on the phone, but I wanted you to be a part of the conversation here too," says Mr. Dupont.

Mami gives me the *contesta* look, but I don't know what to say 'cause there's no question. Not really.

He continues. "But I tell you, Manu-ay-la, you're missing out on your education by being here. Disruptive behavior like what you demonstrated can really set kids back in school."

What am I missing? Double number lines, negative numbers. Yeah, I do suck at that. Math is not something I should miss, but I get this feeling deep down in my gut that standing up for kids in school is more important than $-10 - (-8)$.

"I appreciate how passionate you are about some issues," he says. "But you see, there is a good way and bad way to go about things. I invited your parents here so we could all help you see that there is a better way to go about it, and—"

"And what way would that have been?" asks Mami. "The good way to address the harassment happening against girls in your school?"

My neck cracks a little as I turn and stare at her. Did she really just say that?

Maybe I didn't hear right. She always follows the rules, tells me to never speak up to authority, that surviving sometimes means going unnoticed and just always doing your best so you can rise. Sometimes I've felt like she's wanted me to disappear, to drown in my two-sizes-too-large clothes. To always say *please* and *gracias*, let everyone pass, be good. For the longest time I thought her definition of good meant always doing what was asked.

Mr. Dupont clears his throat in that I'm-angry-and-don't-know-what-to-say kind of way. Then he looks at Dad in a half smile that's more uncomfortable than friendly, but Dad just stares back with a big smile. Mami grabs my hand underneath the table.

"You're lucky I won't expel you, this time," Mr. Dupont says. "Destruction of property is a serious offense."

I swallow hard at the word "expel."

Mami's hand tightens around mine.

"Destruction of property? The mic cord did that. And how is that worse than assault?" I say, my voice shaking a little and my body rising from the chair in a half stand.

Mami pulls me down with her hand. Then she starts talking again. "What has been done about the harassment in school?"

This time, Mr. Dupont is prepared. "I am so glad you asked, Mrs. Semilla. We plan to talk with the boys, and we will be reviewing video camera footage."

But Mami's words make me feel bold as well. "You didn't need to review the camera footage to give A'niya a map so she could find new ways to walk! You didn't review camera footage before switching her locker to the dungeon! And what about the videos still out there?" Smooth. All shakes are out of my voice. "And you didn't review the bus camera footage when some boys ripped my bra, or even confiscate their phones. You just believed them. You always believe them."

Now Mami's holding my hand over the table. I see her eyes shine a little like she's about to cry. She's looking closer at his sweater and then at mine. She gets the same look like when she mispronounces a word or something. Embarrassed. I open my mouth to say something again, but Dad gives me a give-him-a-chance-to-answer look.

"Yes, we gave her a nice, new locker in the basement, Manu-ai-la. Mr. Semilla, that's actually the remodeled part of the building. I'd be happy to give you a tour. I don't think I've seen you at the open houses when we give tours. I assure you all we do not have a harassment problem. This is an isolated incident, and we are working around the clock to implement the best consequences for everyone involved." Mr. Dupont turns to Mami again. "Is there anything going on at home? Any changes that might be causing this behavior?"

Dad shakes his head, and Mami looks offended by the question. "No, not at all," she says.

"Look," says Mr. Dupont, looking at me. "Unfortunately, your actions today caused some destruction of property, and demonstrated disrespect toward staff. We're suspending you for one week. Consider yourself lucky to get away with only a suspension. Pull something like this again, and you could be looking at expulsion, young lady."

"One whole week?" Dad asks, a confused look on his face.

"That's longer than what J.J. got for pulling the fire alarm in the middle of a math test last year, longer than Liam got for ripping the soap dispensers out of the bathrooms 'cause of some stupid social media challenge, that's—"

"Mr. Semilla, this is better than expulsion," Mr. Dupont says, ignoring me. "Manu-ay-la's actions caused a lot of disruption, and we must issue an out-of-school suspension." Then he turns to me. "Think of it as a time to reflect on your actions. Your task is to write a reflection—what happened and what you would do differently next time. You have a five-day suspension. You can come back one week from this Monday."

"But the Speak Up is that Monday! This is so un—"

"Mr. Dupont, we will be on a trip for an important family matter. We will be leaving that Monday. Can she come back a little sooner so she does not have to end the year in this way?" Mami asks.

But Mr. Dupont lifts up his hands and waves the student code of conduct in the air like he's trying to swat away a fly.

I want Mami to say this is unfair, but I guess it's better than expulsion. I didn't pull the fire alarm, I didn't get in a fight, I didn't start a food fight in the cafeteria, I didn't vandalize the bathroom, I definitely didn't slap anyone's butt or grope anyone's boob while they were minding their own business, and I definitely didn't film anything. But I want Mami to yell, call him a pendejo, tell him that this is an injusticia, 'cause that sounds so much more intense than just "not fair."

But nada. She just stares into Mr. Dupont's eyes—the only time I've seen this look on her is in the pictures Tía Beatriz sent.

Mr. Dupont gives me the paper with the reflection prompt. Mami asks if it goes on my school record. He says no, but that high school won't be that nice. She stands to shake his hand, says she understands, and thanks him. Dad does the same.

He walks us out, talks into his walkie-talkie, and heads down the hall.

With six minutes left before the bell rings, Dad, Mami, and I walk up the stairs to grab my backpack. I see things poking out of my locker. Ugh, it must have gotten vandalized. We get closer. Pointy notes are poking out of my locker, like paper airplanes that got stuck. So stupid. I grab and pull them out. I'm about to crumple them up, but then I open one and read through it

For the database.

It's half a page of a girl telling me about kids that are photoshopping her face on gross videos to send around school and post it online. Some new gross app. I give it to Mami. I open the next one. It's from an eighth grader. The town hall was only for seventh grade. She writes that she's being harassed by her ex-boyfriend and his friends on her walk to school. When she told security, they told her it's not harassment if the guy was her boyfriend, and that they couldn't do anything anyways 'cause it's off school property.

I fold it closed before I finish, and then I open the next one. I look through all of them. The notes all talk about incidents where nothing ever happened. Things girls *told* the school about.

I quickly gather them together and stuff them in my pocket. We rush out before the hallway swarm. On the walk to the car, the notes burn in my pocket. If I do nothing about them, I'm not a doer, and pues, I kind of started something, maybe. But if I do something, it's expulsion. And if I get expelled, then Mami would probably disown me. I wouldn't be able to do the Speak Up competition.

"Mami, remember the project I told you about?" I ask.

"Manuela," she says. "We leave in ten days. The tickets are bought. Do you know how expensive and complicated it is to change?"

Dad looks at her, but she doesn't return the look.

"We have something important the day we arrive in Guatemala. Just do your part from here and let Kai and Connie present on that day, and let them go if you win, qué sé yo."

But I started something, and I can't run away from it.

TWENTY-FIVE

WE'RE ALL QUIET on the way home. Not even El Sol 91.1 is on.

I want to ask Mami why she stood up for me like that, but I also don't want her to take it back. Then she reaches behind her seat to grab my hand.

"Manuela, what you did was important."

Important. The word bounces around the car and warms me. My heart is smiling and exploding all at the same time. I'm about to say thank you—

"But you didn't have to make it such a show, Manuela. Ms. Martinez told me everything. TODO. How you ran around the band too. . . ."

Ms. Martinez? She called Mami after the town hall? I realize that's why Mami didn't come in raging. I look down, a little embarrassed. Then I look up at her.

She's laughing! Like, for real, she's laughing. Not the polite laugh she does at school or at the bank when someone tells a bad joke, but a laugh like when someone tells her a joke in Spanish. She gives my hand a squeeze.

I want to ask her a bunch of questions. At least a million and a half things. I could start with the letters, the wall that's existed between us for weeks and weeks now (my whole life, really). Or I could ask her if she was REALLY, ACTUALLY, an ACTUAL feminist. I want to tell her how my Spanish has gotten better with each letter, and that I want her to tell me about Guatemala. I want to one day hear the birds outside my window like they're always talking about. The ones she's always writing and singing songs about. I want to tell her how I want to win Speak Up so bad even though after today I know in my heart that our free pads idea definitely isn't enough.

I could tell her I'm not so against Guatemala as I was before, but I want her hand to stay on mine, 'cause no sé, her touch feels like the first warm day of the year. Maybe even better than what Tía Beatriz felt, all wrapped and linked in other women's arms, and in the strength of their collective. I take it all in. I let her have the last word. That what I did is important. I want to stay in this moment for as long as we can, because it feels good. We both smile. There's nothing like Mami's smile and knowing that she's proud of me even though she doesn't say it.

At home, I rush to my room, open my school computer and a Google Excel sheet. I check the Las Nerdas Google doc to see if they've written to me.

CHECK YOUR EMAIL is all I see.

There're a lot of new messages that I quickly scan to see if any are from A'niya.

Nada.

I open one from Kai, sent two minutes ago. The subject reads: *Nerda Mission.*

I read the email while some pictures load.

Hey, C and K here. There's a sub and he fell asleep with the
newspaper still in his hands. EVERYONE is talking about your
database. What do we do? BTW, Genesis is in French class
right now, but she's obviously IN.

Then I scroll down and see they attached pictures of new sticky
notes from my locker.

#Nomorebasementlockers

A boy pulled my shirt down right
outside of the PE locker rooms. When
I reported it, I got told that spaghetti
straps are against the dress code, and
to change the way I dress and let's
see if it happens again.

I stare at the sticky note picture for a long time. How many more
stories like these are there?

In my Google Excel, I type and delete, type and delete about
five times before finally settling on a title. Then I give Las Nerdas
editing access y todo. I want to write to my disappeared tía and
thank her for the database idea, but there's no time, 'cause Kai

and Connie's icons pop up at the top of the document. Connie's reformatting the columns and making it all pretty 'cause that's Connie.

In our doc, I tell them about all of the letters in my locker right before I went home—the ones they didn't see.

ugh

gross

We have to change our Speak Up project, I type.

Crickets. Well, not even crickets, 'cause crickets at least sing. Connie just sends an exclamation point, and then her icon disappears. Is that a good thing or a bad thing?

Then Kai writes *g2g. Sub woke up*, and she's off. Then logs back on and writes *Nerdas4ever* and logs back off, for real this time. Two minutes pass.

I stay on the doc and switch back to the Excel file. We have six incidents written and it's only been a few hours.

This is our Speak Up project. It has to be. It's not maxi pads and free tampons and more bathroom passes, though that's real important too.

I take out my poster paper. What did Tía Beatriz write on her signs? What did the sign say that Mami was holding in that old picture? What does Tía always say at the end?

CLING! I hear Mami and Dad grabbing sartenes and ollas downstairs in the kitchen. She'll be calling me soon to help, so I go up to the attic while I still have time. The letter stack is getting thin, and I could really use some revolution strategy ideas right now.

I grab the box of letters.

Isabela,

Tomorrow Maribel and I leave for Honduras. Eight other women from here are taking the bus. We're meeting with a group of women who got word about what we are doing. They've been arming a mass protest against the government for trying to cut communities off from their water source, their economy, and livelihood. The government has been targeting many of the women activists. It's crazy how connected it all is. Environmental rights are women's rights. Their struggles are our struggles too. You told me that once, remember?

They're planning something big. We'll march on the highway, write a petition. We'll start there. Between Maribel and me, the whole world will know once we publish what we've been working on. We'll take it to the government, and every news source. They'll have to see us. Our bus leaves at 8 p.m. tomorrow and we'll drive through the night. Thank you, Isabela. If you hadn't done what you did, I wouldn't be here. We can't stay silent.

> *Primero una voz, y luego seremos millones*
> *Beatriz*

The words *They'll have to see us* ring in my soul.

"¡Manuela! ¿Me ayudas?" shouts Mami from downstairs.

I quickly look through the letters, but that's the last one.

What happened to the rest? I thought there were more, but there are just maps, notes of addresses, phone numbers, and names that make no sense to me. And they're in Mami's handwriting. None of it makes sense.

I take all the letters in my hand—the whole stack of years' worth of writing, my only glimpse into Mami's and her sister's past lives. For too long it's been the wall between us, even before I knew they existed. I stuff them in my bag. They're not meant to be up in the attic closed up in a tin box. I hurry down the ladder, missing a rung and sliding down—hard.

"¡Manuela!" Mami shouts again.

I tie a dirty sock over the cut on my leg, return the ladder, and try not to hobble downstairs and into the kitchen.

"Why are you walking funny?" says Mami, shouting over the blender and Dad's whistling.

"It's how I walk," I say. Which is a total lie, but I'm desperate.

Mami asks me for help. She hands me a wooden spoon and motions to the onion jumping and popping in the sartén. She adds garlic and cinnamon, and the smells dance in my nose like the merengue she plays when she's happy and it's just them in the kitchen.

I wait for them to say something . . . to ask me anything . . . but they don't. I let my heart dance to their music, their feet shuffling quickly around each other, and their hands in and out of kitchen cabinets. But my feet stay firmly rooted to the kitchen floor, because something knocks on my brain over and over again and keeps me from moving. I can't let it go. All I keep thinking about are the phone numbers and addresses in Mami's handwriting. Why hasn't she talked to me about the letters? C.C. totally called her a mentirosa and told her about the letters, but nothing.

What is it she can't tell me?

TWENTY-SIX

Seven more days wondering
if an apology to A'niya
is better late than never

Groped, Harassed, and Other *Unfair Nasty Stuff.*

Kai, Connie, Genesis, and I finally settle on the name for the database after we debated all weekend in the Google Excel chat. It feels good (like when you shake all the Jarritos soda bottles at your mean third-cousin's quinceañera party and the fizz explodes on everyone's lacy shiny clothes. It happened once).

I jolt up to Mami opening my curtains.

"No estás de vacaciones," she says.

I groan and look at my alarm clock: 7:45 a.m. There's a ding from my school computer. It's Genesis, sending an email from her phone at 7:45am. Pictures of two new notes taped to my locker this Monday morning, my official first day of suspension. Now that Genesis got her period and she's a woman and all, her parents got her a phone, "para emergencias." I think it's all kinds of unfair, but I'm happy for her, too. I mean, it's a cool phone. Plus, her home screen is a selfie of all the Nerdas.

I click on the image she sent and also open the database. *Anonymous 8th grader* writes that last year two boys from her math class pushed her into the boys' bathroom in between classes and pushed her head down toward *you know where*. Then they said something real gross, laughed, and ran out. She told security, and the next day administration switched *her* math class. But they never talked to the boys, and they got to keep their same schedule.

They should switch THEIR math class! I write to Genesis. *That is so messed up!*

Girl, I know, she responds, almost immediately and attaches another picture.

I click on the next image.

Ur project sucks. UR the sexist one.

Genesis obviously didn't read through all of them before sending. This one is straight up hate mail.

Ugh. Maybe it's the running around and being chased by the principal, or falling off the ladder, or maybe it's falling asleep at my desk last night, but my whole body aches. I cannot get sick. My birthday is next week. The Speak Up competition is next week. Even after we came up with the name for the database, Las Nerdas never responded to me when I said we had to change our project. I lie back down and picture how it's all going to go, but I jump 'cause just then the door flies open and it's Mami, again.

"Mami, I need privacy sometimes," I say.

"Privacy's for gringos. *Levantate*. It's not a day off for you. Finish homework, write your reflection, qué sé yo, or you can come help me downstairs. I took the day off," she says, but she's smiling so I know she's not mad. Hasn't been all weekend. I grab the computer and hesitate, but then grab my bag too. My tía's letters dance at the bottom as I follow her downstairs and to the kitchen.

At the table, my back stops hurting and the hairs on my arms are warmed by the notes of cinnamon, ginger, and thyme in the tea Mami is making for Abuelita (her own homemade cough recipe, and cure for nervousness associated with travel, according to Abuelita). But then I feel Mami's eyes on me, and my heart squeezes a little. I used to think that getting struck by lightning on your quinceañera would probably hurt less (both physically and emotionally) than her piercing eyes. But now I think about how Mami stood up for me, so today I look back at her. Our eyes meet.

"Manuela, how did all of this escalate?" she says, with a long sigh, as if last Friday's town hall has been rolling around in her head all weekend.

Sweat builds and swirls on my forehead, but I've come too far to back out now. I'm a doer.

Taking a deep breath, I say café con pan café con pan café con pan three times in my head like Abuelita told me to do when I need to walk like I'm all grown and brave. I'm pretty sure she stole that from those Mexican songs she's always listening to where they make music with their shoes.

It helps 'cause I say, "I have questions too, Mami." There's no shake in my voice.

Uy, here it comes, I think.

She sits right across from me. "I'm listening."

I am not expecting that, so I sit there like a tonta. I don't know what to say. Then I reach in my bag and the edges of the letters poke the tips of my fingers. I slowly take them out of my bag and place the stack on the table. She looks down at the letters.

I wait for a meteor to hit us, for the earth below and walls around us to shake. I picture a giant sinkhole, and everyone falls through except for this table, and it'll just be me and Mami staring at each other. I wait for it. I wait for her to get angry (in Spanish). I hold the letters tight against my chest and—

Then I think she might cry.

But she smiles. Her eyes sparkle a little, kind of like in the pictures in these letters, in her life before me. And right at this moment, she looks like that woman in them, the one who C.C. called "feminist." The one who chased stories and protested, and wore green revolutionary pants.

"You read all of them?" she says.

I nod. At first, I still can't find the right palabras. But then words flow out nonstop. I tell her that Tía Beatriz called her a feminist, and I didn't know what she meant, and that I want to know, where are the other letters and what are all of these names and addresses in her handwriting, and what is this thing that Mami did that she keeps referencing but won't actually say, and *why are there no more letters*—

"Manuela, are you going to let me tell you?"

"Sorry." My fingers play with the edges of the letters and then tap them against the table. "Mami, are you a feminist?"

She smiles at my question, but swallows and looks out the window, as if the word itself makes her sad.

"You told me once that feminism is peligroso and that bad things happen to feminists and women who call attention to themselves," I say. "Should I stop?"

But no matter her answer, I know I won't. I can't. There are like ten emails in my inbox with stories of girls at my school who have had real gross and degrading and sometimes violent things happen to them and nothing was done. There are even some notes from boys, and it's not hate mail. I started something, and I can't stop, even if she tells me I should. No puedo.

"I know these weren't meant for me, and . . . and have nothing to do with me, but—"

Mami just stares at them and doesn't say anything at first. Then she puts her hand up. "It has everything to do with you, Manuela. I knew they would end up in your hands somehow. Un día."

The idea that these letters aren't dirty secrets, but stories meant for me all along . . .

"Everything to do with me? How?"

"My sister and I were journalism students. We had just graduated and we wanted to write about the femicides going on, even though no one was calling them that. Guatemala signed a peace deal many years back and the civil war had officially ended, but the violence did not. Especially the violence against women. Women were disappearing, being killed, and there was no justice anywhere."

My eyes haven't blinked since she started talking and they start to hurt.

Then Mami tells me about making powerful people mad, and how their friend disappeared while on a trip delivering food and medical supplies to a different town. Her body was found in the jungle. The official report was that she died of an infection. She tells me about disrupting police meetings and interviewing women at roadblocks. She said that even their university cautioned them and said that journalists were supposed to be objective bystanders.

"But anyone who saw what we were seeing knew that wasn't possible," she says.

I sit at the edge of the kitchen chair, feeling the letters come to life at my fingertips.

"Our work got the attention of a collective of journalists working in the northern region of the country and we were offered an opportunity to join them. We accepted. We had bus tickets and our bags packed. But right before we left, we got threats from men in suits. *Hombres del gobierno.* Your dad was working with an NGO, and we had met a few months before. Even *he* started getting death threats. The men who threatened us knew everything about us.

"Your abuelita and my father, who you never met, owned a bookstore and café that on its own became a meeting place for many activists. They broke everything in it and beat her up and told her all the horrible things they would do to us. We had seen it happen to our friends and our colleagues, but nothing could prepare us for it. Abuelita urged us to go, thinking we could escape the violence against journalists and their families happening in the capital."

Tears fill my eyes, and they feel hot against my face. My heart aches at the thought of men in suits threatening Abuelita's life, and of someone sending death threats to Mami and Dad. A familiar pain pulses in my body, the one I felt watching A'niya get assaulted in the hallway, the one I felt when I first learned about Lani, and watching kids crowd around a phone to watch a viral video of a girl being kicked on the ground on her walk home and being called horrible things. It's a feeling I can't name. Mami was scared, and just thinking about that makes my head fill with rage. If I ever go to Guatemala, I am going to go look for those men, and—

"But then I thought of you."

I choke on my breath. "Me?"

"Only your father knew this at the time, but I was pregnant with you," she says. "And somehow the men who threatened us found out. They worked like spies, after all. They threatened to kill me . . . and I thought of you."

And then I think my heart stops completely, at least for a second. "You were pregnant, with me, in Guatemala?"

She nods but doesn't look at me.

"That's when we told the family. Your father was the most nervous. He found an opportunity to leave for the United States, with everyone. But my heart was torn. The week before we were supposed to leave for the United States, Beatriz announced that she was not coming with us. She would be taking the job to join a group of journalists. And for a moment I felt like a quitter. I thought of ways I could still go with her. I tried to imagine so many ways to keep us safe, but I knew it wasn't possible. She urged me to leave with your dad and Abuelita and Gladys to the United States, and I begged her to come with us, but she refused. I never went to see her off the day she left."

My hand is so close to Mami's that I can feel the warmth. I think of all the times her touch on my hand has helped calm me.

"I should have tried harder. If I had, I could have convinced her," she says, and her voice shakes. "I didn't want to stop her from doing important work. But because of that, I also didn't save her. For years, I have thought I should have been on that bus, or I should have convinced her to come with us to this country. But I ran, and I let her go."

Then she picks up the last letter like her fingers memorized its creases.

"We wrote for years, and when I got the last letter, it felt different. I tried to call all of my journalist contacts but no one knew anything at first. Then, weeks later, it was all over the news. A bus on its way to Honduras was hijacked. All the women were taken off, and—"

Mami starts to cry.

I am crying too, for what I know fills the space of her last words. This time, I grab her hand. Her voice steadies.

"Only a few of them survived. Maribel was one of them. They never said the names of the other women. None could be identified afterward."

Then she stops talking. And for the first time, she didn't tell me *you'll understand when you're older.* She told me her story like they were words for me, like it was my story too.

Mami wipes her eyes. "That was ten years ago. I wrote and called every number for years. People we knew told us it was still too dangerous. You were little and I didn't want to risk it. Then, a few months ago, Doña Consuelo's daughter called us."

I remember Doña Consuelo from the letters—the woman who started the database of missing women, from the church office. She tells me Doña Consuelo's daughter packed Tía Beatriz's stuff in boxes and never went through them. One day, she did, for her own daughter, and she had many of Beatriz's things, including Mami's letters, and pictures. Tía Beatriz and her photographer friend, Maribel, were writing a book about femicides in the decades post-civil war. I remember Abuelita's stories about the civil war.

"Manuela, I see so much of her in you and that's why it means so much for me to take you to Guatemala. I know you want to do this project and win, and spending the summer with your friends learning important things is an amazing opportunity, but it means everything to take you. I left so abruptly. I ran, and it's time to go back."

My heart crumbles; I can't believe I ever thought that going to Guatemala was stupid. The pull that I've been feeling toward it for a while now tugs at my gut. I start to daydream about the bird songs they're always talking about.

"The reason we have to go on your birthday is that Guatemala City is opening a museum of resistance and memory in the name of journalists who have been killed, and they are holding a special opening event remembering the activists and journalists on that bus who died. Doña Consuelo will be there, and many of the women who knew Beatriz. The event is our only chance to meet them. To be in the same room as those who loved her. Like Maribel. She was one of the few who survived. ¿Entiendes?"

Her words sit heavy on me. Maribel wouldn't be just a name in letters, but a person right in front of me. I feel like I know her already. I wonder how I would feel if I had to leave my house, my school, Las Nerdas, all of a sudden. And how if I had the opportunity to go back, I would. I'd do everything to go back.

My heart scatters in a million places. "Mami, the Speak Up competition just feels really important," I say. But it sounds like a tontería after everything she just told me. I realize how important this is to her, to return to the place she had to leave so abruptly. To be surrounded by people who can fill gaps in her story in a way no one here can, in a way that even imagination can't.

"Sí, es muy importante," she says, and her eyes are all orgullo about it. She sighs. "Manuela, es tu decisión."

And then it hits me, right in the frente. Technically I wasn't alive, so obvio no one can go blaming me or anything, but I was part of

Mami's decision to leave, good or not. I changed everything for her, just like my decision now will change things for her.

I realize now that everything I am is because of everything they were. Their story is my story, and for the first time, I feel connected to Guatemala. But also to here. Definitely to here.

"You have one week to decide. Just remember, para todo hay consecuencia," she says.

I carry her words for a long time, for like a gazillion eye blinks. I know what she wants me to say, expects me to say.

I know what I have to do.

TWENTY-SEVEN

Six more days worrying
over if I'll make the right decision

It's less than one week till my birthday.

Mami lets Kai and Connie come over after school, even though it's Tuesday and I've barely completed two days of suspension. Connie brings the HI-CHEW candies. Kai brings the Takis and the sticky notes and folded papers. Dad and C.C. sit around us, on standby for any help we need.

"Where's Genesis?" I ask Kai and Connie as they get comfortable at the kitchen table.

They look at each other.

"Her mom didn't let her come . . . you know, school night and all," Kai says.

I get it. Mami's the same, except she's like a new person ever since our conversation. She keeps our cups full of Rosa de Jamaica, and brings out plates of tostadas with smooth frijoles, slices of pickled radishes, red onions and queso fresco crumbled on top.

Connie lays the sticky notes down on the table, and Kai picks up the first one.

I ride bus #1506. I was walking to my seat and some boys put their phones out and took a picture under my skirt. They sent it to each other. They said if I told anyone they would post it on Instagram.

We read the next ones, and the next and the next. Lots of the names we don't recognize, but some we do. Others don't write their names at all. Horrible stories told in tiny sticky notes about girls being harassed on social media; boys sending horrible pictures with girls' faces photoshopped on it; another girl gets hands down her shirt on the school bus. Gross. She never told the bus driver, 'cause they said they would beat her little brother up if she did. And anyways, the bus driver already seems so stressed out with kids throwing stuff at him, that she feels bad to say anything. She doesn't want to be one more thing. And all of it with fingers on phones, ready to hit record.

There're notes after notes of girls feeling bad and small, and not *mujer* at all. There're notes from all grades, even though the town hall was just for seventh grade.

"This one's from Hector," says Kai.

"Hector!?" I grab the green sticky note out of her hand. Hector, who I've known since I was little. It's definitely Hector's handwriting—the words slide off the edge of the paper like ice cream sliding down a cone. And then his name is written all big on the back, maybe 'cause he thought he had to write his name. I blink to make sure I'm seeing it right.

He writes about the gross stuff some boys did to him in the locker room before PE. He tried to get excused from changing into gym clothes so he wouldn't have to go to the lockers. The vice principal told him it's just normal locker room talk and horseplay. He wanted to tell the PE teacher, 'cause he's real nice, but he was too embarrassed. And then I remember the beginning of the year when he started hating PE even though he could run for way longer than anyone else in our grade. My heart aches with guilt and I wish I would have asked him why.

"Look, another guy," says Connie.

We read and our fingers crinkle the colorful pieces of paper with rage and disgust. There are girls who tell of older sisters being told it's not assault if it's a boyfriend, girls being suspended for filing "false reports"'cause there wasn't enough proof, girls being told to cover up next time, and boys feeling too embarrassed to speak out, 'cause, you know, supposedly none of that happens to boys. But it does. It happens to boys at our school, and I didn't realize it till now. Each time, nothing was done. One girl even took it to the school board, but they never answered her. It's all kinds of messed up.

We type the stories up on my school computer. When our hands get tired, we switch off and then someone else starts writing. When we're done sifting through the sticky notes, I open my email.

"Whoa," says Connie. Kai looks over my shoulder. There're about fifteen new unread emails, aside from the seven or so I got the day before.

There's one from A'niya's friend, an eighth grader.

When I got off the bus, some high school boys who live in
my neighborhood started following me on the field in front
of my apartment and they were trying to do stuff. Anyways, I
reported it the next day, but security and the principal told me
that they have a really good relationship with the high school
and that involving them was a big deal and that I should think
about making such a big accusation.
Idk why I wrote this. It just feels good to not keep it to myself
anymore.

I keep scrolling through unread emails, but none are from A'niya.
We get to the last one.

J.J. was having a party because his parents weren't home.
My dad was working late, so I went. They were drinking
something. I had a little bit. J.J. and some other guys tried to
put their hands down my pants. I tried to move away but I was
really dizzy. J.J. did put his hands down my pants and another
kid took a picture and they were circulating that picture among
all the guys. I only know cuz some girl showed me the next day
in the cafeteria. I didn't tell anyone . . . idk, I was drunk and I
guess I know they'll say it was my fault. But I know I didn't want
that to happen. This is weird. Cya.

My head spins and the keyboard is hot against my fingertips. All
of this happening right under our noses all year. Students were getting harassed and groped and assaulted and humiliated and accused
of lying, all year.

I show some of them to Mami as she comes and refills our Rosa de Jamaica.

"Qué terrible," she just keeps saying.

I think of my tía and what she did when interviewing women and listening to their stories for her own articles, how it just wasn't enough and she put down her notebook and joined them in a human chain of women.

"THIS is our project. THIS is Speak Up," I say.

Kai and Connie look up.

"It's not free period products, even though that's real important. We should still fight for that. Let's propose a student-led sexual harassment database. We'll also propose community organization to help us with stuff like education, and resources, and . . . and . . . if adults aren't going to do anything about it, we will. People need to know. Maybe it can help someone feel . . . not so alone. Oh, and we need to do a protest too!"

Connie picks some HI-CHEW out of her teeth. "I don't know about a protest, Mani," she says. "You just got suspended for stealing the mic and all that."

"Yeah," says Kai. "So a protest would definitely be expulsion."

Uy, that sounds like a mala palabra.

We bite into our tostadas, and wash it down with Rosa de Jamaica, the ice clinking against our teeth. We look at all the sticky notes in front of us—the light of the screen shining onto our faces as it starts to get dark outside. This is what we started. How do you go back from this? No sé. You don't, right?

And just like that, Kai says what I'm thinking.

"You started something, and you can't unstart it," she says.

"*We* started something. We're a collective."

Their smiles warm the room, and that's when I decide to tell them. All of it.

With Tía Beatriz's letters now sprawled out on the table, I paraphrase her story the best I can. Months of reading letters reduced to five minutes. I show them newspaper clippings and the pictures taped to the back of the Nerda notebook. They ask my parents about Guatemala and the civil war, and I'm made full by the stories of my parents.

"Mrs. Semilla, please tell me you still have those shoes!" Connie says to my mom.

I laugh, 'cause it's a detail only Connie would focus on.

"OK, fine, I'm inspired. A protest definitely needs to be part of our presentation," Kai says.

"Yeah, that's exactly what I'm thinking," says Connie.

"Look," I say. "I know we'd be risking a lot if we do some big protest. Expulsion for me."

They nod. Connie chews on her nail.

"And getting expelled could mean we don't win, and don't go to New York, and I know New York has meant everything, but sometimes you have to make a choice despite the consequences, right?" I say.

"Mani, you go down, we all go down," says Kai.

I look at Connie, and she's all smiles and nods. She puts her pinkie out for our Nerda handshake. We all go in.

"Plus, we're like revolutionaries now. Revolutionaries don't go to fancy Speak Up revolution summer camps, you know?" says Kai.

We laugh, flap our hands like quetzal wings, and click our thumbnails against our teeth.

"But we CANNOT tell Ms. Martinez or the judges the new plan or that we're switching our project. It'll be a surprise. And the database is something we'll start now, but obviously we'll be working on it all summer. We'll use the protest to announce it." says Kai.

"I have an idea," I say. "Each of these sticky notes is a story. We need to tell these stories. What if we write their stories on these posters and cardboard pieces? Each one of them."

"Yeah, and we can get to school really early and put them all over Mr. Dupont's door!" says Connie.

Abuelita, who's been sitting by the window next to her altares, daydreaming and humming to herself this whole time, taps on the wall and says, "Buena idea, chulitas."

We all laugh a little. I smile, 'cause Connie's always taking things too far, and I hope she never changes.

"What about this," says Kai. "We choose one line from each story, and we write that line on our signs. We can paraphrase too, but we have to keep the essence of each story. I think that would be really impactful."

I write down Kai's ideas on a piece of paper, 'cause she uses sophisticated words like *essence* and *impactful* and I think she's just as smart as her sister and C.C. I smile so hard at my friends my cheeks hurt.

We look at each other. This is bigger than New York.

WE LET OURSELVES DAYDREAM about winning out loud, free like quetzales while we work. Maybe the judges will like it so much that we win, and we can't get expelled. Maybe we'll inspire students across the state to do a similar database at their schools.

Mami brings back old printer paper boxes from work. C.C. and Dad empty old moving boxes and cut them into perfect squares. We use poster paper too. There's a knock on the door and Mami goes to answer it.

"Hola Señora, soy Genesis."

I hear Mami's surprised and happy voice asking Genesis questions as she leads her into the kitchen.

"Hey," Genesis says.

I get up and we hug.

"¿Genesis, vos querés juguito?" Mami asks her.

"OK, gracias, Señora," Genesis says, in perfect Spanish and manners, as she takes a seat and grabs markers and poster paper like she already knows what to do. "My mom has an event at their church tonight. She's picking me up in like an hour, so I just wanted to help a little."

"Yeah!" I say. We catch her up on the plan.

"What's wrong?" I say.

"Look, Mani. I believe in everything you're doing. It's really, really important. And I want to be a part of it," she says. "It's just that . . . I kind of want to do my own thing for the actual project and presentation," she says.

For a second I think my heart stops. "But, you read the sticky notes. You know what's happening. I thought—"

"I'm going to do the compost thing. I've already been talking to the county environmental office. I'm going to try and put a compost bin in every cafeteria in the county! I'm just really interested in composting and recycling and climate change and zero waste, and all that stuff. I always have been. And, Ms. Martinez said it was OK to switch as long as we had some sort of action plan to present to the judges next week. And I do . . ."

"I just . . . I just thought this is really important, and maybe you should read the emails I got. I mean, it's bad. It's—" I trip on my words.

But Genesis doesn't stop or trip on her words. "This doesn't mean I don't want to riot against harassment or anything like that. I am 100 percent into this and will help. It's just that I really think composting is like my niche, you know? And plus, what you're doing is way, way bigger than just a project. I'm in. It's just for Monday, I'll have my own separate presentation."

Ever since Genesis got her period and got all *mujer* and *I have a cell phone* on us, she uses fancy words like *niche*, that I don't really understand. But I try to listen.

"And I've never been out of this state! Well, Honduras . . . but I was little when we moved. All I know is Honduras, kind of, and this place," she says. "I want to win. My whole life I've felt guilty about things and I refuse to feel that anymore. I hope you understand."

I'm not mad. Instead, I feel energy under my feet, and my chest is full. I try to verbalize all the thoughts racing through my head.

"Genesis, yours is bigger than New York too. I want to help with yours as well. We're a collective, remember?"

Maybe part of being a woman is being able to choose things for yourself, and Genesis is choosing, even if it's different from what I'm choosing.

"Nerdas forever?" she says.

I give her the biggest hug. Kai and Connie join. It feels good to have all of the Nerdas in the same safe place, crowded around cardboard cutouts with fragments of different stories—stories that will soon form an even bigger collective.

"OK, let's do this!' Genesis says, and we get back to work. Our fingers are sticky with HI-CHEW and saliva and stained with marker ink and our brains are as full as our hearts—the place our voices come from, ready to burst and fly.

TWENTY-EIGHT

*Five more chances
to stand up for myself*

I USED TO THINK that telling Mami I didn't want to go to church required courage from a deep place. I'd run over a million ways to say it: *I think I'll stay home today and read a book and drink hot chocolate and eat the burnt crispy edges off of plátanos instead of going to church.* I used to think that was THE big choice I had in my life. But now, that decision feels as tiny as choosing between red and blue Takis. Obvio. I didn't think that a way bigger decision—like meteor-size bigger—would be right in front of me, a few days before I turned thirteen.

By Wednesday, the kitchen table still looks like a protest sign factory, and Mami is OK with it.

"Mami," I say, taking her hand in the kitchen.

I swallow. The decision ate at my heart.

"I'm staying. I have to. My school is my community. I'm from here and Guatemala, but I am what I am because of here. Staying to do the Speak Up presentation, whether I win or not, is important to me right now. 'Cause it's not just about winning, Mami. It's about what it means to win. To the girls in my school. Even if it means being expelled." That word feels escandaloso. It's just not something you do. Para nada. "Because of what it means to me, Mami," I say. "To do something."

I look away. In the quiet between us, I hear a voice in my head. Soft at first but then . . . it's música. Chavela Vargas's "Rayando el Sol" and Rebeca Lane's "Este Cuerpo Es Mío" become my theme songs like in movies 'cause that's exactly how I feel: like my words are scratching the sun and I'm about to get burnt and blasted out into the hottest parts of the atmosphere all while fighting for respect for our bodies. But it feels right.

Mami still hasn't said anything. She's quiet for what feels like almost forever. She gently cups my chin in her hand.

"Fine," she says and smiles. "You definitely came from me."

I smile so hard I think my glasses are going to crack off my face. (I kind of hope they do so I can get new ones.)

She hugs me. "C.C. can stay with you. Tía Gladys will be here too, and she can help out. We'll figure it out." Then she holds my chin up so I have to look directly into her eyes. "And if they try and expel you for bringing attention to a very important issue, pues we fight it because that's in our blood."

I see in Mami's eyes the girl in the picture with the sign and bullhorn and fuego—a woman who knew and accepted all consequences.

Kai and Connie come over after school every day and we make more and more signs.

Some people in the environmental planning office agreed to meet with Genesis, and she emailed us selfies of her in front of the building, looking real important and 100 percent mujer. I think she knew for a long time that she would switch, she was just searching for the courage to voice it out loud, and I'm glad she found it.

Even Mami, Dad, Abuelita, Tía, and C.C. help write on the signs now.

"I can't believe you can get suspended for accidentally breaking the school guitars, but not for harassing or assaulting someone," I say to Dad.

"Let it be fuel for your project, Manuela," he says, and I know he's right. When I think about my tía and the community she found in Guatemala, I smile as I look at mine.

I make signs with Rebeca Lane and Audry Funk song titles.

Nos Queremos Vivas #micuerpo.

Kai draws boobs, hands holding them, and writes *Not an invitation, no matter the size.*

My locker has become a wall of confessions and complaints, of pain and hope. It's covered with sticky notes and index cards, and Las Nerdas bring me a new pile of notes every day. Mr. Dupont and Mr. Robertson put up a Caution: Slippery When Wet sign in front of it just so no one would add to it. But a plastic wet floor sign can't stop the revolution. Notes keep coming. Kai, Connie, Genesis, and I read through all of them. Horrible things we didn't even know about.

And the emails keep coming, but none from A'niya.

Finally, we find three boxes. We decorate and name each one the TELL YOUR STORY box in black Sharpie. We gather about thirty cardboard cutouts and sheets of scrap paper, and save another thirty for Friday. I type up instructions, telling people to tell their stories of harassment and lack of accountability and to bring it to the Speak Up and wait for the signal. Kai, Connie, and Genesis put the TELL YOUR STORY boxes in girls' bathrooms at school.

By Friday afternoon, the TELL YOUR STORY box is empty. Every piece of paper or scrap of carboard was taken to write a story.

On Sunday night, I ask Las Nerdas to come over so we can tighten up our plan. The Speak Up presentation with the fancy judges is tomorrow. Tomorrow is also my first day back from suspension, mi cumpleaños, and when my parents and Abuelita leave for Guatemala—all at the same time. Genesis comes over too, even though she's busy getting her own project ready.

We do our Nerdas handshake, and Genesis does it so perfectly, like she's been a Nerda all year. In a way, I guess she has. We just didn't know it.

The four of us look at the signs we've made spread all out across the floor, signs that changed the more we read the notes and emails. Peeling the glue off of my hands, I try not to think too hard about how Mami, Abuelita, and Dad are all leaving tomorrow.

In my room, I stuff extra instructions into my bag to tape on all the bathroom stall doors. Bulging out of the inside pocket, I find the folded-up pieces of paper with Mami's song lyrics and take them out. I read them again even though I read all of them already. In almost each one, the same line:

"'Y un día cantarán.'"
"'Y un día cantarás.'"

One day they will sing. I know from the legends Abuelita is always telling me about that I have to fill in the gaps. One day they will sing again. One day *you* will sing again. I think beyond my school, beyond the kids who think harassment is just a normal part of the school experience. That their bodies being invaded and violated is just part of what it means to be a student in this country. Except it's not. At least it shouldn't be. I think beyond them, of my tía and all the disappeared women she was trying to find out about, write about, whose stories she tried to piece together. I think of her and Maribel who trekked days through jungles just so the world would know something about a woman who had gone missing. They believed that each woman and her story mattered, how each one of them mattered. I know the boys at my school aren't the men who threatened Tía Beatriz and Maribel, or the police boyfriend . . . but how do these men begin? They begin somewhere. And it's the same culture and thinking that supports it, right? I can't help but wonder. I bring the posters upstairs and add Mami's lyrics to them.

#undíacantaremos
#cantaremos

For the quetzal, it's not merely about making noise, but about singing. There's a difference. I think of A'niya, how what happened embarrassed her. It shut her down so much to where she stopped showing up to school. She stopped singing. And I hate thinking this, but I shared her story without her consent, and in a way, I had a part in stopping her from singing. I take out my paper and pen and start writing.

Dear A'niya,
    You asked me not to tell anyone about what happened, and I
violated your trust. I am truly sorry. It was not my place to share

your story. I wanted to stand up for someone but putting your
story out there like that was not the way to do it. I've been
thinking a lot about what it means to stand up, to use your voice
for good. And it's not just yelling stuff out loud. I hope you can
forgive me one day, but I understand if you need more time.

I fold the paper up and put it in my glasses case where I won't lose it. I look at the posters and flyers sprawled out on my bed. Mami's lyrics jumping off the page at me. Quotes from kids' stories, and Rebeca Lane lyrics in my head. I hope that somewhere in a room like mine, or at a kitchen table, at least one person is writing their story on a cardboard flap, a story they had buried deep down, excited for tomorrow.

I grab a black Sharpie. I have work to do.

TWENTY-NINE

Mi cumpleaños

MONDAY MORNING, LIGHT PEEKS through my cortinas and I stretch and take up space.

I ache all over. I guess that's what happens when you turn thirteen and spend a week hunched over making revolutionary posters.

I get out of bed extra early, 'cause I hear the *zip zip* of Mami and Dad closing suitcases.

Everyone is sitting around the kitchen table and they rush over to hug me when I get to the bottom step. I'm smothered in kisses and hugs and *feliz cumpleaños* and *happy birthdays*.

Mami got up early to take the flan out of the fridge, set it perfectly on a platter, and drizzle the caramelized sugar. The refrigerator door has every address, phone number, hospital, *everything*. She is repeating instructions over and over again to C.C. Then she hugs us both real hard, and says, "Cuidense, we'll be back in a couple of weeks! Don't cause any bad trouble, only the good kind," and winks.

Abuelita sits in her chair by the Santa Ana statues. She's dressed like she's getting a bautizo at church or something. My

Sharpie-stained fingers run through her freshly curled hair and I bend down to give her a kiss. "Te voy a extrañar, Abuelita," I say.

She puts both my hands in hers and looks up at my eyes. "Feliz cumpleaños, chulita." She does the sign of the cross on my forehead. "What I want for you is to have no missing parts. To be a full you. Build your full *you* this summer, chulita."

"It's only a few weeks, Abuelita," I remind her, shrugging it off, but I glow in her moment of lucidity.

C.C. helps carry out suitcases, and Tía Gladys helps Abuelita get in the car. Then it's just me and my parents.

Dad hands me a cup of coffee, and I can tell it has less milk, just like he makes it for everyone else. I take a sip, and think, this is what it tastes like to be *toda una mujer.*

I set the coffee down as Mami hands me a present. "We'll bring you back more from Guatemala, but we wanted to give you this first."

I carefully unfold her perfect wrapping job. Then lift the top of what seems like a clothing box.

It's the white pants.

I look up at her, mouth wide open, and I get escalofríos all over my arms.

"I found the ones with the least amount of rips," Mami says.

I lift the pants up and swear they shine in the early morning sun coming in through the kitchen window. I look at the tag. It's my size! OK, maybe one size bigger, but still! I hug the pants and then hug both of them.

"Apurate pues que vas a llegar tarde," Mami says, so I rush upstairs to change.

I grab the box of signs we made all week. Kai and Connie already took a lot of them. On my way out, I fight back the tears poking at my eyes as I hug my parents and Mami repeats instructions and emergency situations and to never be away from C.C. or Tía Gladys this next month, and that even though Tía Gladys will be working and busy, that I can always call her and that anything I need signed, she is authorized to sign.

"Y una cosa más," Mami says.

Fear eats at my stomach. What if I get expelled and Mami's not there to pick me up? I think of consecuencias. Expulsion sounds like a palabrota.

"Buena suerte, mi revolucionaria," she says.

The tears actually come this time.

Tía's words—*Primero una voz, y luego seremos millones*—dance on the tip of my tongue.

By the time I get to school, I try to shake how strange it feels after missing a whole week. Instead, I focus on this giant wedgie that's been forming since the bus ride here. The last thing I need on my birthday is my greasy handprint on my butt from birthday champurradas. No gracias. Not today, 'cause I'm a woman now. Kind of.

I wonder if I should run to the locker room before the rush of kids and find someone else's nasty gym shorts. But I fight the feeling, 'cause I remember what Abuelita told me this morning. *You are a woman today. If you want to be treated like one, you have to walk like the underwear you're wearing is yours.*

(Don't ask me what that means. Like I said, some things just don't translate that well.)

In one hand I'm carrying the box of signs, so with the other, I pull up the white pants to readjust them, but it only makes the wedgie worse.

My whole life I've wanted to turn thirteen. I've been waiting for this day. They say that the morning you turn thirteen, you realize what womanhood is all about. And by "they" I mean Abuelita, 'cause she totally said that last night, and she's been hyping me up about this day almost as much as I have. I keep expecting to feel what womanhood is all about, waiting for it to click. Her words from this morning ring in my ear: *I just want you to know your full self.*

I take a deep breath. Familiar smells hit my nose. The Speak Up banner hangs above the auditorium, next to balloons high enough that no kid can jump up and pull them down. The hallway is buzzing with presentation talk. The panel judges have already arrived and administrators are giving them tours.

"BUUUUUURP!" a boy to my left in the seventh-grade hall lets out the biggest belch right in my face, as I walk to my locker.

I want to throw up, but I can't 'cause I don't want to mess up these pants, or the signs I'm carrying around in this box. I will not mess up my first day of being thirteen.

Some girls look at me, and then quickly down. I think of all the anonymous notes I got and wonder how many of these faces wrote to me. I try to make eye contact, but they keep walking. But then a girl walks by, nods at me. Wedged under her armpit is a cardboard cutout with writing I can't make out.

Then two more girls walk toward me and they put up two fingers. I think they're flicking me off—it almost looks like the gross V gesture the boys use—but they're for real doing *the peace sign*. In their other hands are paper signs tucked under their arms. I don't catch what the signs say, but I recognize the paper from our TELL YOUR STORY boxes.

"Eleven forty-seven. We're ready!" one of them says as she walks past me.

"Thank you," the other one says.

They get lost in the sea of backpacks before I can say anything. I turn the corner, and see my locker at the end of the hall. Sticky notes jut out of it like confetti. I hear a few kids say "Happy birthday!" I recognize girls from the sticky notes and emails. Then another girl gives me the peace sign again. I don't know what to do so I scrunch my nose and tilt my head. I do the peace sign back. It's supposed to look cool, but I'm not sure if it does.

I get to my locker. #nomorebasementlockers, #micuerpo, #keepyourhandstoyourself, #endharassmentculture are written all over it in blue, pink, yellow, green sticky notes. I can't believe it. It's been over a week and the notes never stopped.

All the things girls have to go through when they're still kids . . . and not just girls . . . maybe it gets even worse when you're older. But maybe, I don't know, *saying something* means it won't. Maybe this is what Abuelita was talking about. Maybe this is what it means to be a woman. Seeing all of these notes and hashtags, I start to feel more comfortable in what I'm wearing. I feel more comfortable being me.

Kai, Connie, and Genesis come running down the hallway with balloons and some of the protest signs tucked under their arms.

"Happy birthday!" says Connie.

"Mani, no offense, but we can celebrate later. We've got business," says Kai.

Smiling, I can't think of a better way to celebrate. We strategize where we'll put the signs and flyers.

"So, we'll do it like we said last night, OK?" I open the box and show them the additions to our posters, and Mami's song lyrics.

"Eleven forty-seven," I confirm.

The three of them nod.

"Remember," I say. "This is bigger than the presentation or project. This is the real thing. Nerdas come first."

"Las Nerdas forever," Genesis says, in a half laugh half smile.

Another girl walks by, flashing a peace sign with her fingers held out in front of her. I wait for her to round the corner.

When she's out of sight, I say, "Girls keep giving me the peace sign."

Kai laughs and puts her arm around me. "You mean the V sign?"

V? I think. Then it hits me . . .

"Yeah, not a peace sign, silly! It's a V! Girls have taken it back from the boys! They're reapplying it," says Connie.

"You mean reappropriating it," says Kai. "You know, like *reclaiming* it. They started doing it last week."

Two more girls do it as they walk past us.

I stretch my arm out and do it back. Kai and Connie giggle.

The late bell rings. We all jump.

"Hand out the flyers, but, like, real low-key, 'cause if administration reads them too closely, they'll shut it down," I say. Our flyers have tampons and pads drawn all over them so it looks like it's just flyers for our free feminine hygiene product revolution. Don't get me wrong, that's still important too.

I see them read over the new additions—Mami's lyrics. Smiles are across their faces, so I know I'm good.

"According to the Speak Up schedule, presentations start at eleven thirty," says Kai.

We all nod as I hand them signs and flyers to distribute in the bathrooms. Then they're off, shoving some flyers into kids' hands on their way to class.

I walk all the way down to the basement and into the bathroom, and I set a new TELL YOUR STORY box with ready-made signs right by the door so no one can miss it. I take out one of the signs I made last night and tape it on the wall with an arrow pointing down toward the box.

Tell your story. Tell others' stories.
Didn't get a chance to make one? Grab one here!
END THE CULTURE OF ASSAULT AND HARASSMENT
NOW! SHOW UP WITH YOUR SIGN AT 11:47!

I look in the mirror of the quiet basement bathroom. My jeans feel tight and thick against my skin. I look at the door, and hope that no one walks in. I stick my hand down the back side of my pants and pick out the wedgie and pull the underwear to the edges of my butt. Better. Once out of the bathroom, I feel powerful walking down the hallways. Something tells me it's not just the jeans. Something inside me feels powerful. Maybe it's knowing that kids in my school—some I don't even know—are ready. Abuelita's words last night rattle around in my bones till they settle. I walk like I just became a mujer.

The warning bell rings. I quickly stick flyers in lockers and give some to kids scattering to class. I pass out a few more flyers before I walk into first period health. Mr. Jones is making stacks of paper on his desk but drops them when the Pledge starts blasting through the intercom. A'niya's empty seat reminds me of the letter in my glasses case. Maybe it's that, or the smell of Sharpies, Takis, and the usual farts, but I start to feel a little sick to my stomach. I ask to use the bathroom, even though I was just there.

On the toilet, I roll up my pants so that they don't touch the floor and hold them out as far away as possible so they don't touch the nasty toilet seat. I sit there for like five minutes. Nothing. Maybe it's just nerves about the protest.

I give it another minute. Nothing. I take out the flyers and duct tape from my bag, and start to put them up on the door.

#nomorebasementlockers
#keepyourhandstoyourself
#nomoreblame
#bodiesarenotslutty
#holdmenaccountable
#micuerpoesmío
#undíacantaremos
11:47a.m. Find a sign. Grab it, and meet
in front of auditorium. March with us. Tell your story.

Eleven forty-seven is a weird time to schedule a protest, but that's when our "Free Period Product Campaign" presentation is scheduled.

My hands sweat a little. I'm not gonna lie, I'm scared of expulsion. But I started something and I'm not gonna run. Today is our day to win. Well, it's about so much more. People who have put their stories out there are expecting something big, and I'm not going to miss it for some little stomachache.

I give up and wash my hands.

I walk toward the creepy abandoned storage closet next to A'niya's locker, 'cause I know Kai stashed a few signs there. Then I see there are some things written in Sharpie on her locker. I look closer.

SLUT

LOSER

My fists tighten. I take our best sign and am about to tape it up to cover the vandalism when I hear, "What are you doing?"

I turn around and A'niya is standing right in front of me.

A big knot forms in my stomach. I know I messed up with her. I'm searching for the right words. A million thoughts race through my head. I even want to ask her why she's skipping first period, but I don't want her to call me a tonta. I reach into my bag and take out my glasses case. I fumble to get it open, and take out the letter I wrote to her. She's looking at my pants 'cause she knows those are totally the ones she has and yes I copied her. *¿Y qué?* I want to say, but I don't. I'm waiting to see how mad she is, 'cause there're degrees of enojada, you know?

"A'niya, I'm really sorry. I am not going to explain why I did what I did, because then it's not a real apology. But I wrote you a letter, and I hope you read it when you're ready," I say without taking a breath.

She picks something out of her nails and yanks the letter out of my hand and unfolds it. She stares at it for a while and I wonder if she's really reading it, but I see her eyeballs move, so she's gotta be. She folds the letter back up and stuffs it in her back pocket. Then she grabs the flyer out of my hand. I stand there all quiet, not sure what she's going to do.

"What kind of event starts at eleven forty-seven?" she asks.

"Well, protest—" I start rambling, talking nonstop. About the protest, about the database, about the notes, about how I didn't mean to call her out, and—

"Chill, Mani," she says, with her hand right up against my mouth. "You sound like a washing machine, all mumbling and annoying. And I'm not gonna lie, I was like real hurt."

"I know, I'm sorry, I—"

"Uh, excuse me, I wasn't done."

I stop talking. This is the moment she's going to make me rethink this whole thing. I'm going to go home crying, I won't go through with it. We could just stick to our original plan. I mean, free tampons and pads are important. Do I run like Mami ran all those years ago, 'cause she was protecting my future? No puedo. So I take a deep breath, because I can't back down no matter what she says. I started something and I can't unstart it. I decide to fly straight into it, my quetzal wings made of brightly colored sticky note stories.

But then she says, "What you're doing . . . it's real important and stuff, even if you don't win. And in a weird way I'm glad I could help inspire it. And I kind of want to say thank you, but also not really 'cause you're so annoying. Kinda cool, but you know, annoying cool. And I forgive you. It wasn't right, but it took guts too. And I admire that."

"You forgive me?"

"Yeah, you need your ears cleaned? Don't make me take it back," she says, handing the flyer back to me.

I want to hug her so bad, but we're not really hugging friends yet.

I hand her a sign, but she laughs. "I made my own," she says. "It's in my locker. Later, puta."

It's like hearing the sugar for the flan bubble pop: magic.

I smile and say, "Later, puta," back.

"No, only I say it."

"Oh. Yeah, sorry."

She turns and we walk our separate ways. The bell rings. Second period is starting. I grab the signs against my chest, preparing for a tormenta, but my voice is clear, maybe for the first time ever.

THIRTY

WE ALL PILE INTO the auditorium for the Speak Up presentations. In the seats, a sea of girls wear dresses and skirts and suits. Boys wear khakis and some even wear ties. Everyone rehearses their speeches on fresh printer paper and their voices sound like cicadas buzzing throughout the room. They all look like they're focused, daydreaming hard about a summer in New York.

We sit through one presentation after another.

Genesis covers herself in eggshells and banana peels with apple skin for hair. It's cute, smart, and kind of weird. She talks about how soon there will be no more space in landfills. She explains what composting is and promises composting bags to each student in order to reduce food waste during lunch. She even made colorful laminated signs to put around the school building explaining what can and can't be composted. It's a clean, organized system, and it creates change. Real change.

She's good. Like really good. The judges stand and applaud. Her smile radiates. I clap so hard that my hands sting.

"We're up next, Mani," says Kai.

I thought I'd be daydreaming about winning and going to New York. About not having to make my bed right away for the first time in forever. About Kai and Connie and me eating hot dogs from street corner vendors like people do on TV.

But that's not what I'm thinking about as the judges wave us to the stage. I'm thinking about the letters and emails and sticky notes. Of A'niya being hidden in the basement like what Corey and Mason did to her was her fault.

It wasn't her fault.

It wasn't C.C.'s fault for what happened to her.

And it wasn't my tía's—

"Ma-nuhuaila Semilla, Kai Espinoza, Connie Salar. Title of project: Free and Universal Feminine Hygiene Products in Every Bathroom. Come to the stage and take it away, ladies," a judge in a suit and bow tie says.

Some of the judges smile and nod like it's a real good idea. Pues, it is. But it's just not the idea we're going to talk about today. Uy, here we go.

We sit still for a moment. It's 11:45. Two more minutes till the time we told everyone.

I turn to Kai and Connie. "Nerdas forever," I say.

Then I stand from my seat.

"Groped in the stairwell," I say, but my voice shakes a little and not everyone hears. I clear my throat. "Groped in the stairwell. Administration said sorry, the cameras weren't working that day."

The judges look confused. They look at each other, then back at me.

Kai stands and says, "Jumped on her walk home from school. Video went viral. Kid who knocked her down got one day of in-school suspension. Nothing happened to the filmers."

Then Connie joins us. "Assaulted by ex-boyfriend. Told it wasn't assault."

Then Genesis stands from one of the chairs in the audience. "Told her body was mature for a sixth grader and that was an invitation for unwanted touching."

We take turns saying, out loud, others' stories like we are sound amplifiers.

"What is going on?" I hear a judge say. The judges are trying to talk to our teachers who are sitting to the left of the audience.

"What's going on?" I say, as if on the heels of his words. "These are only some of the things that the students here at school have to go through. For our project, we created a database of harassment incidents in our community to raise awareness. Kids should be able to get home without wondering if they're the next targets of these assaults. We should be able to get an education without fearing for our bodies. We should be able to attend school safely. It is no one's right to touch us, or spread sexually violent content about us. And these behaviors . . . this acceptance of violence, this culture of harassment . . . it starts here and it needs to end here. We want accountability. It ends here."

The quiver from my voice is gone.

I look over at Ms. Martinez, who's all sonrisas. So are some of the PE teachers standing next to her.

I rehearsed my speech with C.C. a thousand times. I know it by heart, better than I know the chorus to Chavela Vargas and Rebeca Lane songs.

My arms, which were heavy with the weight of carrying the poster box earlier, now feel light as they spring up with the first sign. It has a border of pads, tampons, *V*'s and glitter. Hashtags like #noplaceforbodyviolence, #donttouchme, and #harassmentfreeschool fill the middle.

Whispers, gasps, and laughter explode throughout the auditorium.

Then, silence.

Kai, Connie, Genesis, and I are the only ones standing.

Then, someone from the crowd yells, "What she was wearing is never a reason!"

Someone else yells, "No body violence at school!"

Three people stand. Then another. Two of the four lift up signs. Then I can't tell where the voices are coming from. I hear shouting outside.

"No more basement lockers! Respect! Accountability!"

Then more signs pop up from the crowd.

Kai looks at me. "Ready?"

I nod.

We lift our signs higher and start marching toward the door.

"Young ladies!" one of the judges yells.

In the hallway, I can see several students holding signs, yelling, "No more creepy basement lockers!"

"No more blaming clothing!"

"No more blaming body type!"

"School is a place where my body should be respected!"

"And where respect of others' bodies should be taught!" someone responds.

About twenty people walk out of the auditorium behind us.

"Where are we going?" several of them ask me. They look at me like I have answers. I'm about to say I don't know, but for once, I really know.

"To every class!" I say. "We speak up at every class. And then we all walk out together!"

We rush toward the auditorium exit.

"Everybody stay where you are!" Mr. Robertson yells as he tries to keep everyone inside the auditorium, but isn't able to.

I am in front of about thirty people. Then thirty-five, then forty. We yell.

"No more basement lockers! Culture of harassment stops HERE!"

Other kids walk out of the bathroom. We see sixth and eighth graders who have walked out of their classrooms. Girls who wrote to me are next to me, behind me, all around me. They are chanting, some are singing. Then I see A'niya. She stands next to me and lifts her sign and starts yelling, "No more basement lockers!"

I blink 'cause I'm not sure if this is real.

I stand straight, like Abuelita told me to do, the grip around my chest uncurls, like a wing opening.

I stop talking. I stop chanting. I listen to the sound around me, like it's the song of the morning birds Abuelita and Tía and Mami talk about. It's music all around me. I think about Tía Beatriz, how she must have felt in her first school protest and how that led to bigger things. Real protests.

But this feels real. This is real. This is my community and I expect more of it, for me. For the girl next to me. Even for the girl who won't share her Takis with me. Even for the girls who sometimes say mean things to me. For everyone.

Then I stop. I feel queasy. My stomachache is back. Maybe it's the emotions. I turn the corner, but Mr. Dupont is standing there with security and a few of the panel judges, some still looking confused, expecting a different presentation. Mr. Dupont even has his bus loop bullhorn. Behind me are about fifty kids with signs. It's like a standoff.

"Ms. Semilla, you are risking expulsion!" Mr. Dupont says.

I hear several people in the crowd say, "Boo," and I stand straight, like Abuelita tells me to do.

But then someone yells from the back.

"Then expel us too!"

"Yeah!"

Signs go up and down like in the protests in the faded pictures in the attic, like in the videos C.C. shows me of the protests she goes to.

"Listen up, ladies," Mr. Dupont says, all incómodo, the way Abuelita says men get when they feel threatened. "I appreciate the passion for this project, but I think it's gone a little too far."

"Too far?" And that's when I realize my voice is so strong and loud that it quiets my side of the hallway. And everyone waits. I turn around. They're waiting for me. "Too far is getting your bra snapped and ripped on the bus, but YOU are the one that gets in trouble. And instead of speaking up, people film," I say.

"Or being shamed for your body and being told you invite touching and harassment," a girl shouts from behind me.

Some of the panel judges look at me, like they're listening. Like actually listening. One of them is even taking notes.

But before I can say anything, a girl's voice raises down the hallway. It's Jordyn from health and English class. "Too far is having mean sexual jokes about you on social media and the school telling you it can't do anything about what happens off school grounds." Then she looks at me and gives an awkward wave. I smile.

"Too far is being told the shape of your body invited unwanted gropes," a girl shouts, but I can't even see who it is.

Then I hear a familiar voice on the other side of the hallway, close to Mr. Dupont.

"Too far is getting away with things just because you're a boy."

I can't believe it. It's Gonzalo.

He's holding his own handmade sign. Some boys look at him like he's an alien, but others clap.

Now other judges are writing things down in a notebook. Another woman types something on her phone. Mr. Dupont puts his bullhorn down, but then Mr. Robertson grabs the bullhorn out of his hands.

"How about a town hall? We can discuss all of this when you're ready—" he says.

"We're ready now," I say. "We want a culture of respect. We want a specific harassment report, not just a combined one with bullying. And we want to be heard and believed."

The judges look at Mr. Dupont and Mr. Robertson. They look at each other. Ms. Martinez stands on her toes to look over some tall eighth graders. She's not holding any signs, but her eyes hold a thousand signs.

Mr. Dupont grips his bullhorn like he just needs to say the word and I'm expelled. Boom. Basta. Ya. I'm gone. Future ruined, right? What happens to kids who get expelled? Will Mami have to move, again?

And that's when I feel it. Like I just sat in someone's lunch of Ramen noodle soup.

I look down between my thighs and there's a dark red spot on my white jeans.

I look up and stare at the crowd. They stare back.

The panel judge who was taking notes puts her pen hand to her mouth in that ay-pobrecita kind of way.

Uy, I think. I am the last person I want to be right now.

I am too frozen to cry. My heart beats in my ears. This is worse than what happened to Genesis. For a second, I want to disappear. I wish I had flushed myself down the toilet earlier. I want a giant meteor to come crashing down on this hallway, but just on me.

Mr. Dupont and Mr. Robertson are both on their walkie-talkies, but every sound is just a buzz in my ear right now.

Do I have such mala suerte that I could be expelled and get my period all over my brand-new white jeans, all on the same day, on my birthday?

I search for Las Nerdas in the crowd, but nada. All I hear is my pulse, and my heart jumping around inside of me.

THIRTY-ONE

A GIRL BEHIND ME WHO obviously hasn't noticed shouts, "What are we waiting for!"

I stand for a real long time, for the period to make me feel like a woman. Like, Sunday-morning-line-at-Sabor-de-Mi-Tierra type long. (Mami doesn't mind how long we wait, 'cause she says the vegetables are the freshest there, but watching her run her fingers over the limes and pretty rows of green and orange guicoys, I know it's 'cause she wants to touch things that only days before touched Guatemala.) Yeah, longer than that.

"What next, Mani?"

A sixth grader I recognize from my bus looks up at me. She doesn't seem to care that period blood is soaking my new pants in front of everyone. She's carrying a protest sign that's way bigger than she is, on it a fragment of a story that happened to her sister.

My face is all flushed as I stand there waiting for the meteor to hit and BOOM! I'd be transformed right in front of everyone's eyes. Into toda una mujer. I look down. I wait for bigger boobs. I wait for my legs to start doing some new walk that says *I'm a jefa*, or . . . something. Anything. I wait. I watch.

But solutions don't magically fall from the sky no matter how many santos I pray to. Feeling like a woman isn't instant like a meteor explosion. It slow cooks like Christmas tamales, or like that pozole that Abuelita used to make and say was Guatemalan even though I told her so many times pozole is Mexican, to which she responded, *Guatemalans invented the calendar, chulita. You doubt their ability to make pozole?* That's the thing about Abuelita, you can't tell her something ISN'T Guatemalan.

We're out of places to go. The contest judges are scattered around in the hallway, and they look like they're trying to figure out if this is our project or if this is real. It's both, I guess.

I fight the ache in my stomach that's pulling me to want to curl up in a corner. I don't know how much time I have. I picture my period streaming down my pant leg and messing up the floors and no one will be able to get out 'cause they'll start slipping all over the place. Uy, I think. Getting your period *does* make you all dramatic.

That's when I hear it.

"Ew!" It's Mason and Corey, with J.J. behind them.

Then I hear "Ouch" and "Watch it!" through the crowd and that's when I see her.

Genesis is elbowing her way through people.

She takes off her green cardigan sweater with glittery buttons all over it, and bits of leftover eggshells. "Here," she whispers. "You were there for me, remember?"

The old me would have taken it and prayed to all the santos to take me far, far away. But something feels different. The tightness squeezing my body and holding me in place starts to uncurl. Around me a blur of cardboard with pieces, but together they make a whole story. A collective. And that's when it comes to me from a deep, deep place.

"We are a collective!" I yell.

Some repeat. Then more.

Kai, Connie, and A'niya push their way through the crowd to me and Genesis. They look down, then all slowly look up with their mouths open. Connie looks at Kai and gives her the *do-something!* look, and Genesis keeps pushing the sweater at me. Everyone is looking at my pants.

But before anyone can say anything else, something deep inside me takes over. Or maybe I do. It's like all the blood rushes to my feet 'cause I start to feel unstuck. I breathe in all the smells: sweaty feet, Sharpies, Axe, sour gum chewed for hours. And it all wraps me like a blanket, like warm atol hitting every bone on its way down to your stomach. It feels like I've been holding my breath this whole time and I let it out in one exhale.

I move toward Corey. I raise my fist and look directly in his eyes, even though I have to look up a little, 'cause he's way taller than me. I don't care, 'cause I'm a woman.

"¡Primero una voz, y luego seremos millones!" I yell.

Silence.

Then I look around. "¡Una voz y seremos millones!" I yell, in a quetzal voice Abuelita would be proud of. In a quetzal voice *I* am proud of. It floats over the signs of all of our stories.

Silence.

Then a roar.

Roars and whistles, like we all turned to pressure cookers or something.

"¡Una voz y seremos millones!" some yell back.

Only a handful of kids understand, and the ones who don't, pues, it doesn't matter, 'cause it's still for them. Those words are for everyone. Todos, you know?

A girl behind me raises her fist and yells, "Yeah! Girl power!"

Then it's like a flood. Everyone starts.

"More accountability!"

"No more basement lockers!"

"Zero tolerance for harassment!"

"¡Una voz y seremos millones!"

Even boys join in. I catch a glimpse of Hector's face and his arm stretched wide with a sign. My fist is still raised, and I yell, "We see you!" and everyone repeats it.

A girl behind me yells, "No more basement lockers as victim blaming!" Everyone repeats it. The words aren't perfect and they don't rhyme like they do at the protests C.C. goes to, but they're raw and honest and they make sense.

We walk, ignoring the bell indicating class just ended. We raise our posters and fists and keep walking and chanting until it feels like the whole school is here. Some teachers try to tell kids to go to class, but then they give up. Others sneak in a few claps; I see them mouth the chants.

I hear Mr. Dupont yell into his bullhorn, "Manu-aila Se-mila, in my office NOW!"

But I ignore him. I open the exit doors and lead everyone onto the soccer field, 'cause you know, we promised a walkout.

We sit on the grass. Sixth graders with seventh graders. Eighth graders with sixth graders.

Kids are talking, laughing, telling stories. Hugging. Eighth grade girls come up to me and tell me about the first time they got their periods.

Mr. Dupont and Mr. Robertson stand on the steps talking to the panel judges. Security is out on the field, but they don't tell us to go back inside. There's too many of us. I stopped counting. We stay there for a long time, until we hear the last bell of the day. And when the bell rings, we all rush back in, arm in arm, to grab our stuff out of our lockers and head to the bus loop.

Kai, Connie, Genesis, A'niya, and I walk down the seventh-grade hallway. I want to say people part for us, but then I'd be a mentirosa. We have to elbow our way through a little bit. But a lot of people give us high fives and shake our shoulders. Even more stick their arms out and give us the V peace signs. It's an energy I've never felt, better than reaching page 100 on our Nerda Manifesto. We float. Our smiles are so big that our faces hurt. We pick up and clean up whatever we can on our way out, 'cause we're children of immigrants and if we don't, we are *ingratas malcriadas consentidas*.

We walk out to the bus loop like it's any other day, except it's not. We skipped classes, that means unexcused absences. And it's the first time in Nerda history that we walk the hallways completely silent. Maybe we each think of what we'll do this summer. We daydream. We wonder if we won, in more ways than one.

At the bus loop, Genesis puts her head on my shoulder. "Hey," she says. "Whoever wins . . . WE won."

But we both know there's NO way I won. I smile, the signs now feeling like extensions of my arms.

"I know my project wasn't about justice and—" she starts, but I cut her off.

"It is, though," I say. "Every project was important. Plus, a healthier planet and less food waste is better for women, so it's like all connected." I think of my tía's last letter, when she was about to board a bus to Honduras, because she saw a connection—an hilo—between the stories there and those in Guatemala, between environmental protection and the right of women to live free from violence.

"Environmental rights are women's rights. Thanks for helping me see that." I know I'm mad plagiarizing my tía, but I don't think she'd mind.

I imagine C.C. saying something like that, but I stop thinking about her. *I* would say something like that too.

Mason and Corey don't get on the bus that day. Their other friends are quiet and keep their hands to themselves the whole ride. When Gonzalo gets on, I give him the nod, and he does it back. Maybe next time, there might even be a we're-cool-now smile. We're close to Genesis's stop, and she grabs her stuff. We do the Nerda handshake.

"Nerdas for life," she says.

"Nerdas for life," I say.

The two more stops to my house are long. I look down at my pants. The bloody spot starts to feel cold. The energy keeps me floating for a while, but then I think: the Guatemala trip is gone. Our summer plans are gone, for sure. We were too much for the judges, but I'm OK with too much. And then the word *expulsion* starts to creep up on me, but whatever happens, I want to think it was all worth it.

I think of what I'll say to my parents when they call me after they land. I think about what I'll tell C.C. and Tía Gladys right now or where to even start. I think about what else we can do this summer while my parents are gone.

When I get home, I open the door, bracing myself for an empty house.

My parents, Tía, Abuelita, and C.C. are all sitting around the table, their big smiles turning to gasps as they look down and stare at my pants. I'm frozen still at the doorway, expecting them to rush over and make a scene.

We stare at each other for a while.

"Camarada," says Abuelita. "How bad is it out there?"

Abuelita is in another place and another year right now. I brought her to a time of uprisings and protests. I give her a kiss on the cheek and say, "Hola, Abuelita."

"No, Mamita, it's Manuela. She just got back from school. And looks like she just got her period all over her new white pants. Ay Dios mio," Mami says.

"¡A Manuela! Toda una mujercita," Abuelita says, and then starts singing a song about a girl who leaves for the city and comes back a woman and all the men in town want to talk to her, but she would rather spend her day playing guitar. Her singing carries me around the table, saludando everyone, waiting for an explanation.

"Felicitaciones," my tía and Mami both say at the same time. I expect the usual picking apart my body that always happens, but they don't say anything.

"Why are you guys still here?" I finally manage to ask.

They all look at each other and then at Mami. Mami motions upstairs, and we go. I go to the bathroom and change out of my pants.

No amount of white vinegar or bleach will take this stain away. I let it soak anyways in the bathtub.

In my room, Mami is sitting on my bed and motions for me to sit next to her. She's holding an old picture album and a folder. Then she puts a ticket for Guatemala City, Guatemala in my hand. The ticket is for five days from now. I look up at her, confused.

"We're all going. I changed our tickets and got you and C.C. one," she says.

"But how did you know I wasn't going to win? Or did you think I would choose Guatemala in the end?"

There is a hurt in my voice and she senses it, 'cause she's Mami and all. "Manuela, projects like yours are never meant to win," she says.

"What? But—"

"Let me finish. Projects like yours are never set up to win, but they are meant to matter beyond anything you can measure, beyond a competition, and their impact lasts more than a prize or summer camp. People like us don't win in the ways most people think of winning. People are scared of what you want, Manuela. And they should be because what you want is something they should want. Something your tía wanted so much."

We both turn our heads to watch a bird land on the branch right outside my window.

Abuelita, Tía, and, Mami are always talking about how the birds in Guatemala sound different, how they have different songs for different parts of the day and how much they miss those sounds. I understand what she's saying.

She puts the book in my lap. I open it, and it is filled with pictures of her sister. In the first one, she is standing next to the pila, a big cement sink in a small courtyard. Her hands are filled with soap and she's laughing. There is a volcano in the background.

"El Volcán de Fuego," she says. "And that is where we always washed our clothes when I was your age." She points to the cement sink in the picture. "My father built that by hand. It is where we washed everything by hand. We'd scrub our clothes against the cement. Sometimes we would accidentally cut our fingers. And over there we had neighbors, and they always used to climb the wall to throw rotten mangoes from the mango tree."

"I've rarely ever heard you or Abuelita talk about him," I say.

"He was killed the week before we had to grab everything and leave. We quickly realized that the threats were real," she says.

I picture Mami, long black hair in her face, like me, hanging up wet clothes, her fingers getting all wrinkly from the water, dreaming of what she would be.

Then she switches to Spanish seamlessly and starts telling me about their neighborhood and stories about her sister and father. Normally I would have shut her out, but I follow. We've never really talked in full Spanish. My Spanish still isn't perfect, but her story feels like when I'm listening to Chavela Vargas or rapping the chorus of Rebeca Lane's and Audry Funk's songs about respecting girls' bodies and futures. It's like I understand everything, even the words I don't know.

Today feels different. My quetzal voice flaps in my chest like wings, and I guess this is what it feels like. Once you have it, it's always there.

I look up at her. "Why are you always so scared?"

"There is a part of me that wanted you to lose. It's also why I've made you wear such loose stuff. I have had this fear that attention can lead to violence and death and I wanted you to be unseen, to be protected. But that is not protection. I gave you advice I would have hated when I was your age. I thought living here you would have come out different than me and your aunt, but you inherited all of us, plus everything that is uniquely yours. You are your own person. But that fear—my fear—isn't letting you grow into who you are supposed to be."

And I realize just then that Mami is still figuring out womanhood too, and maybe it's something that's constantly evolving.

She sees me. I was part of her story and my tía's story and Abuelita's and C.C.'s and all the kids who put notes in my locker and sent emails. We're all part of the same story.

"¿Qué pasa?" she asks, picking up my chin.

"You're going to miss it . . . the ceremony," I say. "Getting there five days later means you'll miss the event honoring the women on that bus."

Thirteen years ago Mami left Guatemala, because of me. She ran. She made a decision that she felt was best for me. And now she's sacrificing a real important moment, again, for me. They're all sacrificing something big . . . for me. Mami's life has been one sacrifice after another. I feel a tight squeeze around my heart and start to cry. She won't get to hear her sister's name said to a big crowd of people who knew her, who heard some of her last words. She won't get to meet the women who spent her last years, months, days, and hours with her. And I won't either. Maybe one here and one there, but not all in the same room.

Mami hardens her grip on my chin and says, "Estoy muy orgullosa de ti."

And that's when I realize she knew the consequences all along. It was her choice to make, and she made it. And I see it now, what

C.C. and Tía Beatriz had said all along about how Mami is a feminist, even though her feminism doesn't look like mine all the time.

I smile, but I still can't find words for what I feel right now.

"I'm sorry about the jeans," I say.

"Esta bien. They were on sale," she says. Her eyes sparkle a little, and I realize for the first time that Mami's life didn't start when I was born. She had a whole other life before me.

"I am so proud of how you are figuring out womanhood," she says, laughing a little, but I know she means it. Her laugh is loud and warm, and in sync with the song of birds outside of my window that fills the room.

"Felicidades again," she says, hugging me before heading downstairs.

And I know she's talking about my period and becoming a woman and all of that. For so long it's all that I wanted. And I want to tell her, that this isn't what makes me feel like a woman, but I can't contain all the emotions rushing through my body or quite find the right set of words right now.

Being a woman isn't about periods and body size or shape or how anyone sees you. It's just different for everyone, and that's OK.

For me, it's about fighting. Fighting against all the things that keep us down for being women, like the disrespect of and violence against women's bodies.

I sit in my room alone, and look out the window at the bird that's still there. I picture Mami and Tía Beatriz sitting in the room they shared, daydreaming hard like the Nerdas and I do, about things so different, but so similar at the same time. They shared a dream but could not have imagined how different their paths would be. Or maybe they could, and they accepted consecuencias of their different choices.

Hay que aceptar las consecuencias, Abuelita used to say. But I think it's less about acceptance and more about confronting . . . how do you turn your story into a song?

Mami saw me and I saw her. She was part of my story, but I was also part of hers. Our stories don't end. They're long and connected, like the strongest hilo, and I am influenced by the things unsaid, by dreams left in bus tragedies on mountainsides, and it's my job to make something out of what comes from that. My sueños are hers and theirs all wrapped in one.

THIRTY-TWO

Five days after mi cumpleaños,
a.k.a. the day I found my quetzal voice
and became a mujer

WE DON'T GET IN TROUBLE. I don't get expelled. We don't win the trip to New York.

But our protest has parents asking questions the rest of week— our last week as seventh graders. It has news people asking to share the videos kids posted on TV. The new student board of education member asked me to help her come up with new demands against school harassment. It's so much, I have Dad helping me respond to all the requests.

Kai cut her hair short—exactly how she wanted. Her parents are still learning to accept. She also asked for a family meeting and talked about getting therapy for Lani—that what happened to her isn't normal and that they should talk about it and stop treating it like a secret to be ashamed of.

So we did kind of win, because our protest meant something.

One of the Speak Up judges contacted my parents and asked to talk to me. She runs a violence awareness and prevention center. One of the things the center does is teach teenagers about body safety and respect. She asked if Las Nerdas wanted to work with them this summer to come up with trainings for their middle school education programs. The judge said our presentation gave her an idea to start a youth navigator program to train teenagers to advocate for respect for bodies, make schools more accountable, but also provide talks for families at community centers. She said we'd get community service hours, and even official T-shirts!

When I told Mami about it, she gave me the choice, again. I thought about it. This would be real, actionable change that would make a difference. I told Las Nerdas that they'd have to update me and that I'd join in the next cohort, 'cause this time I was choosing Guatemala.

NOW I AM IN THE LAST place I thought I would be—the airport.

They're announcing everything in English and Spanish and the sounds feel like missing pieces of a puzzle clicking together in my ear. I look at Dad reading the newspaper someone left on the seat he now sits in. He looks up at me and smiles.

Abuelita is praying the rosary, but she has a sparkle in her eyes, and I know what that means. She's about to start singing, but maybe this time, no one will try to silence her. Maybe this time, others will join in, because she is a short flight closer to where it all started.

I look around and we're in a room full of people with stories and memories and songs. C.C. sits on the footrest with my tía's feet on her lap. She's massaging her aches and pains away. Doña Marta says it's from the heartache of bad relationships and feminist daughters with no plans to marry. But I think it's from years of working on her feet in those warehouses where they kept speeding up the conveyer belt and her hands and feet couldn't keep up, messing up her hands and feet for a long time. Unfairness comes in so many forms.

(I'm a woman now so I can say these things with certainty.)

Then there's Mami. She stands with her hands on her hips by the window that looks out on to where the planes land and take off. I've never really noticed her hair. It's a black river. How many secrets have nestled there? The weight they must carry. She watches the planes take off and land and I hope all the guilt she's been carrying all these years starts to dissolve like the caramelo over my birthday flan.

I think of what I would have said if I could have met Tía Beatriz. Not just through letters. Maybe words wouldn't have been enough. But maybe it's like when you first take a bite of mango smothered in salt, lime, and spicy Tajín flakes—are there any words to describe the goodness?

I still ask myself what kind of world it is where women disappear on buses and are too scared to go to school. Where kids my age film an attack instead of helping or speaking up. But it's also one where women protest and sing and remold their lives and fight against unfairness in their own ways. It's about making hard choices, *sin importar las consecuencias*. I guess that's why her letters could have so much sadness and so much joy at the same time.

I think of my tía and how, for a few years, we lived under the same sun. She thought of me before I knew she existed. She said my name and she was part of my story before I ever considered the depth of my story and history. We were connected—in story and sound. What would I say to her? Nada, I guess. Not at first. I'd like to think we would all sit at the same round table and drink the same coffee—mine with a little more milk. We would listen to the sounds of the birds they're always talking about (the ones God made just for Guatemala and Guatemala alone, according to Abuelita).

But that's the thing about birds. Some migrate, and then they come back, and their sound and stories are theirs wherever they go. It's kinda like they're always home. And as for the quetzal birds— the actual ones majestically hiding in the rain forest—one day maybe they really will sing again.

ACKNOWLEDGMENTS

THE FACT THAT you are reading this page is a dream come true for me. This book started as a messy and fragmented short story. I owe infinite gratitude to the people who took these fragments at their different stages and helped me turn it into a novel.

Thank you to my family. Especially my parents, for your endless support and advice. For your strength and your stories. For reading to me early on and beginning my love of books that I have carried with me throughout my life. For giving me the gift of a bilingual home, and for taking me to Guatemala and making sure it was a part of my identity and memories. For instilling the belief that a creative endeavor is a worthwhile endeavor. Shoutout to my tías, for answering my endless questions about words in Spanish.

To my husband, Steven, for always encouraging me. For asking me the question on a rainy walk that inspired me to write the short story that later became this book. Thank you for reminding me that one of the first things I ever told you was that I wanted to be a writer. Te quiero.

To my daughters, for letting me squeeze in a writing desk next to your own "work stations" and listening to me read my revisions out loud to you. For letting my stories share the boundless love and time I have for both of you.

To my in-laws, Vern and Bob, for caring about my writing and always cheering me on.

Thank you to the educators who shaped my life and my love of reading and writing. Thank you for always making me feel like I had something to say. To my high school creative writing class, Erewhon, where I first imagined myself as a writer. To my college professors who introduced me to authors and books that have changed my life, and who taught me about women's movements in Latin America, a theme that always finds its way into my stories. Special shoutout to Dr. Angelo Robinson—I am so grateful that we can be on this publishing journey together, but above all, thank you for our friendship and shared love of poetry.

To my friends who believe in me and listen to me write out loud during car rides, and who celebrate every success. To those who read early chapters and offered invaluable feedback. Special shoutout to Catalina Bartlett and Ricardo Martínez, wildly talented writers themselves, who helped shape those early chapters.

To Las Hermanas Mentorship Program, SCBWI, The Highlights Foundation's Latinx Writers Symposium, The Writer's Center, the Maryland Writer's Conference, the Kweli Color of Children's Literature Conference, and the talented writers I met at each of these places and form part of my writing community.

To my fellow writers in the Writer's Center's year-long short story workshop, who read the earliest version of this book when it was an unfinished short story. Thank you to Dr. Ivelisse Rodriguez, brilliant teacher and writer. You were the first person to tell me this little story should be a novel. Thank you for your thorough and brilliant edits, questions and comments that dug deep into the soul of each story. I am so thankful for you for teaching me craft and opening so many doors. You are pivotal in my writing journey. Taking your class feels like one of the most important choices I have ever made!

To Sandra Cisneros, Ruth Behar and the Macondo Writers Workshop. What a joyful and powerful week of writing! I am so lucky my first chapter passed through your brilliant minds and hands.

To my agent, Ellen Goff. I am so grateful for you! Thank you for loving Mani and seeing her potential from the start. I am so happy I signed up for a 10-minute critique slot with you at the Maryland Writer's Conference. You understood the heart of this story even when all you initially saw were 10 messy pages! Thank you for the months and rounds of edits, and for answering all of my endless questions. I couldn't ask for a better agent!

To my editor, Irene Vázquez, for taking Mani to the next level. For your brilliant edits, for pushing me to make her voice shine beyond what I had imagined and helping me identify the central question Mani is asking herself: what does a feminist look like? Thank you for helping me bring to life the journey of a girl who is figuring out how to truly sing in the world. Mani is truly in the best hands. I am grateful for the whole team at Levine Querido and Chronicle Books: Antonio Gonzalez Cerna, Kerry Taylor, Danielle Maldonado, and Freesia Blizard. I feel lucky and proud that this story is among all the incredible stories you put out into the world. Thank you to Rosa Colón Guerra for this bold and stunning cover. Thank you to copyeditor Johanie Martinez-Cools and proofreader Meghan Maria McCullough.

To e.E. Charlton-Trujillo, my Musas mentor, without whom this book would not exist. For helping me choose novel over short story collection. For the accountability I needed in order to get this done. For asking me to send you one chapter every Sunday night, and if I didn't, I knew to expect an email! For your reading homework assignments, and your lessons on craft. For your humor and your friendship. I continue to learn so much from you. For the hours you and Gia put into "the letter." I have never laughed so hard. Thank you for being the first person to tell me that Mani's voice belonged in the world, and for advocating for her. And of course, for letting me know when I had reached my Takis limit.

To the place where I was born, Guatemala. The memories of drinking café con leche and listening to birds around a table full of family, stories, and the crispiest plátanos inspired the sounds and smells that made their way into this story. I acknowledge the activists and journalists all over Guatemala and Central America who are fighting to end violence against women; your incredible work is a model in this global struggle.

Finally, to my readers. Thank you for choosing this book and joining Mani in her journey to find her quetzal voice.

ABOUT THE AUTHOR

ANNA LAPERA teaches middle school by day and writes stories about girls stepping into their power in the early hours of the morning. She is a member of Las Musas, a 2022 Macondista and *Kweli Journal* mentee, and has received support from Tin House, *Kweli Journal* and SCBWI. When she's not writing, you can find her visiting trails and coffee shops in Silver Spring, Maryland, where she lives with her family. *Mani Semilla Finds Her Quetzal Voice* is her debut novel. You can find her online at annalaperawriter.com

SOME NOTES
ON THIS BOOK'S PRODUCTION

Art for the jacket was created by Rosa Colón Guerra. The text was
set by Westchester Publishing Services, in Danbury, CT, in Perpetua.
The display was set in Abadi. The book was printed on 78 gsm Yunshidai
Ivory uncoated woodfree FSC™-certified paper and bound in China.

Production supervised by Freesia Blizard
Book interiors designed by Patrick Collins
Editor: Irene Vázquez
Managing Editor: Danielle Maldonado

LEVINE QUERIDO